THE
NEBULA
AWARDS
19

THE NEBULA AWARDS #19

EDITED BY
Marta Randall

ARBOR HOUSE
New York

The Library of Congress cataloged this serial as follows:

The Nebula awards.—No. 18——New York [N.Y.]: Arbor House, c1983–
   v.; 22 cm.
   Annual.
   Vols. for 1983–   published for the Science Fiction Writers of
      America.
Continues: Nebula award stories (1982)
   ISSN 0741-5567 = The Nebula awards.

   1. Science fiction, American—Periodicals.   I. Science Fiction
Writers of America.
PS648.S3N38   813'.0876'08—dc19   83-647399
Library of Congress   [8404]   AACR 2   MARC-S

Manufactured in the United States of America

10 9 8 7 6 5 4 3 2 1

Contents

Introduction
by *Marta Randall*

The Science Fiction Writers of America was founded twenty years ago to provide a voice to science fiction writers in their professional dealings, to battle injustices, and to deal with the unromantic, behind-the-scenes, but absolutely necessary details of a professional's career. Over these past two decades the organization has been remarkably effective in its efforts, from forcing the repeal of unjust contracts to conducting successful audits, and has been termed the most effective writer's organization in the country. Why, then, involve itself with the process of handing out awards?

The answer, I think, lies in the history of American science fiction. The genre found its popular genesis during the pulp years, published in magazines printed on cheap stock, complete with garish covers often featuring bug-eyed monsters and scantily clad females in obvious need of rescue; not the sort of packaging calculated to generate respect, and for decades s.f. remained a literary stepchild, considered *prima facie* undeserving of critical attention. To be honest, this reputation was not entirely undeserved. The pulps were often stuffed with hack work, formula stories written with little concern for such minutia as characterization, theme, and literary value. These less-than-shining efforts frequently hid works of true literary value which crept into the magazines' pages, and s.f.'s mainstream reputation as a field of inept stories ineptly written became entrenched in the critical mind.

In the 1980s s.f. took a turn for the popular, generated in part by the television and film media, and in 1983 works of science fiction suddenly appeared on *The New York Times* bestseller lists. Nonetheless, there are still mainstream publications that discriminate against science fiction or known science fiction writers, and reviewers who ignore the field except in those rare instances when one actually reads within the genre and reports in astonishment that the works of Writer X cannot possibly be science fiction because they are much too good.

Not too surprisingly, science fiction fans and professionals reacted to this exclusion by an exclusion of their own. Barred from participation in the self-congratulations of the mainstream literary establishment, s.f. generated self-congratulatory forms of its own, in the Hugo and Nebula awards. Annually we gather to celebrate ourselves, to award those works we feel to be at the apex of our field, to wine and dine each other, to renew our professional friendships, and, not incidentally, to warn of new professional outrages and oil our weaponry.

The Hugo Awards, given at the annual World Science Fiction Convention, are chosen by a vote of science fiction fans and readers; the Nebulas are chosen by the writers themselves and represent the choice of professionals in the field.

During the awards year, which runs from January through December, members of the Science Fiction Writers of America recommend stories and novels to their fellow writers. As the year progresses, the number of recommendations mounts; those works with the most recommendations appear on a preliminary ballot, and the works garnering the most votes then appear on the final ballot. Additionally, a Nebula jury exists to bring to the members' attention works appearing outside of the field's usual publications, and has the power to add one further work to each of the four award categories (novel, novella, novellette, and short story). The final Nebula ballot goes to active members of the organization, that is, to professional science fiction and fantasy writers.

The results of this process, for works published in 1983, appear in these pages.

Hardfought

by Greg Bear

Greg Bear, winner of two Nebulas for 1983, brings a varied background to his writing. Born in San Diego, California, he has lived in Alaska and the Far East and is once more in southern California. Greg has worked as a part-time lecturer at the San Diego Space Museum and as a technical writer, reflecting his interest in physics, astronomy, and history. His novels include Heigira, Beyond Heaven's River, *and* Strength of Stones. *His short fiction has been collected in* The Wind from a Burning Woman, *published by Arkham House. He and his wife Astrid edit the Science Fiction Writers of America* Forum.

Herewith, Hardfought, *winner of the Nebula for best novella of 1983.*

In the Han Dynasty, historians were appointed by royal edict to write the history of Imperial China. They alone were the arbiters of what would be recorded. Although various emperors tried, none could gain access to the ironbound chest in which each document was placed after it was written. The historians preferred to suffer death rather than betray their trust.

At the end of each reign the box would be opened and the documents published, perhaps to benefit the next emperor. But for these documents, Imperial China, to a large extent, has no history.

The thread survives by whim.

*

Humans called it the medusa. Its long twisted ribbons of gas strayed across fifty parsecs, glowing blue, yellow, and carmine. Its central core was a ghoulish green flecked with watery black. Half a dozen protostars circled in the core,

10

and as many more dim conglomerates pooled in dimples in the nebula's magnetic field. The Medusa was a huge womb of stars—and disputed territory.

Whenever Prufrax looked at it in displays or through the ship's ports, it seemed malevolent, like a zealous mother showing an ominous face to protect her children. Prufrax had never had a mother, but she had seen them in some of the fibs.

At five, Prufrax was old enough to know the *Mellangee's* mission and her role in it. She had already been through four ship-years of indoctrination. Until her first battle she would be educated in both the Know and the Tell. She would be exercised and trained in the Mocks; in sleep she would dream of penetrating the huge red-and-white Senexi seedships and finding the brood mind. "Zap, Zap," she went with her lips, silent so the tellman wouldn't think her thoughts were straying.

The tellman peered at her from his position in the center of the spherical classroom. Her mates stared straight at the center, all focusing somewhere around the tellman's spiderlike teaching desk, waiting for the trouble, some fidgeting. "How many branch individuals in the Senexi brood mind?" he asked. He looked around the classroom. Peered face by face. Focused on her again. "Pru?"

"Five," she said. Her arms ached. She had been pumped full of moans the wake before. She was already three meters tall, in elfstate, with her long, thin limbs not nearly adequately fleshed out and her fingers still crisscrossed with the surgery done to adapt them to the gloves.

"What will you find in the brood mind?" the tellman pursued, his impassive face stretched across a hammerhead as wide as his shoulders. Some of the fems thought tellmen were attractive. Not many—and Pru was not one of them.

"Yoke," she said.

"What is in the brood-mind yoke?"

"Fibs."

"More specifically? And it really isn't all fib, you know."

"Info. Senexi data."

"What will you do?"

"Zap," she said smiling.

"Why, Pru?"

"Yoke has team gens-memory. Zap yoke, spill the life of the team's five branch inds."

"Zap the brood, Pru?"

"No," she said solemnly. That was a new instruction, only in effect since her class's inception. "Hold the brood for the supreme overs." The tellman did not say what would be done with the Senexi broods. That was not her concern.

"Fine," said the tellman. "You tell well, for someone who's always half-journeying."

Brainwalk, Prufrax thought to herself. Tellman was fancy with the words, but to Pru, what she was prone to do during Tell was brainwalk, seeking out her future. She was already five, soon six. Old. Some saw Senexi by the time they were four.

"Zap, Zap," she went with her lips.

Aryz skidded through the thin layer of liquid ammonia on his broadest pod, considering his new assignment. He knew the Medusa by another name, one that conveyed all the time and effort the Senexi had invested in it. The protostar nebula held few mysteries for him. He and his four branch-mates, who along with the all-important brood mind comprised one of the six teams aboard the seedship, had patrolled the nebula for ninety-three orbits, each orbit—including the timeless periods outside status geometry—taking some one hundred and thirty human years. They had woven in and out of the tendrils of gas, charting the infalling masses and exploring the rocky accretion disks of stars entering the main sequence. With each measure and update, the brood minds refined their view of the nebula as it would be a hundred generations hence when the Senexi plan would finally mature.

The Senexi were nearly as old as the galaxy. They had achieved spaceflight during the time of the starglobe when the galaxy had been a sphere. They had not been a quick or brilliant race. Each great achievement had taken thousands of generations, and not just because of their material handicaps. In those times elements heavier than helium had been rare, found only around stars that had greedily absorbed huge amounts of primeval hydrogen, burned fierce and blue and exploded early, permeating the ill-defined galactic arms with carbon and nitrogen, lithium and oxygen. Elements heavier than iron had been almost nonexistent. The biologies of cold gas-giant worlds had developed with a much smaller palette of chemical combinations in producing the offspring of the primary Population II stars.

Aryz, even with the limited perspective of a branch ind, was aware that, on the whole, the humans opposing the seedship were more adaptable, more vital. But they were not more experienced. The Senexi with their billions of years had often matched them. And Aryz's perspective was expanding with each day of his new assignment.

In the early generations of the struggle, Senexi mental stasis and cultural inflexibility had made them avoid contact with the Population I species. They had never begun a program of extermination of the younger, newly life-forming worlds; the task would have been monumental and probably useless. So when spacefaring cultures developed, the Senexi had retreated, falling back into the redoubts of old stars even before engaging with the new kinds. They had retreated for three generations, about thirty thousand human years, raising their broods on cold nestworlds around red dwarfs, conserving, holding back for the inevitable conflicts.

As the Senexi had anticipated, the younger Population I races had found need of even the aging groves of the galaxy's first stars. They had moved in savagely, voraciously, with all the strength and mutability of organisms evolved from a richer soup of elements. Biology had, in some ways, evolved in its own right and superseded the Senexi.

Aryz raised the upper globe of his body, with its five silicate eyes arranged in a cross along the forward surface. He had memory of those times, and times long before, though his team hadn't existed then. The brood mind carried memories selected from the total store of nearly twelve billion years' experience; an awesome amount of knowledge, even to a Senexi. He pushed himself foward with his rear pods.

Through the brood mind Aryz could share the memories of a hundred thousand past generations, yet the brood mind itself was younger than its branch individuals. For a time in their youth, in their liquid-dwelling larval form, the branch inds carried their own sacs of data, each a fragment of the total necessary for complete memory. The branch inds swam through ammonia seas and wafted through thick warm gaseous zones, protoplasmic blobs three to four meters in diameter, developing their personalities under the weight of the past—and not even a complete past. No wonder they were inflexible, Aryz thought. Most branch inds were aware enough to see that—especially when they were allowed to compare histories with the Population I species, as he was doing—but there was nothing to be done. They were content the way they were. To change would be unspeakably repugnant. Extinction was preferable . . . almost.

But now they were pressed hard. The brood mind had begun a number of experiments. Aryz's team had been selected from the seedship's contingent to oversee the experiments, and Aryz had been chosen as the chief investigator. Two orbits past, they had captured six human embryos in a breeding device, as well as a highly coveted memory storage center. Most Senexi engagements had been with humans for the past three or four generations. Just as the Senexi dominated Population II species, humans were ascendant among their kind.

Experiments with the human embryos had already been conducted. Some had been allowed to develop normally; others had been tampered with, for reasons Aryz was not aware of. The tamperings had not been very successful.

The newer experiments, Aryz suspected, were going to take a different direction, and the seedship's actions now focused on him; he believed he would be given complete authority over the human shapes. Most branch inds would have dissipated under such a burden, but not Aryz. He found the human shapes rather interesting, in their own horrible way. They might, after all, be the key to Senexi survival.

The moans were toughening her elfstate. She lay in pain for a wake, not daring to close her eyes; her mind was changing and she feared sleep would be the end of her. Her nightmares were not easily separated from life; some, in fact, were sharper.

Too often in sleep she found herself in a Senexi trap, struggling uselessly, being pulled in deeper, her hatred wasted against such power. . . .

When she came out of the rigor, Prufrax was given leave by the subordinate tellman. She took to the *Mellangee*'s greenroads, walking stiffly in the shallow gravity. Her hands itched. Her mind seemed almost empty after the turmoil of the past few wakes. She had never felt so calm and clear. She hated the Senexi double now; once for their innate evil, twice for what they had made her overs put her through to be able to fight them. Logic did not matter. She was calm, assured. She was growing more mature wake by wake. Fight-budding, the tellman called it, hate coming out like bloom, synthesizing the sunlight of his teaching into pure fight.

The greenroads rose temporarily beyond the labyrinth shields and armor of the ship. Simple transparent plastic and steel geodesic surfaces formed a lacework over the gardens, admitting radiation necessary to the vegetation growing along the paths. No machines scooted one forth and inboard here. It was necessary to walk. Walking was luxury and privilege.

Prufrax looked down on the greens to each side of the paths without much comprehension. They were *beautiful.* Yes, one should say that, think that, but what did it mean? Pleasing? She wasn't sure what being pleased meant, outside of thinking Zap. She sniffed a flower that, the signs explained, bloomed only in the light of young stars not yet fusing. They were near such a star now, and the greenroads were shiny black and electric green with the blossoms. Lamps had been set out for other plants unsuited to such darkened conditions. Some technic allowed suns to appear in selected plastic panels when viewed from certain angles. Clever, the technicals.

She much preferred the looks of a technical to a tellman, but she was common in that. Technicals required brainflex, tellmen cargo capacity. Technicals were strong and ran strong machines, like in the adventure fibs, where technicals were often the protags. She wished a technical were on the greenroads with her. The moans had the effect of making her receptive—what she saw, looking in mirrors, was a certain shine in her eyes—but there was no chance of a breeding liaison. She was quite unreproductive in this moment of elfstate. Other kinds of meetings were not unusual.

She looked up and saw a figure at least a hundred meters away, sitting on an allowed patch near the path. She walked casually, gracefully as possible with the stiffness.

Not a technical, she saw soon, but she was not disappointed. Too calm.

"Over," he said as she approached.

"Under," she replied. But not by much—he was probably six or seven ship years old and not easily classifiable.

"Such a fine elfstate," he commented. His hair was black. He was shorter than she, but something in his build reminded her of the glovers. She accepted his compliment with a nod and pointed to a spot near him. He motioned for her to sit, and she did so with a whuff, massaging her knees.

"Moans?" he asked.

"Bad stretch," she said.

"You're a glover." He was looking at the fading scars on her hands.

"Can't tell what you are," she said.

"Noncombat," he said. "Tuner of the mandates."

She knew very little about the mandates, except that law decreed every ship carry one, and few of the crew were ever allowed to peep. "Noncombat, hm?" she mused. She didn't despise him for that; one never felt strong negatives for a crew member. She didn't feel much of anything. Too calm.

"Been working on ours this wake," he said. "Too hard, I guess. Told to walk." Overzealousness in work was considered an erotic trait aboard the *Mellangee*. Still, she didn't feel too receptive toward him.

"Glovers walk after a rough growing," she said.

He nodded. "My name's Clevo."

"Prufrax."

"Combat soon?"

"Hoping. Waiting forever."

"I know. Just been allowed access to the mandate for a half-dozen wakes. All new to me. Very happy."

"Can you talk about it?" she asked. Information about the ship not accessible in certain rates was excellent barter.

"Not sure," he said, frowning. "I've been told caution."

"Well, I'm listening."

He could come from glover stock, she thought, but probably not from technical. He wasn't very muscular, but he wasn't as tall as a glover, or as thin, either.

"If you'll tell me about gloves."

With a smile she held up her hands and wriggled the short, stumpy fingers. "Sure."

The brood mind floated weightless in its tank, held in place by buffered carbon rods. Metal was at a premium aboard the Senexi ships, more out of tradition than actual material limitations. From what Aryz could tell, the Senexi used metals sparingly for the same reason—and he strained to recall the small dribbles of information about the human past he had extracted from the memory store—for the same reason **that the Romans of old Earth regarded farming as the only truly noble occupation—**

Farming being the raising of *plants* for food and raw materials. *Plants* were analogous to the freeth Senexi ate in their larval youth, but the freeth were not green and sedentary.

There was always a certain fascination in stretching his mind to encompass human concepts. He had had so little time to delve deeply—and that was good, of course, for he had been set to answer specific questions, not mire himself in the whole range of human filth.

He floated before the brood mind, all these thoughts coursing through his tissues. He had no central nervous system, no truly differentiated organs except those that dealt with the outside world—limbs, eyes, permea. The brood mind, however, was all central nervous system, a thinly buffered sac of viscous fluids about ten meters wide.

"Have you investigated the human memory device yet?" the brood mind asked.

"I have."

"Is communication with the human shapes possible for us?"

"We have already created interfaces for dealing with their machines. Yes, it seems likely that we can communicate."

"Does it occur to you that in our long war with humans, we have made no attempt to communicate before?"

This was a complicated question. It called for several qualities that Aryz, as a branch ind, wasn't supposed to have. Inquisitiveness, for one. Branch inds did not ask questions. They exhibited initiative only as offshoots of the brood mind.

He found, much to his dismay, that the question had occurred to him. "We have never captured a human memory store before," he said, by way of incomplete answer. "We could not have communicated without such an extensive source of information."

"Yet, as you say, even in the past we have been able to use human machines."

"The problem is vastly more complex."

The brood mind paused. "Do you think the teams have been prohibited from communicating with humans?"

Aryz felt the closest thing to anguish possible for a branch ind. Was he being considered unworthy? Accused of conduct inappropriate to a branch ind? His loyalty to the brood mind was unshakeable. "Yes."

"And what might our reasons be?"

"Avoidance of pollution."

"Correct. We can no more communicate with them and remain untainted than we can walk on their worlds, breathe their atmosphere." Again, silence. Aryz lapsed into a mode of inactivity. When the brood mind re-addressed him, he was instantly aware.

"Do you know how you are different?" it asked.

"I am not . . ." Again, hesitation. Lying to the brood mind was impossible for him. What snared him was semantics, a complication in the radiated signals between them. He had not been aware that he was different; the brood mind's question suggested he might be. But he could not possibly face up to the fact and analyze it all in one short time. He signaled his distress.

"You are useful to the team," the brood mind said. Aryz calmed instantly. His thoughts became sluggish, receptive. There was a possibility of redemption. But how was he different? "You are to attempt communication with the shapes yourself. You will not engage in any discourse with your fellows while you are so involved." He was banned. "And after completion of this mission and transfer of certain facts to me, you will dissipate."

Aryz struggled with the complexity of the orders. "How am I different, worthy of such a commission?"

The surface of the brood mind was as still as an undisturbed pool. The indistinct black smudges that marked its radiating organs circulated slowly within the interior, then returned, one above the other, to focus on him. "You will grow a new branch ind. It will not have your flaws, but, then again, it will not be useful to me should such a situation come a second time. Your dissipation will be a relief, but it will be regretted."

"How am I different?"

"I think you know already," the brood mind said. "When the time comes, you will feed the new branch ind all your memories but those of human contact. If you do not survive to that stage of its growth, you will pick your fellow who will perform that function for you."

A small pinkish spot appeared on the back of Aryz's globe. He floated forward and placed his largest permeum against the brood mind's cool surface. The key and command were passed, and his body became capable of reproduction. Then the signal of dismissal was given. He left the chamber.

Flowing through the thin stream of liquid ammonia lining the corridor, he felt ambiguously stimulated. His was a position of privilege and anathema. He had been blessed—and condemned. Had any other branch ind experienced such a thing?

Then he knew the brood mind was correct. He was different from his fellows. None of them would have asked such questions. None of them could have survived the suggestion of communicating with human shapes. If this task hadn't been given to him, he would have had to dissipate anyway.

The pink spot grew larger, then began to make greyish flakes. It broke through the skin, and casually, almost without thinking, Aryz scraped it off against a bulkhead. It clung, made a radio-frequency emanation something like a sigh, and began absorbing nutrients from the ammonia.

Aryz went to inspect the shapes.

She was intrigued by Clevo, but the kind of interest she felt was new to her. She was not particularly receptive. Rather, she felt a mental gnawing as if she were hungry or had been injected with some kind of brain moans. What Clevo told her about the mandates opened up a topic she had never considered before. How did all things come to be—and how did she figure in them?

The mandates were quite small, Clevo explained, each little more than a cubic meter in volume. Within them was the entire history and culture of the human species, as accurate as possible, culled from all existing sources. The mandate in each ship was updated whenever the ship returned to a contact station. It was not likely the *Mellangee* would return to a contact station during their lifetimes, with the crew leading such short lives on the average.

Clevo had been assigned small tasks—checking data and adding ship records—that had allowed him to sample bits of the mandate. "It's mandated that we have records," he explained, "and what we have, you see, is *man-data*." He smiled. "That's a joke," he said. "Sort of."

Prufrax nodded solemnly. "So where do we come from?"

"Earth, of course," Clevo said. "Everyone knows that."

"I mean, where do *we* come from—you and I, the crew."

"Breeding division. Why ask? You know."

"Yes." She frowned, concentrating. "I mean, we don't come from the same place as the Senexi. The same way."

"No, that's foolishness."

She saw that it was foolishness—the Senexi were different all around. What was she struggling to ask? "Is their fib like our own?"

"Fib? History's not a fib. Not most of it, anyway. Fibs are for unreal. History is overfib."

She knew, in a vague way, that fibs were unreal. She didn't like to have their comfort demeaned, though. "Fibs are fun," she said. "They teach Zap."

"I suppose," Clevo said dubiously. "Being noncombat, I don't see Zap fibs."

Fibs without Zap were almost unthinkable to her. "Such dull," she said.

"Well, of course you'd say that. I might find Zap fibs dull—think of that?"

"We're different," she said. "Like Senexi are different."

Clevo's jaw hung open. "No way. We're crew. We're human. Senexi are . . ." He shook his head as if fed bitters.

"No, I mean . . ." She paused, uncertain whether she was entering unallowed territory. "You and I, we're fed different, given different moans. But in a big way we're different from Senexi. They aren't made, nor act, as you and I. But . . ." Again it was difficult to express. She was irritated. "I don't want to talk to you anymore."

A tellman walked down the path, not familiar to Prufrax. He held out his hand for Clevo, and Clevo grasped it. "It's amazing," the tellman said, "how you two gravitate to each other. Go, elfstate," he addressed Prufrax. "You're on the wrong greenroad."

She never saw the young researcher again. With glover training under way, the itches he aroused soon faded, and Zap resumed to overplace.

The Senexi had ways of knowing humans were near. As information came in about fleets and individual cruisers less than one percent nebula diameter distant, the seedship seemed warmer, less hospitable. Everything was UV with anxiety, and the new branch ind on the wall had to be shielded by a special silicate cup to prevent distortion. The brood mind grew a corniculum automatically, though the toughened outer membrane would be of little help if the seedship was breached.

Aryz had buried his personal confusion under a load of work. He had penetrated the human memory store deeply enough to find instructions on its use. It called itself a *mandate* (the human word came through the interface as a correlated series of radiated symbols), and even the simple preliminary directions were difficult for Aryz. It was like swimming in another family's private sea, though of course infinitely more alien; how could he connect with experiences never had, problems and needs never encountered by his kind?

He could speak some of the human languages in several radio frequencies, but he hadn't yet decided how he was going to produce modulated sound for the human shapes. It was a disturbing prospect. What would he vibrate? A permeum could vibrate subtly—such signals were used when branch inds joined to form the brood mind—but he doubted his control would ever be subtle enough. Sooner expect a human to communicate with a Senexi by controlling the radiations of its nervous system! The humans had distinct organs within their breathing passages that produced the vibrations; perhaps those structures could be mimicked. But he hadn't yet studied the dead shapes in much detail.

He observed the new branch ind once or twice each watch period. Never before had he seen an induced replacement. The normal process was for two brood minds to exchange plasm and form new team buds, then to exchange and nurture the buds. The buds were later cast free to swim as individual larvae. While the larvae often swam through the liquid and gas atmosphere of a Senexi world for thousands, even tens of thousands of kilometers, inevitably they returned to gather with the other buds of their team. Replacements were selected from a separately created pool of "generic" buds only if one or more originals had been destroyed during their wanderings. The destruction of a complete team meant reproductive failure.

In a mature team, only when a branch ind was destroyed did the brood mind induce a replacement. In essence, then, Aryz was already considered dead.

Yet he was still useful. That amused him, if the Senexi emotion could be called amusement. Restricting himself from his fellows was difficult, but he filled the time by immersing himself, through the interface, in the mandate.

The humans were also connected with the mandate through their surrogate parent, and in this manner they were quiescent.

He reported infrequently to the brood mind. Until he had established communication, there was little to report.

And throughout his turmoil, like the others he could sense a fight was coming. It could determine the success or failure of all their work in the nebula. In the grand scheme, failure here might not be crucial. But the Senexi had taken the long view too often in the past. Their age and experience—their calmness—were working against them. How else to explain the decision to communicate with human shapes? Where would such efforts lead? If he succeeded.

And he knew himself well enough to doubt he would fail.

He could feel an affinity for them already, peering at them through the thick glass wall in their isolated chamber, his skin paling at the thought of their heat, their poisonous chemistry. A diseased affinity. He hated himself for it. And reveled in it. It was what made him particularly useful to the team. If he was defective, and this was the only way he could serve, then so be it.

The other branch inds observed his passings from a distance, making no judgments. Aryz was dead, though he worked and moved. His sacrifice had been fearful. Yet he would not be a hero. His kind could never be emulated.

It was a horrible time, a horrible conflict.

She floated in language, learned it in a trice; there were no distractions. She floated in history and picked up as much as she could, for the source seemed inexhaustible. She tried to distinguish between eyes-open—the barren, pale grey-brown chamber with the thick green wall, beyond which floated a murky roundness—and eyes-shut, when she dropped back into language and history with no fixed foundation.

Eyes-open, she saw the Mam with its comforting limbs and its soft voice, its tubes and extrusions of food and its hissings and removal of waste. Through Mam's wires she learned. Mam also tended another like herself, and another, and one more unlike any of them, more like the shape beyond the green wall.

She was very young, and it was all a mystery.

At least she knew her name. And what she was supposed to do. She took small comfort in that.

They fitted Prufrax with her gloves, and she went into the practice chamber, dragged by her gloves almost, for she hadn't yet knitted her plug-in nerves in the right index digit and her pace control was uncertain.

There, for six wakes straight, she flew with the other glovers back and forth across the dark spaces like elfstate comets. Constellations and nebula aspects flashed at random on the distant walls, and she oriented to them like a night-flying bird. Her glovemates were Ornin, an especially slender male, and Ban, a red-haired female, and the special-projects sisters Ya, Trice, and Damu, new from the breeding division.

When she let the gloves have their way, she was freer than she had ever felt before. Did the gloves really control? The question wasn't important. Control was somewhere uncentered, behind her eyes and beyond her fingers, as if she were drawn on a beautiful silver wire where it was best to go. Doing what was best to go. She barely saw the field that flowed from the grip of the thick, solid gloves or felt its caressing, life-sustaining influence. Truly, she hardly saw or felt anything but situations, targets, opportunities, the success or failure of the Zap. Failure was an acute pain. She was never reprimanded for failure; the reprimand was in her blood, and she felt like she wanted to die. But then the opportunity would improve, the Zap would succeed, and everything around her—stars, Senexi seedship, the *Mellangee,* everything— seemed part of a beautiful dream all her own.

She was intense in the Mocks.

Their initial practice over, the entry play began.

One by one, the special-projects sisters took their hyperbolic formation. Their glove fields threw out extensions, and they combined force. In they went, the mock Senexi seedship brilliant red and white and UV and radio and hateful before them. Their tails swept through the seedship's outer shields and swirled like long silky hair laid on water; they absorbed fantastic energies, grew bright like violent little stars against the seedship outline. They were engaged in the drawing of the shields, and sure as topology, the spirals of force had to have a dimple on the opposite side that would iris wide enough to let in glovers. The sisters twisted the forces, and Prufrax could see the dimple stretching out under them—

The exercise ended. The elfstate glovers were cast into sudden dark. Prufrax came out of the mock unprepared, her mind still bent on the Zap. The lack of orientation drove her as mad as a moth suddenly flipped from night to day. She careened until gently mitted and channeled. She flowed down a tube, the field slowly neutralizing, and came to a halt still gloved, her body jerking and tingling.

"What the breed happened?" she screamed, her hands beginning to hurt.

"Energy conserve," a mechanical voice answered. Behind Prufrax the other elfstate glovers lined up in the catch tube, all but the special-projects sisters. Ya, Trice, and Damu had been taken out of the exercise early and replaced by simulations. There was no way their functions could be mocked. They entered the tube ungloved and helped their comrades adjust to the overness of the real.

As they left the mock chamber, another batch of glovers, even younger and fresher in elfstate, passed them. Ya held her hands up, and they saluted in return. "Breed more every day," Prufrax grumbled. She worried about having so many crew she'd never be able to conduct a satisfactory Zap herself. Where would the honor of being a glover go if everyone was a glover?

She wriggled into her cramped bunk, feeling exhilarated and irritated. She replayed the Mocks and added in the missing Zap, then stared gloomily at her small narrow feet.

Out there the Senexi waited. Perhaps they were in the same state as she—ready to fight, testy at being reined in. She pondered her ignorance, her inability to judge whether such things were even possible among the enemy.

She thought of the researcher, Clevo. "Blank," she murmured. "Blank, blank." Such thoughts were unnecessary, and humanizing Senexi was unworthy of a glover.

Aryz looked at the instrument, stretched a pod into it, and willed. Vocal human language came out the other end, thin and squeaky in the helium atmosphere. The sound disgusted and thrilled him. He removed the instrument from the gelatinous strands of the engineering wall and pushed it into his interior through a stretched permeum. He took a thick draft of ammonia and slid to the human shapes chamber again.

He pushed through the narrow port into the observation room. Adjusting his eyes to the heat and bright light beyond the transparent wall, he saw the round mutated shape first—the result of their unsuccessful experiments. He swung his sphere around and looked at the others.

For a time he couldn't decide which was uglier—the mutated shape or the normals. Then he thought of what it would be like to have humans tamper with Senexi and try to make them into human forms. . . . He looked at the round human and shrunk as if from sudden heat. Aryz had had nothing to do with the experiments. For that, at least, he was grateful.

Apparently, even before fertilization, human buds—eggs—were adapted for specific roles. The healthy human shapes appeared sufficiently different—discounting *sexual* characteristics—to indicate some variation in function. They were four-podded, two-opticked, with auditory apparatus and olfactory organs mounted on the *head,* along with one permeum, the *mouth.* At least, he thought, they were hairless, unlike some of the other Population I species Aryz had learned about in the mandate.

Aryz placed the tip of the vocalizer against a sound-transmitting plate and spoke.

"Zello," came the sound within the chamber. The

mutated shape looked up. It lay on the floor, great bloated stomach backed by four almost useless pods. It usually made high-pitched sounds continuously. Now it stopped and listened, straining on the tube that connected it to the breed-supervising device.

"Hello," replied the male. It sat on a ledge across the chamber, having unhooked itself.

The machine that served as surrogate parent and instructor stood in one corner, an awkward parody of a human, with limbs too long and head too small. Aryz could see the unwillingness of the designing engineers to examine human anatomy too closely.

"I am called—" Aryz said, his name emerging as a meaningless stretch of white noise. He would have to do better than that. He compressed and adapted the frequencies. "I am called Aryz."

"Hello," the young female said.

"What are your names?" He knew that well enough, having listened many times to their conversations.

"Prufrax," the female said. "I'm a glover."

The human shapes contained very little genetic memory. As a kind of brood marker, Aryz supposed they had been equipped with their name, occupation, and the rudiments of environmental knowledge. This seemed to have been artificially imposed; in their natural state, very likely, they were born almost blank. He could not, however, be certain, since human reproductive chemistry was extaordinarily subtle and complicated.

"I'm a teacher, Prufrax," Aryz said. The logic structure of the language continued to be painful to him.

"I don't understand you," the female replied.

"You teach me, I teach you."

"We have the Mam," the male said, pointing to the machine. "She teaches us." The Mam, as they called it, was hooked into the mandate. Withholding that from the humans—the only equivalent, in essence, to the Senexi sac

of memory—would have been unthinkable. It was bad
enough that humans didn't come naturally equipped with
their own share of knowledge.

"Do you know where you are?" Aryz asked.

"Where we live," Prufrax said. "Eyes-open."

Aryz opened a port to show them the stars and a portion
of the nebula. "Can you tell where you are by looking out
the window?"

"Among the lights," Prufrax said.

Humans, then, did not instinctively know their positions
by star patterns as other Population I series did.

"Don't talk to it," the male said. "Mam talks to us." Aryz
consulted the mandate for some understanding of the
name they had given to the breed-supervising machine.
Mam, it explained, was probably a natural expression for
womb-carrying parent. Aryz severed the machine's power.

"Mam is no longer functional," he said. He would have
the engineering wall put together another less identifiable
machine to link them to the mandate and to their nutrition. He wanted them to associate comfort and com-
pleteness with nothing but himself.

The machine slumped, and the female shape pulled
herself free of the hookup. She started to cry, a reaction
quite mysterious to Aryz. His link with the mandate had
not been intimate enough to answer questions about the
wailing and moisture from the eyes. After a time the male
and female lay down and became dormant.

The mutated shape made more soft sounds and tried to
approach the transparent wall. It held up its thin arms as if
beseeching. The others would have nothing to do with it;
now it wished to go with him. Perhaps the biologists had
partially succeeded in their attempt at transformation;
perhaps it was more Senexi than human.

Aryz quickly backed out through the port, into the cool
and security of the corridor beyond.

*   *   *

It was an endless orbital dance, this detection and matching of course, moving away and swinging back, deceiving and revealing, between the *Mellangee* and the Senexi seedship. It was inevitable that the human ships should close in; human ships were faster, knew better the higher geometries.

Filled with her skill and knowledge, Prufrax waited, feeling like a ripe fruit about to fall from the tree. At this point in their training, just before the application, elfstates were very receptive. She was allowed to take a lover, and they were assigned small separate quarters near the outer greenroads.

The contact was satisfactory, as far as it went. Her mate was an older glover named Kumnax, and as they lay back in the cubicle, soothed by air-dance fibs, he told her stories about past battles, special tactics, how to survive.

"Survive?" she asked puzzled.

"Of course." His long brown face was intent on the view of the greenroads through the cubicle's small window.

"I don't understand," she said.

"Most glovers don't make it," he said patiently.

"I will."

He turned to her. "You're six," he said. "You're very young. I'm ten. I've seen. You're about to be applied for the first time, you're full of confidence. But most glovers won't make it. They breed thousands of us. We're expendable. We're based on the best glovers of the past, but even the best don't survive."

"I will," Prufrax repeated, her jaw set.

"You always say that," he murmured.

Prufrax stared at him for a moment.

"Last time I knew you," he said, "you kept saying that. And here you are, fresh again."

"What last time?"

"Master Kumnax," a mechanical voice interrupted.

He stood, looking down at her. "We glovers always have

big mouths. They don't like us knowing, but once we know, what can they do about it?"

"You are in violation," the voice said. "Please report to **S.**"

"But now, if you last, you'll know more than the tellman tells."

"I don't understand," Prufrax said slowly, precisely, looking him straight in the eye.

"I've paid my debt," Kumnax said. "We glovers stick. Now I'm going to get my punishment." He left the cubicle. Prufrax didn't see him again before her first application.

The seedship buried itself in a heating protostar, raising shields against the infalling ice and stone. The nebula had congealed out of a particularly rich cluster of exploded fourth- and fifth-generation stars, thick with planets, the detritus of which now fell on Aryz's ship like hail.

Aryz had never been so isolated. No other branch ind addressed him; he never even saw them now. He made his reports to the brood mind, but even there the reception was warmer and warmer, until he could barely endure to communicate. Consequently—and he realized this was part of the plan—he came closer to his charges, the human shapes. He felt more sympathy for them. He discovered that even between human and Senexi there could be a bridge of need—the need to be useful.

The brood mind was interested in one question: how successfully could they be planted aboard a human ship? Would they be accepted until they could carry out their sabotage, or would they be detected? Already Senexi instructions were being coded into their teachings.

"I think they will be accepted in the confusion of an engagement," Aryz answered. He had long since guessed the general outlines of the brood mind's plans. Communication with the human shapes was for one purpose only; to use them as decoys, insurgents. They were weapons.

Knowledge of human activity and behavior was not an end in itself; seeing what was happening to him, Aryz fully understood why the brood mind wanted such study to proceed no further.

He would lose them soon, he thought, and his work would be over. He would be much too human-tainted. He would end, and his replacement would start a new existence, very little different from Aryz—but, he reasoned, adjusted. The replacement would not have Aryz's peculiarity.

He approached his last meeting with the brood mind, preparing himself for his final work, for the ending. In the cold liquid-filled chamber, the great red-and-white sac waited, the center of his team, his existence. He adored it. There was no way he could criticize its action.

Yet—

"We are being sought," the brood mind radiated. "Are the shapes ready?"

"Yes," Aryz said. "The new teaching is firm. They believe they are fully human." And, except for the new teaching, they were. "They defy sometimes." He said nothing about the mutated shape. It would not be used. If they won this encounter, it would probably be placed with Aryz's body in a fusion torch for complete purging.

"Then prepare them," the brood mind said. "They will be delivered to the vector for positioning and transfer."

Darkness and waiting. Prufrax nested in her delivery tube like a freshly chambered round. Through her gloves she caught distant communications murmurs that resembled voices down hollow pipes. The *Mellangee* was coming to full readiness.

Huge as her ship was, Prufrax knew that it would be dwarfed by the seedship. She could recall some hazy details about the seedship's structure, but most of that information was stored securely away from interference by her conscious mind. She wasn't even positive what the tactic would be. In the Mocks, that at least had been clear. Now such information either had not been delivered or had waited in inaccessible memory, to be brought forward by the appropriate triggers.

More information would be fed to her just before the launch, but she knew the general procedure. The seedship was deep in a protostar, hiding behind the distortion of geometry and the complete hash of electromagnetic energy. The *Mellangee* would approach, collide if need be. Penetrate. Release. Find. Zap. Her fingers ached. Sometime before the launch she would also be fed her final moans—the tempers—and she would be primed to leave elfstate. She would be a mature glover. She would be a woman.

If she returned

will return

she could become part of the breed, her receptivity would end in ecstasy rather than mild warmth, she would contribute second state, naturally born glovers. For a moment she was content with the thought. That was a high honor.

Her fingers ached worse.

The tempers came, moans tiding in, then the battle data. As it passed into her subconscious, she caught a flash of—

Rocks and ice, a thick cloud of dust and gas glowing red but seeming dark, no stars, no constellation guides this time. The beacon came on. That would be her only way to orient once the gloves stopped inertial and locked onto the target.

The seedship
was like
a shadow within a shadow
twenty-two kilometers across, yet
carrying
only six

teams

LAUNCH *She flies!*

Data: the *Mellangee* has buried herself in the seedship, ploughed deep into the interior like a carnivore's muzzle looking for vitals.

Instruction: a swarm of seeks is dashing through the seedship, looking for the brood minds, for the brood chambers, for branch inds. The glovers will follow.

Prufrax sees herself clearly now. She is the great avenging comet, bringer of omen and doom, like a knife moving through the glass and ice and thin, cold helium as if they weren't there, the chambered round fired and tearing at hundreds of kilometers an hour through the Senexi vessel, following the seeks.

The seedship cannot withdraw into higher geometries now. It is pinned by the *Mellangee*. It is hers.

Information floods her, pleases her immensely. She swoops down orange-and-grey corridors, buffeting against the walls like a ricocheting bullet. Almost immediately she comes across a branch ind, sliding through the ammonia film against the outrushing wind, trying to reach an armored cubicle. Her first Zap is too easy, not satisfying, nothing like what she thought. In her wake the branch ind becomes scattered globules of plasma. She plunges deeper.

Aryz delivers his human charges to the vectors that will launch them. They are equipped with simulations of the human weapons, their hands encased in the hideous grey gloves.

The seedship is in deadly peril; the battle has almost been lost at one stroke. The seedship cannot remain whole. It must self-destruct, taking the human ship with it, leaving only a fragment with as many teams as can escape.

The vectors launch the human shapes. Aryz tries to determine which part of the ship will be elected to survive; he must not be there. His job is over, and he must die.

The glovers fan out through the seedship's central hollow, demolishing the great cold drive engines, bypassing the shielded fusion flare and the reprocessing plant, destroying machinery built before their Earth was formed.

The special-projects sisters take the lead. Suddenly they are confused. They have found a brood mind, but it is not heavily protected. They surround it, prepare for the Zap—

It is sacrificing itself, drawing them in to an easy kill and away from another portion of the seedship. Power is concentrating elsewhere. Sensing that, they kill quickly and move on.

Aryz's brood mind prepares for escape. It begins to wrap itself in flux bind as it moves through the ship toward the frozen fragment. Already three of its five branch inds are dead; it can feel other brood minds dying. Aryz's bud replacement has been killed as well.

Following Aryz's training, the human shapes rush into corridors away from the main action. The special-projects sisters encounter the decoy male, allow it to fly with them . . . until it aims its weapons. One Zap almost takes out Trice. The others fire on the shape immediately. He goes to his death weeping, confused from the very moment of his launch.

The fragment in which the brood mind will take refuge encompasses the chamber where the humans had been nurtured, where the mandate is still stored. All the other brood minds are dead, Aryz realizes; the humans have swept down on them so quickly. What shall he do?

Somewhere, far off, he feels the distressed pulse of another branch ind dying. He probes the remains of the seedship. He is the last. He cannot dissipate now; he must ensure the brood mind's survival.

Prufrax, darting through the crumbling seedship, searching for more opportunities, comes across an injured glover. She calls for a mediseek and pushes on.

The brood mind settles into the fragment. Its support system is damaged; it is entering the time-isolated state, the flux bind, more rapidly than it should. The seals of foamed electric ice cannot quite close off the fragment before Ya, Trice, and Damu slip in. They frantically call for bind-cutters and preservers; they have instructions to capture the last brood mind, if possible.

But a trap falls upon Ya, and snarling fields tear her from her gloves. She is flung down a dark disintegrating shaft, red cracks opening all around as the seedship's integrity fails. She trails silver dust and freezes, hits a barricade, shatters.

The ice seals continue to close. Trice is caught between them and pushes out frantically, blundering into the region of the intensifying flux bind. Her gloves break into hard bits, and she is melded into an ice wall like an insect trapped on the surface of a winter lake.

Damu sees that the brood mind is entering the final phase of flux bind. After that they will not be able to touch it. She begins a desperate Zap

and is too late.

Aryz directs the subsidiary energy of the flux against her. Her Zap deflects from the bind region, she is caught in an interference pattern and vibrates until her tiniest particles stop their knotted whirlpool spins and she simply becomes

space and searing light.

The brood mind, however, has been damaged. It is losing information from one portion of its anatomy. Desperate for storage, it looks for places to hold the information before the flux bind's last wave.

Aryz directs an interface onto the brood mind's surface. The silvery pools of time-binding flicker around them both. The brood mind's damaged sections transfer their data into the last available storage device—the human mandate.

Now it contains both human and Senexi information.

The silvery pools unite, and Aryz backs away. No longer can he sense the brood mind. It is out of reach but not yet safe. He must propel the fragment from the remains of the seedship. Then he must wrap the fragment in its own flux bind, cocoon it in physics to protect it from the last ravages of the humans.

Aryz carefully navigates his way through the few remaining corridors. The helium atmosphere has almost completely dissipated, even there. He strains to remember all the procedures. Soon the seedship will explode, destroying the human ship. By then they must be gone.

Angry red, Prufrax follows his barely sensed form, watching him behind barricades of ice, approaching the moment of a most satisfying Zap. She gives her gloves their way

and finds a shape behind her, wearing gloves that are not gloves, not like her own, but capable of grasping her in tensed fields, blocking the Zap, dragging them together. The fragment separates, heat pours in from the protostar cloud. They are swirled in their vortex of power, twin locked comets—one red, one sullen grey.

"Who are you?" Prufrax screams as they close in on each other in the fields. Their environments meld. They grapple. In the confusion, the darkening, they are drawn out of the cloud with the fragment, and she sees the other's face.

Her own.

The seedship self-destructs. The fragment is propelled from the protostar, above the plane of what will become planets in their orbits, away from the crippled and dying *Mellangee.*

Desperate, Prufrax uses all her strength to drill into the fragment. Helium blows past them, and bits of dead branch inds.

Aryz catches the pair immediately in the shapes chamber, rearranging the fragment's structure to enclose them with the mutant shape and mandate. For the moment he has time enough to concentrate on them. They are dangerous. They are almost equal to each other, but his shape is weakening faster than the true glover. They float, bouncing from wall to wall in the chamber, forcing the mutant to crawl into a corner and howl with fear.

There may be value in saving the one and capturing the other. Involved as they are, the two can be carefully dissected from their fields and induced into a crude kind of sleep before the glover has a chance to free her weapons. He can dispose of the gloves—fake and real—and hook them both to the Mam, reattach the mutant shape as well. Perhaps something can be learned from the failure of the experiment.

The dissection and capture occur faster than the planning. His movement slows under the spreading flux bind. His last action, after attaching the humans to the Mam, is to make sure the brood mind's flux bind is properly nested within that of the ship.

The fragment drops into simpler geometries.

It is as if they never existed.

The battle was over. There were no victors. Aryz became aware of the passage of time, shook away the sluggishness, and crawled through painfully dry corridors to set the environmental equipment going again. Throughout the fragment, machines struggled back to activity.

How many generations? The constellations were unrecognizable. He made star traces and found familiar spectra and types, but advanced in age. There had been a malfunction in the overall flux bind. He couldn't find the nebula where the battle had occurred. In its place were comfortably middle-aged stars surrounded by young planets.

Aryz came down from the makeshift observatory. He

slid through the fragment, established the limits of his new home, and found the solid mirror surface of the brood mind's cocoon. It was still locked in flux bind, and he knew of no way to free it. In time the bind would probably wear off—but that might require life spans. The seedship was gone. They had lost the brood chamber, and with it the stock.

He was the last branch ind of his team. Not that it mattered now; there was nothing he could initiate without a brood mind. If the flux bind was permanent—as sometimes happened during malfunction—then he might as well be dead.

He closed his thoughts around him and was almost completely submerged when he sensed an alarm from the shapes chamber. The interface with the mandate had turned itself off; the new version of the Mam was malfunctioning. He tried to repair the equipment, but without the engineer's wall he was almost helpless. The best he could do was rig a temporary nutrition supply through the old human-form Mam. When he was done, he looked at the captive and the two shapes, then at the legless, armless Mam that served as their link to the interface and life itself.

She had spent her whole life in a room barely eight by ten meters, and not much taller than her own height. With her had been Grayd and the silent round creature whose name—if it had any—they had never learned. For a time there had been Mam, then another kind of Mam not nearly as satisfactory. She was hardly aware that her entire existence had been miserable, cramped, in one way or another incomplete.

Separated from them by a transparent partition, another round shape had periodically made itself known by voice or gesture.

Grayd had kept her sane. They had engaged in conspiracy. Removing themselves from the interface—what she called "eyes-shut"—they had held on to each other, tried to make sense out of what they knew instinctively, what was fed them through the interface, and what the being beyond the partition told them.

First they knew their names, and they knew that they were glovers. They knew that glovers were fighters. When Aryz passed instruction through the interface on how to fight, they had accepted it eagerly but uneasily. It didn't seem to jibe with instructions locked deep within their instincts.

Five years under such conditions had made her introspective. She expected nothing, sought little beyond experience in the eyes-shut. Eyes-open with Grayd seemed scarcely more than a dream. They usually managed to ignore the peculiar round creature in the chamber with them; it spent nearly all its time hooked to the mandate and the Mam.

Of one thing only was she completely sure. Her name was Prufrax. She said it in eyes-open and eyes-shut, her only certainty.

Not long before the battle, she had been in a condition resembling dreamless sleep, like a robot being given instructions. The part of Prufrax that had taken on personality during eyes-shut and eyes-open for five years had been superseded by the fight instructions Aryz had programmed. She had flown as glovers must fly (though the gloves didn't seem quite right). She had fought, grappling (she thought) with herself, but who could be certain of anything?

She had long since decided that reality was not to be sought too avidly. After the battle she fell back into the mandate—into eyes-shut—all too willingly.

And what matter? If eyes-open was even less comprehensible than eyes-shut, why did she have the nagging feeling eyes-open was so compelling, so necessary? She tried to forget.

But a change had come to eyes-shut, too. Before the battle, the information had been selected. Now she could wander through the mandate at will. She seemed to smell the new information, completely unfamiliar, like a whiff of ocean. She hardly knew where to begin. She stumbled across:

—that all vessels will carry one, no matter what their size or class, just as every individual carries the map of a species. The mandate shall contain all the information of our kind, including accurate and uncensored history, for if we have learned anything, it is that censored and untrue accounts distort the eyes of the leaders. Leaders must have access to the truth. It is their responsibility. Whatever is told those who work under the leaders, for whatever reason, must not be believed by the leaders. Unders are told lies. Leaders must seek and be provided with accounts as accurate as possible, or we will be weakened and fall—

What wonderful dreams the leaders must have had. And they possessed some intrinsic gift called *truth,* through the use of the *mandate.* Prufrax could hardly believe that. As she made her tentative explorations through the new fields of eyes-shut, she began to link the word *mandate* with what she experienced. That was where she was.

And she alone. Once, she had explored with Grayd. Now there was no sign of Grayd.

She learned quickly. Soon she walked along a beach on Earth, then a beach on a world called Myriadne, and other beaches, fading in and out. By running through the entries rapidly, she came up with a blurred *eidos* and so learned what a beach was in the abstract. It was a boundary between one kind of eyes-shut and another, between water and land, neither of which had any corollary in eyes-open.

Some beaches had sand. Some had clouds—the *eidos* of clouds was quite attractive. And one—

had herself running scared, screaming.

She called out, but the figure vanished. Prufrax stood on a beach under a greenish-yellow star, on a world called Kyrene, feeling lonelier than ever.

She explored farther, hoping to find Grayd, if not the figure that looked like herself. Grayd wouldn't flee from her. Grayd would—

The round thing confronted her, its helpless limbs twitching. Now it was her turn to run, terrified. Never before had she met the round creature in eyes-shut. It was mobile; it had a purpose. Over land, clouds, trees, rocks, wind, air, equations, and an edge of physics she fled. The farther she went, the more distant from the round one with hands and small head, the less afraid she was.

She never found Grayd.

The memory of the battle was fresh and painful. She remembered the ache of her hands, clumsily removed from the gloves. Her environment had collapsed and been replaced by something indistinct. Prufrax had fallen into a deep slumber and had dreamed.

The dreams were totally unfamiliar to her. If there was a left-turning in her arc of sleep, she dreamed of philosophies and languages and other things she couldn't relate to. A right-turning led to histories and sciences so incomprehensible as to be nightmares.

It was a most unpleasant sleep, and she was not at all sorry to find she wasn't really asleep.

The crucial moment came when she discovered how to slow her turnings and the changes of dream subject. She entered a pleasant place of which she had no knowledge but which did not seem threatening. There was a vast expanse of water, but it didn't terrify her. She couldn't even identify it as water until she scooped up a handful. Beyond the water was a floor of shifting particles. Above both was an open expanse, not black but obviously space, drawing her eyes into intense pale blue-green. And there was that figure she had encountered in the seedship. Herself. The figure pursued. She fled.

Right over the boundary into Senexi information. She knew then that what she was seeing couldn't possibly come from within herself. She was receiving data from another source. Perhaps she had been taken captive. It was possible she was now being forcibly debriefed. The tellman had discussed such possibilities, but none of the glovers had been taught how to defend themselves in specific situations. Instead it had been stated—in terms that brooked no second thought—that self-destruction was the only answer. So she tried to kill herself.

She sat in the freezing cold of a red-and-white room, her feet meeting but not touching a fluid covering on the floor. The information didn't fit her senses—it seemed blurred, inappropriate. Unlike the other data, this didn't allow participation or motion. Everything was locked solid.

She couldn't find an effective means of killing herself. She resolved to close her eyes and simply will herself into dissolution. But closing her eyes only moved her into a deeper or shallower level of deception—other categories, subjects, visions. She couldn't sleep, wasn't tired, couldn't die.

Like a leaf on a stream, she drifted. Her thoughts untangled, and she imagined herself floating on the water called ocean. She kept her eyes open. It was quite by accident that she encountered:

Instruction. Welcome to the introductory use of the mandate. As a noncombat processor, your duties are to maintain the mandate, provide essential information for your overs, and, if necessary, protect or destroy the mandate. The mandate is your immediate over. If it requires

maintenance, you will oblige. Once linked with the mandate, as you are now, you may explore any aspect of the information by requesting delivery. To request delivery, indicate the core of your subject—

Prufrax! she shouted silently. What is Prufrax?

A voice with different tone immediately took over.

Ah, now that's quite a story. I was her biographer, the organizer of her life tapes (ref. GEORGE MACKNAX), and knew her well in the last years of her life. She was born in the Ferment 26468. Here are selected life tapes. Choose emphasis. Analyses follow.

—Hey! Who are you? There's someone here with me. . . .

—Shh! Listen. Look at her. Who is she?

They looked, listened to the information.

—Why, she's *me* . . . sort of.

—She's *us*.

She stood two and a half meters tall. Her hair was black and thick, though cut short; her limbs well-muscled though drawn out by the training and hormonal treatments. She was seventeen years old, one of the few birds born in the solar system, and for the time being she had a chip on her shoulder. Everywhere she went, the birds asked about her mother, Jay-ax. "You better than her?"

Of course not! Who could be? But she was good; the instructors said so. She was just about through training, and whether she graduated to hawk or remained bird she would do her job well. Asking Prufrax about her mother was likely to make her set her mouth tight and glare.

On Mercior, the Grounds took up four thousand hectares and had its own port. The Grounds was divided into Land, Space, and Thought, and training in each area was mandatory for fledges, those birds embarking on hawk training. Prufrax was fledge three. She had passed Land—

Greg Bear
though she loathed downbound fighting—and was two years into Space. The tough part, everyone said, was not passing Space, but lasting through four years of Thought after the action in nearorbit and planetary.

Prufrax was not the introspective type. She could be studious when it suited her. She was a quick study at weapon maths, physics came easy when it had a direct application, but theory of service and polinstruc—which she had sampled only in prebird courses—bored her.

Since she had been a little girl, no more than five—

—Five! Five what?

and had seen her mother's ships and fightsuits and fibs, she had known she would never be happy until she had ventured far out and put a seedship in her sights, had convinced a Senexi of the overness of end—

—The Zap! She's talking the Zap!

—What's that?

—You're me, you should know.

—I'm not you, and we're not her.

The Zap, said the mandate, and the data shifted.

"Tomorrow you receive your first implants. These will allow you to coordinate with the zero-angle phase engines and find your targets much more rapidly than you ever could with simple biologic. The implants, of course, will be delivered through your noses—minor irritation and sinus trouble, no more—into your limbic system. Later in your training, hookups and digital adapts will be installed as well. Are there any questions?"

"Yes, sir." Prufrax stood at the top of the spherical classroom, causing the hawk instructor to swivel his platform. "I'm having problems with the zero-angle phase maths. Reduction of the momenta of the real."

Other fledge threes piped up that they, too, had had trouble with those maths. The hawk instructor sighed. "We don't want to install cheaters in all of you. It's bad enough needing implants to supplement biologic. Individual learn-

ing is much more desirable. Do you request cheaters?"
That was a challenge. They all responded negatively, but
Prufrax had a secret smile. She knew the subject. She just
took delight in having the maths explained again. She
could reinforce an already thorough understanding.
Others not so well versed would benefit. She wasn't wasting time. She was in the pleasure of her weapon—the
weapon she would be using against the Senexi.

"Zero-angle phase is the temporary reduction of the
momenta of the real." Equations and plexes appeared before each student as the instructor went on. "Nested un-
reals can conflict if a barrier is placed between the participator princip and the assumption of the real. The
effectiveness of the participator can be determined by a
convenience model we call the angle of phase. Zero-angle
phase is achieved by an opaque probability field according
to modified Fourier of the separation of real waves. This
can also be caused by the reflection of the beam—an effective counter to zero-angle phase, since the beam is always
compoundable and the compound is always time-reversed.
Here are the true gedanks—"

—Zero-angle phase. She's learning the Zap.

—She hates them a lot, doesn't she?

—The Senexi? They're Senexi.

—I think . . . eyes-open is the world of the Senexi. What
does that mean?

—That we're prisoners. You were caught before me.

—Oh.

The news came as she was in recovery from the implant.
Seedships had violated human space again, dropping
cuckoos on thirty-five worlds. The worlds had been young
colonies, and the cuckoos had wiped out all life, then tried
to reseed with Senexi forms. The overs had reacted by
sterilizing the planet's surfaces. No victory, loss to both
sides. It was as if the Senexi were so malevolent they didn't
care about success, only about destruction.

She hated them. She could imagine nothing worse.

Prufrax was twenty-three. In a year she would be qualified to hawk on a cruiser/raider. She would demonstrate her hatred.

Aryz felt himself slipping into endthought, the mind set that always preceded a branch ind's self-destruction. What was there for him to do? The fragment had survived, but at what cost, to what purpose? Nothing had been accomplished. The nebula had been lost, or he supposed it had. He would likely never know the actual outcome.

He felt a vague irritation at the lack of a spectrum of responses. Without a purpose, a branch ind was nothing more than excess plasm.

He looked in on the captive and the shapes, all hooked to the mandate, and wondered what he would do with them. How would humans react to the situation he was in? More vigorously, probably. They would fight on. They always had. Even without leaders, with no discernible purpose, even in defeat. What gave them such stamina? Were they superior, more deserving? If they were better, then was it right for the Senexi to oppose their triumph?

Aryz drew himself tall and rigid with confusion. He had studied them too long. They had truly infected him. But here at least was a hint of purpose. A question needed to be answered.

He made preparations. There were signs the brood mind's flux bind was not permanent, was in fact unwinding quite rapidly. When it emerged, Aryz would present it with a judgment, an answer.

He realized, none too clearly, that by Senexi standards he was now a raving lunatic.

He would hook himself into the mandate, improve the somewhat isolating interface he had used previously to search for selected answers. He, the captive, and the shapes would be immersed in human history together.

They would be like young suckling on a Population I mother-animal—just the opposite of the Senexi process, where young fed nourishment and information into the brood mind.

The mandate would nourish, or poison. Or both.

—Did she love?
—What—you mean, did she receive?
—No, did she—we—I—give?
—I don't know what you mean.
— wonder if *she* would know what I mean. . . .

Love, said the mandate, and the data proceeded.

Prufrax was twenty-nine. She had been assigned to a cruiser in a new program where superior but untested fighters were put into thick action with no preliminary. The program was designed to see how well the Grounds prepared fighters; some thought it foolhardy, but Prufrax found it perfectly satisfactory.

The cruiser was a million-ton raider, with a hawk contingent of fifty-three and eighty regular crew. She would be used in a second-wave attack, following the initial hardfought.

She was scared. That was good; fright improved basic biologic, if properly managed. The cruiser would make a raid into Senexi space and retaliate for past cuckooseeding programs. They would come up against thornships and seedships, likely.

The fighting was going to be fierce.

The raider made its final denial of the overness of the real and pip-squeezed into an arduous, nasty sponge space. It drew itself together again and emerged far above the galactic plane.

Prufrax sat in the hawks wardroom and looked at the simulated rotating snowball of stars. Red-coded numerals flashed along the borders of known Senexi territory, signifying old stars, dark hulks of stars, the whole ghostly home region where they had first come to power when the terrestrial sun had been a mist-wrapped youngster. A green arrow showed the position of the raider.

She drank sponge-space supplements with the others but felt isolated because of her firstness, her fear. Everyone seemed so calm. Most were fours or fives—on their fourth or fifth battle call. There were ten ones and an upper scatter of experienced hawks with nine to twenty-five battles behind them. There were no thirties. Thirties were rare in combat; the few that survived so many engagements were plucked off active and retired to PR service under the polinstructors. They often ended up in fibs, acting poorly, looking unhappy.

Still, when she had been more naive, Prufrax's heros had been a man-and-woman thirty team she had watched in fib after fib—Kumnax and Arol. They had been better actors than most.

Day in, day out, they drilled in their fightsuits. While the crew bustled, hawks were put through implant learning, what slang was already calling the Know, as opposed to the Tell, of classroom teaching. Getting background, just enough to tickle her curiosity, not enough to stimulate morbid interest.

—There it is again. Feel?

—I know it. Yes. The round one, part of eyes-open . . .

—Senexi?

—No, brother without name.

—Your . . . brother?

—No . . . I don't know.

—Can it hurt us?

—It never has. It's trying to talk to us.

Leave us alone!

—It's going.

Still, there were items of information she had never received before, items privileged only to the fighters, to assist them in their work. Older hawks talked about the past, when data had been freely available. Stories circulated in the wardroom about the Senexi, and she managed to piece together something of their origins and growth.

Senexi worlds, according to a twenty, had originally been large, cold masses of gas circling bright young suns nearly metal-free. Their gas-giant planets had orbited the suns at hundreds of millions of kilometers and had been dusted by the shrouds of neighboring dead stars; the essential elements carbon, nitrogen, silicon, and fluorine had gathered in sufficient quantities on some of the planets to allow Population II biology.

In cold ammonia seas, lipids had combined in complex chains. A primal kind of life had arisen and flourished. Across millions of years, early Senexi forms had evolved. Compared with evolution on earth, the process at first had moved quite rapidly. The mechanisms of procreation and evolution had been complex in action, simple in chemistry.

There had been no competition between life forms of different genetic bases. On Earth, much time had been spent selecting between the plethora of possible ways to pass on genetic knowledge.

And among the early Senexi, outside of predation there had been no death. Death had come about much later, self-imposed for social reasons. Huge colonies of protoplasmic individuals had gradually resolved into the team-forms now familiar.

Soon information was transferred through the budding of branch inds; cultures quickly developed to protect the integrity of larvae, to allow them to regroup and form a new brood mind. Technologies had been limited to the rare heavy materials available, but the Senexi had expanded for a time with very little technology. They were well adapted to their environment, with few predators and no need to hunt, absorbing stray nutrients from the atmosphere and from layers of liquid ammonia. With perceptions attuned to the radio and microwave frequencies, they had before long turned groups of branch inds into radio telescope chains, piercing the heavy atmosphere and probing the universe in great detail, especially the very active center of the young galaxy. Huge jets of matter, streaming from other galaxies and emitting high-energy radiation, had provided laboratories for their vicarious observations. Physics was a primitive science to them.

Since little or no knowledge was lost in breeding cycles, cultural growth was rapid at times; since the dead weight of knowledge was often heavy, cultural growth often slowed to a crawl.

Using water as a building material, developing techniques that humans still understood imperfectly, they prepared for travel away from their birthworlds.

Prufrax wondered, as she listened to the older hawks, how humans had come to know all this. Had Senexi been captured and questioned? Was it all theory? Did anyone really know—anyone she could ask?

—She's weak.

—Why weak?

—Some knowledge is best for glovers to ignore. Some questions are best left to the supreme overs.

—Have you thought that in here, you can answer her questions, our questions?

—No. No. Learn about me—us—first.

In the hour before engagement, Prufrax tried to find a place alone. On the raider this wasn't difficult. The ship's size was overwhelming for the number of hawks and crew aboard. There were many areas where she could put on an environs and walk or drift in silence, surrounded by the dark shapes of equipment wrapped in plexerv. There was so much about ship operations she didn't understand, hadn't been taught. Why carry so much excess equipment, weapons—far more than they'd need even for replacements? She could think of possibilities—superiors on Mercior wanting their cruisers to have flexible mission capabilities, for one—but her ignorance troubled her less than *why* she was ignorant. Why was it necessary to keep fighters in the dark on so many subjects?

She pulled herself through the cold G-less tunnels, feeling slightly awked by the loneness, the quiet. One tunnel angled outboard, toward the hull of the cruiser. She hesitated, peering into its length with her environs beacon, when a beep warned her she was near another crew member. She was startled to think someone else might be as curious as she. The other hawks and crew, for the most part, had long outgrown their need to wander and regarded it as birdish. Prufrax was used to being different— she had always perceived herself, with some pride, as a bit of a freak. She scooted expertly up the tunnel, spreading her arms and tucking her legs as she would in a fightsuit.

The tunnel was filled with a faint milky green mist, absorbing her environs beam. It couldn't be much more than a couple of hundred meters long, however, and it was quite straight. The signal beeped louder.

Ahead she could make out a dismantled weapons blister. That explained the fog: a plexerv aerosol diffused in the low pressure. Sitting in the blister was a man, his environs glowing a pale violet. He had deopaqued a section of the blister and was staring out at the stars. He swiveled as she approached and looked her over dispassionately. He seemed to be a hawk—he had fightform, tall, thin with brown hair above hull-white skin, large eyes with pupils so dark she might have been looking through his head into space beyond.

"Under," she said as their environs met and merged.

"Over. What are you doing here?"

"I was about to ask you the same."

"You should be getting ready for the fight," he admonished.

"I am. I need to be alone for a while."

"Yes." He turned back to the stars. "I used to do that, too."

"You don't fight now?"

He shook his head. "Retired. I'm a researcher."

She tried not to look impressed. Crossing rates was almost impossible. A bitalent was unusual in the service.

"What kind of research?" she asked.

"I'm here to correlate enemy finds."

"Won't find much of anything, after we're done with the zero phase."

It would have been polite for him to say, "Power to that," or offer some other encouragement. He said nothing.

"Why would you want to research them?"

"To fight an enemy properly, you have to know what they are. Ignorance is defeat."

"You research tactics?"

"Not exactly."

"What, then?"

"You'll be in a tough hardfought this wake. Make you a proposition. You fight well, observe, come to me and tell me what you see. Then I'll answer your questions."

"Brief you before my immediate overs?"

"I have the authority," he said. No one had ever lied to her; she didn't even suspect he would. "You're eager?"

"Very."

"You'll be doing what?"

"Engaging Senexi fighters, then hunting down branch inds and brood minds."

"How many fighters going in?"

"Twelve."

"Big target, eh?"

She nodded.

"While you're there, ask yourself—what are they fighting for? Understand?"

"I—"

"Ask, what are they fighting for. Just that. Then come back to me."

"What's your name?"

"Not important," he said. "Now go."

She returned to the prep center as the sponge-space warning tones began. Overhawks went among the fighters in the lineup, checking gear and giveaway body points for mental orientation. Prufrax submitted to the molded sensor mask being slipped over her face. "Ready!" the overhawk said. "Hardfought!" He clapped her on the shoulder. "Good luck."

"Thank you, sir." She bent down and slid into her fightsuit. Along the launch line, eleven other hawks did the same. The overs and other crew left the chamber, and twelve red beams delineated the launch tube. The fightsuits automatically lifted and aligned on their individual beams. Fields swirled around them like silvery tissue in moving water, then settled and hardened into cold scintillating walls, pulsing as the launch energy built up.

The tactic came to her. The ship's sensors became part of her information net. She saw the Senexi thornship— twelve kilometers in diameter, cuckoos lacing its outer hull like maggots on red fruit, snakes waiting to take them on.

She was terrified and exultant, so worked up that her body temperature was climbing. The fightsuit adjusted her balance.

At the count of ten and nine, she switched from biologic to cyber. The implant—after absorbing much of her thought processes for weeks—became Prufrax.

For a time there seemed to be two of her. Biologic continued, and in that region she could even relax a bit, as if watching a fib.

With almost dreamlike slowness, in the electronic time of cyber, her fightsuit followed the beam. She saw the stars and oriented herself to the cruiser's beacon, using both for reference, plunging in the sword-flower formation to as-

sault the thornship. The cuckoos retreated in the vast red
hull like worms withdrawing into an apple. Then hundreds of tiny black pinpoints appeared in the closest quad-
rant to the sword flower.

Snakes shot out, each piloted by a Senexi branch ind.
"Hardfought!" she told herself in biologic before that portion gave over completely to cyber.

Why were we flung out of dark
through ice and fire, a shower
of sparks? a puzzle;
Perhaps to build hell.

We strike here, there;
Set brief glows, fall through
and cross round again.

By our dimming, we see what
Beatitude we have.
In the circle, kindling
together, we form an
exhausted Empyrean.
We feel the rush of
igniting winds but still
grow dull and wan.

New rage flames, new light,
dropping like sun through muddy
ice and night and fall
Close, spinning blue and bright.
In time they, too,
Tire. Redden.
We join, compare pasts
cool in huddled paths,
turn grey.

And again.
We are a companion flow

of ash, in the slurry,
out and down.
We sleep.

Rivers form above and below.
Above, iron snakes twist,
clang and slice, chime,
helium eyes watching, seeing
Snowflake hawks,
signaling adamant muscles and
energy teeth. What hunger
compels our venom spit?

It flies, strikes the crystal
flight, making mist grey-green
with ammonia rain.

Sleeping, we glide,
and to each side
unseen shores wait
with the moans of an unseen tide.

—She wrote that. We. One of her—our poems.
—Poem?
—A kind of fib, I think.
—I don't see what it says.
—Sure you do! She's talking hardfought.
—The Zap? Is that all?
—No, I don't think so.
—Do you understand it?
—Not all . . .

She lay back in the bunk, legs crossed, eyes closed, feeling the receding dominance of the implant—the overness of cyber—and the almost pleasant ache in her back. She had survived her first. The thornship had retired, severely damaged, its surface seared and scored so heavily it would never release cuckoos again.

It would become a hulk, a decoy. Out of action. *Satisfaction / out of action / Satisfaction . . .*

Still, with eight of the twelve fighters lost, she didn't quite feel the exuberance of the rhyme. The snakes had fought very well. Bravely, she might say. They lured, sacrificed, cooperated, demonstrating teamwork as fine as that in her own group. Strategy was what made the cruiser's raid successful. A superior approach, an excellent tactic. And perhaps even surprise, though the final analysis hadn't been posted yet.

Without those advantages, they might have all died.

She opened her eyes and stared at the pattern of blinking lights in the ceiling panel, lights with their secret codes that repeated every second, so that whenever she looked at them, the implant deep inside was debriefed, reinstructed. Only when she fought would she know what she was now seeing.

She returned to the tunnel as quickly as she was able. She floated up toward the blister and found him there, surrounded by packs of information from the last hard-fought. She waited until he turned his attention to her.

"Well?" he said.

"I asked myself what they are fighting for. And I'm very angry."

"Why?"

"Because I don't know. I *can't* know. They're Senexi."

"Did they fight well?"

"We lost eight. Eight." She cleared her throat.

"Did they fight well?" he repeated, an edge in his voice.

"Better than I was ever told they could"

"Did they die?"

"Enough of them."

"How many did you kill?"

"I don't know." But she did. Eight.

"You killed eight," he said, pointing to the packs. "I'm analyzing the battle now."

"You're behind what we read, what gets posted?" she asked.

"Partly," he said. "You're a good hawk."

"I knew I would be," she said, her tone quiet, simple.

"Since they fought bravely—"

"How can Senexi be brave?" she asked sharply.

"Since," he repeated, "they fought bravely, why?"

"They want to live, to do their . . . work. Just like me."

"No," he said. She was confused, moving between extremes in her mind, first resisting, then giving in too much. "They're Senexi. They're not like us."

"What's your name?" she asked, dodging the issue.

"Clevo."

Her glory hadn't even begun yet, and already she was well into her fall.

Aryz made his connection and felt the brood mind's emergency cache of knowledge in the mandate grow up around him like ice crystals on glass. He stood in a static scene. The transition from living memory to human machine memory had resulted in either a coding of data or a reduction of detail; either way, the memory was cold, not dynamic. It would have to be compared, recorrelated, if that would ever be possible.

How much human data had had to be dumped to make space for this?

He cautiously advanced into the human memory, calling up topics almost at random. In the short time he had been away, so much of what he had learned seemed to have faded or become scrambled. Branch inds were supposed to have permanent memory; human data, for one reason or another, didn't take. It required so much effort just to begin to understand the different modes of thought.

He backed away from sociological data, trying to remain within physics and mathematics. There he could make conversions to fit his understanding without too much strain.

Then something unexpected happened. He felt the brush of another mind, a gentle inquiry from a source made even stranger by the hint of familiarity. It made what passed for a Senexi greeting, but not in the proper form, using what one branch ind of a team would radiate to a fellow; a gross breach, since it was obviously not from his team or even from his family. Aryz tried to withdraw. How was it possible for minds to meet in the mandate? As he retreated, he pushed into a broad region of incomprehensible data. It had none of the characteristics of the other human regions he had examined.

—This is for machines, the other said. —Not all cultural data is limited to biologic. You are in the area where programs and cyber designs are stored. They are really accessible only to a machine hooked into the mandate.

—What is your family? Aryz asked, the first step-question in the sequence Senexi used for urgent identity requests.

—I have no family. I am not a branch ind. No access to active brood minds. I have learned from the mandate.

—Then what are you?

—I don't know, exactly. Not unlike you.

Aryz understood what he was dealing with. It was the mind of the mutated shape, the one that had remained in the chamber, beseeching when he approached the transparent barrier.

—I must go now, the shape said. Aryz was alone again in the incomprehensible jumble. He moved slowly, carefully, into the Senexi sector, calling up subjects familiar to him. If he could encounter one shape, doubtless he could encounter the others—perhaps even the captive.

The idea was dreadful—and fascinating. So far as he knew, such intimacy between Senexi and human had never happened before. Yet there was something very Senexi-like in the method, as if branch inds attached to the brood mind were to brush mentalities while searching in the ageless memories.

The dread subsided. There was little worse that could happen to him, with his fellows dead, his brood mind in flux bind, his purpose uncertain.

What Aryz was feeling, for the first time, was a small measure of *freedom*.

The story of the original Prufrax continued.

In the early stages she visited Clevo with a barely concealed anger. His method was aggravating, his goals never precisely spelled out. What did he want with her, if anything?

And she with him? Their meetings were clandestine, though not precisely forbidden. She was a hawk one now with considerable personal liberty between exercises and engagements. There were no monitors in the closed-off reaches of the cruiser, and they could do whatever they wished. The two met in areas close to the ship's hull, usually in weapons blisters that could be opened to reveal the stars; there they talked.

Prufrax was not accustomed to prolonged conversation. Hawks were not raised to be voluble, nor were they selected for their curiosity. Yet the exhawk Clevo talked a great deal and was the most curious person she had met, herself included, and she regarded herself as uncharacteristically curious.

Often he was infuriating, especially when he played the "leading game," as she called it. Leading her from one question to the next, like an instructor, but without the trappings or any clarity of purpose. "What do you think of your mother?"

"Does that matter?"

"Not to me."

"Then why ask?"

"Because you matter."

Prufrax shrugged. "She was a fine mother. She bore me with a well-chosen heritage. She raised me as a hawk candidate. She told me her stories."

"Any hawk I know would envy you for listening at Jayax's knee."

"I was hardly at her knee."

"A speech tactic."

"Yes, well, she was important to me."

"She was a preferred single?"

"Yes."

"So you have no father."

"She selected without reference to individuals."

"Then you are really not that much different from a Senexi."

She bristled and started to push away. "There! You insult me again."

"Not at all. I've been asking one question all this time, and you haven't even heard. How well do you know the enemy?"

"Well enough to destroy them." She couldn't believe that was the only question he'd been asking. His speech tactics were very odd.

"Yes, to win battles, perhaps. But who will win the war?"

"It'll be a long war," she said softly, floating a few meters from him. He rotated in the blister, blocking out a blurred string of stars. The cruiser was preparing to shift out of status geometry again. "They fight well."

"They fight with conviction. Do you believe them to be evil?"

"They destroy us."

"We destroy them."

"So the question," she said, smiling at her cleverness, "is who began to destroy?"

"Not at all," Clevo said. "I suspect there's no longer a clear answer to that. Our leaders have obviously decided the question isn't important. No. We are the new, they are the old. The old must be superseded. It's a conflict born in the essential difference between Senexi and humans."

"That's the only way we're different? They're old, we're not so old? I don't understand."

"Nor do I, entirely."

"Well, finally!"

"The Senexi," Clevo continued, unperturbed, "long ago needed only gas-giant planets like their homeworlds. They lived in peace for billions of years before our world was formed. But as they moved from star to star, they learned uses for other types of worlds. We were most interested in rocky Earth-like planets. Gradually we found uses for gas giants, too. By the time we met, both of us encroached on the other's territory. Their technology is so improbable, so unlike ours, that when we first encountered them we thought they must come from another geometry."

"Where did you learn all this?" Prufrax squinted at him suspiciously.

"I'm no longer a hawk," he said, "but I was too valuable just to discard. My experience was too broad, my abilities too useful. So I was placed in research. It seems a safe place for me. Little contact with my comrades." He looked directly at her. "We must try to know our enemy, at least a little."

"That's dangerous," Prufrax said, almost instinctively.

"Yes, it is. What you know, you cannot hate."

"We must hate," she said. "It makes us strong. Senexi hate."

"They might," he said. "But, sometime, wouldn't you like to . . . sit down and talk with one, after a battle? Talk with a fighter? Learn its tactic, how it bested you in one move, compare—"

"No!" Prufrax shoved off rapidly down the tube. "We're shifting now. We have to get ready."

—She's smart. She's leaving him. He's crazy.

—Why do you think that?

—He would stop the fight, end the Zap.

—But he was a hawk.

—And hawks became glovers, I guess. But glovers go wrong, too. Like you.

—?

—Did you know they used you? How you were used?

—That's all blurred now.

—She's doomed if she stays around him. Who's that?

—Someone is listening with us.

—Recognize?

—No, gone now.

The next battle was bad enough to fall into the hell-fought. Prufrax was in her fightsuit, legs drawn up as if about to kick off. The cruiser exited sponge space and plunged into combat before sponge-space supplements could reach full effectiveness. She was dizzy, disoriented. The overhawks could only hope that a switch from biologic to cyber would cure the problem.

She didn't know what they were attacking. Tactic was flooding the implant, but she was only receiving the wash of that; she hadn't merged yet. She sensed that things were confused. That bothered her. Overs did not feel confusion.

The cruiser was taking damage. She could sense at least that, and she wanted to scream in frustration. Then she was ordered to merge with the implant. Biologic became cyber. She was in the Know.

The cruiser had reintegrated above a gas-giant planet. They were seventy-nine thousand kilometers from the upper atmosphere. The damage had come from ice mines—chunks of Senexi-treated water ice, altered to stay in sponge space until a human vessel integrated nearby. Then they emerged, packed with momentum and all the residual instability of an unsuccessful exit into status geometry. Unsuccessful for a ship, that is—very successful for a weapon.

The ice mines had given up the overness of the real within range of the cruiser and had blasted out whole sections of the hull. The launch lanes had not been damaged. The fighters lined up on their beams and were peppered out into space, spreading in the classic sword flower.

The planet was a cold nest. Over didn't know what the atmosphere contained, but Senexi activity had been high in the star system, concentrating on this world. Over had decided to take a chance. Fighters headed for the atmosphere. The cruiser began planting singularity eggs. The eggs went ahead of the fighters, great black grainy ovoids that seemed to leave a trail of shadow—the wake of a birthing disruption in status geometry that could turn a gas giant into a short-lived sun.

Their time was limited. The fighters would group on entry sleds and descend to the liquid water regions where Senexi commonly kept their upwelling power plants. The fighters would first destroy any plants, look into the liquid ammonia regions to search for hidden cuckoos, then see what was so important about the world.

She and five other fighters mounted the sled. Growing closer, the hazy clear regions of the atmosphere sparkled with Senexi sensors. Spiderweb beams shot from the six sleds to down the sensors. Buffet began. Scream, heat, then a second flower from the sled at a depth of two hundred kilometers. The sled slowed and held station. It would be their only way back. The fightsuits couldn't pull out of such a large gravity well.

She descended deeper. The pale, bloated beacon of the red star was dropping below the second cloudtops, limning the strata in orange and purple. At the liquid ammonia level she was instructed to key in permanent memory of all she was seeing. She wasn't "seeing" much, but other sensors were recording a great deal, all of it duly processed in her implant. "There's life here," she told herself. Indigenous life. Just another example of Senexi disregard for basic decency: they were interfering with a world developing its own complex biology.

The temperature rose to ammonia vapor levels, then to liquid water. The pressure on the fightsuit was enormous, and she was draining her stores much more rapidly than expected. At this level the atmosphere was particularly thick with organics.

Senexi snakes rose from below, passed them in altitude, then doubled back to engage. Prufrax was designated the deep diver; the others from her sled would stay at this level in her defense. As she fell, another sled group moved in behind her to double the cover.

She searched for the chracteristic radiation curve of an upwelling plant. At the lower boundary of the liquid water level, below which her suit could not safely descend, she found it.

The Senexi were tapping the gas giant's convection from greater depths than usual. Above the plant, almost indetectable, was another object with an uncharacteristic curve. They were separated by ten kilometers. The power plant was feeding its higher companion with tight energy beams.

She slowed. Two other fighters, disengaged from the brief skirmish above, took positions as backups a few dozen kilometers higher than she. Her implant searched for an appropriate tactic. She would avoid the zero-angle phase for the moment, go in for reconnaissance. She could feel sound pouring from the plant and its companion—rhythmic, not waste noise, but deliberate. And homing in on that sound were waves of large vermiform organisms, like chains of gas-filled sausage. They were dozens of meters long, two meters at their greatest thickness, shaped vaguely like the Senexi snake fighters. The vermiforms were native, and they were being lured into the uppermost floating structure. None were emerging. Her backups spread apart, descended, and drew up along her flanks.

She made her decision almost immediately. She could see a pattern in the approach of the natives. If she fell into the pattern, she might be able to enter the structure unnoticed.

—It's a grinder. She doesn't recognize it.

—What's a grinder?

—She should make the Zap! It's an ugly thing; Senexi use them all the time. Net a planet with grinders, like a cuckoo, but for larger operations.

The creatures were being passed through separator fields. Their organics fell from the bottom of the construct, raw material for new growth—Senexi growth. Their heavier elements were stored for later harvest.

With Prufrax in their midst, the vermiforms flew into the separator. The interior was hundreds of meters wide, lead-white walls with flat grey machinery floating in a dust haze, full of hollow noise, the distant bleats of vermiforms being slaughtered. Prufrax tried to retreat, but she was caught in a selector field. Her suit bucked and she was whirled violently, then thrown into a repository for examination. She had been screened from the separator; her plan to record, then destroy, the structure had been foiled by an automatic filter.

"Information sufficient." Command logic programmed into the implant before launch was now taking over. "Zero-angle phase both plant and adjunct." She was drifting in the repository, still slightly stunned. Something was fading. Cyber was hissing in and out; the over logic-commands were being scrambled. Her implant was malfunctioning and was returning control to biologic. The selector fields had played havoc with all cyber functions, down to the processors in her weapons.

Cautiously she examined the down systems one by one, determining what she could and could not do. This took as much as thirty seconds—an astronomical time on the implant's scale.

She still could use the phase weapon. If she was judicious and didn't waste her power, she could cut her way out of the repository, maneuver and work with her escorts to destroy both the plant and the separator. By the time they returned to the sleds, her implant might have rerouted itself and made sufficient repairs to handle defense. She had no way of knowing what was waiting for her if—when—she escaped, but that was the least of her concerns for the moment.

She tightened the setting of the phase beam and swung her fightsuit around, knocking a cluster of junk ice and silty phosphorescent dust. She activated the beam. When she had a hole large enough to pass through, she edged the suit forward, beamed through more walls and obstacles, and kicked herself out of the repository into free fall. She swiveled and laid down a pattern of wide-angle beams, at the same time relaying a message on her situation to the escorts.

The escorts were not in sight. The separator was beginning to break up, spraying debris through the almost opaque atmosphere. The rhythmic sound ceased, and the crowds of vermiforms began to disperse.

She stopped her fall and thrust herself several kilometers higher—directly into a formation of Senexi snakes. She had barely enough power to reach the sled, much less fight and turn her beams on the upwelling plant.

Her cyber was still down.

The sled signal was weak. She had no time to calculate its direction from the inertial guidance cyber. Besides, all cyber was unreliable after passing through the separator.

Why do they fight so well? Clevo's question clogged her

thoughts. Cursing, she tried to blank and keep all her faculties available for running the fightsuit. *When evenly matched, you cannot win against your enemy unless you understand them. And if you truly understand, why are you fighting and not talking?* Clevo had never told her that—not in so many words. But it was part of a string of logic all her own.

Be more than an automaton with a narrow range of choices. Never underestimate the enemy. Those were old Grounds dicta, not entirely lost in the new training, but only emphasized by Clevo.

If they fight as well as you, perhaps in some ways they fight-think like you do. Use that.

Isolated, with her power draining rapidly, she had no choice. They might disregard her if she posed no danger. She cut her thrust and went into a diving spin. Clearly she was on her way to a high-pressure grave. They would sense her power levels, perhaps even pick up the lack of field activity if she let her shields drop. She dropped the shields. If they let her fall and didn't try to complete the kill—if they concentrated on active fighters above—she had enough power to drop into the water-vapor regions, far below the plant, and silently ride a thermal into range. With luck, she could get close enough to lay a web of zero-angle phase and take out the plant.

She had minutes in which to agonize over her plan. Falling, buffeted by winds that could knock her kilometers out of range, she spun like a vagrant flake of snow.

She couldn't even expend the energy to learn if they were scanning her, checking out her potential.

Perhaps she underestimated them. Perhaps they would be that much more thorough and take her out just to be sure. Perhaps they had unwritten rules of conduct like the ones she was using, taking hunches into account. Hunches were discouraged in Grounds training—much less reliable than cyber.

She fell. Temperature increased. Pressure on her suit began to constrict her air supply. She used fighter trancing to cut back on her breathing.

Fell.

And broke the trance. Pushed through the dense smoke of exhaustion. Planned the beam web. Counted her reserves. Nudged into an updraft beneath the plant. The thermal carried her, a silent piece of paper in a storm, drifting back and forth beneath the objective. The huge field intakes pulsed above, lightning outlining their invisible extension. She held back on the beam.

Nearly faded out. Her suit interior was almost unbearably hot.

She was only vaguely aware of laying down the pattern. The beams vanished in the murk. The thermal pushed her through a layer of haze, and she saw the plant, riding high above clear-atmosphere turbulence. The zero-angle phase had pushed through the field intakes, into their source nodes and the plant body, surrounding it with bright blue Tcherenkov. First the surface began to break up, then the middle layers, and finally key supports. Chunks vibrated away with the internal fury of their molecular, then atomic, then particle disruption. Paraphrasing Grounds description of beam action, the plant became less and less convinced of its reality. "Matter dreams," an instructor had said a decade before. "Dreams it is real, maintains the dream by shifting rules with constant results. Disturb the dreams, the shifting of the rules results in inconstant results. Things cannot hold."

She slid away from the updraft, found another, wondered idly how far she would be lifted. Curiosity at the last. Let's just see, she told herself; a final experiment.

Now she was cold. The implant was flickering, showing signs of reorganization. She didn't use it. No sense expanding the amount of time until death. No sense—

at all.

The sled, maneuvered by one remaining fighter, glided up beneath her almost unnoticed.

Aryz waited in the stillness of a Senexi memory, his thinking temporarily reduced to a faint susurrus. What he waited for was not clear.

—Come.

The form of address was wrong, but he recognized the voice. His thoughts stirred, and he followed the nebulous presence out of Senexi territory.

—Know your enemy.

Prufrax . . . the name of one of the human shapes sent out against their own kind. He could sense her presence in the mandate, locked into a memory store. He touched on the store and caught the essentials—the grinder, the up-draft plant, the fight from Prufrax's viewpoint.

—Know how your enemy knows you.

He sensed a second presence, similar to that of Prufrax. It took him some time to realize that the human captive was another form of the shape, a reproduction of the . . .

Both were reproductions of the female whose image was in the memory store. Aryz was not impressed by threes—Senexi mysticism, what had ever existed of it, had been preoccupied with fives and sixes—but the coincidence was striking.

—Know how your enemy sees you.

He saw the grinder processing organics—the vermiform natives—in preparation for a widespread seeding of deuterium gatherers. The operation had evidently been conducted for some time; the vermiform populations were greatly reduced from their usual numbers. Vermiforms were a common type-species on gas giants of the sort depicted. The mutated shape nudged him into a particular channel of the memory, that which carried the original Prufrax's emotions. She had reacted with *disgust* to the Senexi procedure. It was a reaction not unlike what Aryz

might feel when coming across something forbidden in
Senexi behavior. Yet eradication was perfectly natural,
analogous to the human cleansing of *food* before *eating*.

—It's in the memory. The vermiforms are intelligent.
They have their own kind of civilization. Human action on
this world prevented their complete extinction by the
Senexi.

—So what matter they were *intelligent?* Aryz responded.
They did not behave or think like Senexi, or like any
species Senexi find compatible. They were therefore not
desirable. Like humans.

—You would make humans extinct?
We would protect ourselves from them.

—Who damages whom most?

Aryz didn't respond. The line of questioning was incomprehensible. Instead he flowed into the memory of Prufrax, propelled by another aspect of complete freedom,
confusion.

The implant was replaced. Prufrax's damaged limbs and
skin were repaired or regenerated quickly, and within four
wakes, under intense treatment usually reserved only for
overs, she regained all her reflexes and speed. She re-
quested liberty of the cruiser while it returned for repairs.
Her request was granted.

She first sought Clevo in the designated research area.
He wasn't there, but a message was, passed on to her by a
smiling young crew member. She read it quickly:

"You're free and out of action. Study for a while, then
come find me. The old place hasn't been damaged. It's less
private, but still good. Study! I've marked highlights."

She frowned at the message, then handed it to the crew
member, who duly erased it and returned to his duties.
She wanted to talk with Clevo, not study.

But she followed his instructions. She searched out
highlighted entries in the ship's memory store. It was not

nearly as dull as she had expected. In fact, by following the highlights, she felt she was learning more about Clevo and about the questions he asked.

Old literature was not nearly as graphic as fibs, but it was different enough to involve her for a time. She tried to create imitations of what she read, but erased them. Nonfib stories were harder than she suspected. She read about punishment, duty; she read about places called heaven and hell, from a writer who had died tens of thousands of years before. With ed supplement guidance, she was able to comprehend most of what she read. Plugging the store into her implant, she was able to absorb hundreds of volumes in an hour.

Some of the stores were losing definition. They hadn't been used in decades, perhaps centuries.

Halfway through, she grew impatient. She left the research area. Operating on another hunch, she didn't go to the blister as directed, but straight to memory central, two decks inboard the research area. She saw Clevo there, plugged into a data pillar, deep in some aspect of ship history. He noticed her approach, unplugged, and swiveled on his chair. "Congratulations," he said, smiling at her.

"Hardfought," she acknowledged, smiling.

"Better than that, perhaps," he said.

She looked at him quizzically. "What do you mean, better?"

"I've been doing some illicit tapping on over channels."

"So?"

—He *is dangerous!*

"You've been recommended."

"For what?"

"Not for hero status, not yet. You'll have a good many more fights before that. And you probably won't enjoy it when you get there. You won't be a fighter then."

Prufrax stood silently before him.

"You may have a valuable genetic assortment. Overs think you behaved remarkably well under impossible conditions."

"Did I?"

He nodded. "Your type may be preserved."

"Which means?"

"There's a program being planned. They want to take the best fighters and reproduce them—clone them—to make uniform top-grade squadrons. It was rumored in my time—you haven't heard?"

She shook her head.

"It's not new. It's been done; off and on, for tens of thousands of years. This time they believe they can make it work."

"You were a fighter, once," she said. "Did they preserve your type?"

Clevo nodded. "I had something that interested them, but not, I think, as a fighter."

Prufrax looked down at her stubby-fingered hands. "It was grim," she said. "You know what we found?"

"An extermination plant."

"You want me to understand them better. Well, I can't. I refuse. How can they do such things?" She looked disgusted and answered her own questions. "Because they're Senexi."

"Humans," Clevo said, "have done much the same, sometimes worse."

"No!"

—No!

"Yes," he said firmly. He sighed. "We've wiped Senexi worlds, and we've even wiped worlds with intelligent species like our own. Nobody is innocent. Not in this universe."

"We were never taught that."

"It wouldn't have made you a better hawk. But it might

make a better human of you, to know. Greater depth of character. Do you want to be more aware?"

"You mean, study more?"

He nodded.

"What makes you think *you* can teach me?"

"Because you thought about what I asked you. About how Senexi thought. And you survived where some other hawk might not have. The overs think it's in your genes. It might be. But it's also in your head."

"Why not tell the overs?"

"I have," he said. He shrugged. "I'm too valuable to them, otherwise I'd have been busted again, a long time ago."

"They wouldn't want me to learn from you?"

"I don't know," Clevo said. "I suppose they're aware you're talking to me. They could stop it if they wanted. They may be smarter than I give them credit for." He shrugged again. "Of course they're smart. We just disagree at times."

"And if I learn from you?"

"Not from me, actually. From the past. From history, what other people have thought. I'm really not any more capable than you . . . but I know history, small portions of it. I won't teach you so much, as guide."

"I did use your questions," Prufrax said. "But will I ever need to use them—think that way—again?"

Clevo nodded. "Of course."

—You're quiet.

—She's giving in to him.

—She gave in a long time ago.

—She should be afraid.

—Were you—we—ever really afraid of a challenge?

—No.

—Not Senexi, not forbidden knowledge.

—Someone listens with us. Feel—

Clevo first led her through the history of past wars, judging that was appropriate considering her occupation. She was attentive enough, though her mind wandered; sometimes he was didactic, but she found she didn't mind that much. At no time did his attitude change as they pushed through the tangle of the past. Rather her perception of his attitude changed. Her perception of herself changed.

She saw that in all wars, the first stage was to dehumanize the enemy, reduce the enemy to a lower level so that he might be killed without compunction. When the enemy was not human to begin with, the task was easier. As wars progressed, this tactic frequently led to an underestimation of the enemy, with disastrous consequences. "We aren't exactly underestimating the Senexi," Clevo said. "The overs are too smart for that. But we refuse to understand them, and that could make the war last indefinitely."

"Then why don't the overs see that?"

"Because we're being locked into a pattern. We've been fighting for so long, we've begun to lose ourselves. And it's getting worse." He assumed his didactic tone, and she knew he was reciting something he'd formulated years before and repeated to himself a thousand times. "There is no war so important that to win it, we must destroy our minds."

She didn't agree with that; losing the war with the Senexi would mean extinction, as she understood things.

Most often they met in the single unused weapons blister that had not been damaged. They met when the ship was basking in the real between sponge-space jaunts. He brought memory stores with him in portable modules, and they read, listened, experienced together. She never placed a great deal of importance in the things she learned; her interest was focused on Clevo. Still, she learned.

The rest of her time she spent training. She was aware of a growing isolation from the hawks, which she attributed to her uncertain rank status. Was her genotype going to be preserved or not? The decision hadn't been made. The more she learned, the less she wanted to be singled out for honor. Attracting that sort of attention might be dangerous, she thought. Dangerous to whom, or what, she could not say.

Clevo showed her how hero images had been used to indoctrinate birds and hawks in a standard of behavior that was ideal, not realistic. The results were not always good; some tragic blunders had been made by fighters trying to be more than anyone possibly could or refusing to be flexible.

The war was certainly not a fib. Yet more and more the overs seemed to be treating it as one. Unable to bring about strategic victories against the Senexi, the overs had settled in for a long war of attrition and were apparently bent on adapting all human societies to the effort.

"There are overs we never hear of, who make decisions that shape our entire lives. Soon they'll determine whether or not we're even born, if they don't already."

"That sounds paranoid," she said, trying out a new word and concept she had only recently learned.

"Maybe so."

"Besides, it's been like that for ages—not knowing all our overs."

"But it's getting worse," Clevo said. He showed her the projections he had made. In time, if trends continued unchanged, fighters and all other combatants would be treated more and more mechanically, until they became the machines the overs wished them to be.

—No.

—Quiet. How does he feel toward her?

It was inevitable that as she learned under his tutelage,

he began to feel responsible for her changes. She was an excellent fighter. He could never be sure that what he was doing might reduce her effectivenes. And yet he had fought well—despite similar changes—until his billet switch. It had been the overs who had decided he would be more effective, less disruptive, elsewhere.

Bitterness over that decision was part of his motive. The overs had done a foolish thing, putting a fighter into research. Fighters were tenacious. If the truth was to be hidden, then fighters were the ones likely to ferret it out. And pass it on. There was a code among fighters, seldom revealed to their immediate overs, much less to the supreme overs parsecs distant in their strategospheres. What one fighter learned that could be of help to another had to be passed on, even under penalty. Clevo was simply following that unwritten rule.

Passing on the fact that, at one time, things had been different. That war changed people, governments, societies, and that societies could effect an enormous change on their constituents, especially now—change in their lives, their thinking. Things could become even more structured. Freedom of fight was a drug, an illusion—

—No!

used to perpetuate a state of hatred.

"Then why do they keep all the data in stores?" she asked. "I mean, you study the data, everything becomes obvious."

"There are still important people who think we may want to find our way back someday. They're afraid we'll lose our roots, but—"

His face suddenly became peaceful. She reached out to touch him, and he jerked slightly, turning toward her in the blister. "What is it?" she asked.

"It's not organized. We're going to lose the information. Ship overs are going to restrict access more and more. Eventually it'll decay, like some already has in these stores.

I've been planning for some time to put it all in a single unit—"

—*He* built the mandate!

"and have the overs place one on every ship, with researchers to tend it. Formalize the loose scheme still in effect, but dying. Right now I'm working on the fringes. At least I'm allowed to work. But soon I'll have enough evidence that they won't be able to argue. Evidence of what happens to societies that try to obscure their histories. They go quite mad. The overs are still rational enough to listen; maybe I'll push it through." He looked out the transparent blister. The stars were smudging to one side as the cruiser began probing for entrances to sponge space. "We'd better get back."

"Where are you going to be when we return? We'll all be transferred."

"That's some time removed. Why do you want to know?"

"I'd like to learn more."

He smiled. "That's not your only reason."

"I don't need someone to tell me what my reasons are," she said testily.

"We're so reluctant," he said. She looked at him sharply, irritated and puzzled. "I mean," he continued, "we're hawks. Comrades. Hawks couple like *that.*" He snapped his fingers. "But you and I sneak around it all the time."

Prufrax kept her face blank.

"Aren't you receptive toward me?" he asked, his tone almost teasing.

"You're so damned superior. Stuffy," she snapped.

"Aren't you?"

"It's just that's not all," she said, her tone softening.

"Indeed," he said in a barely audible whisper.

In the distance they heard the alarms.

—It was never any different.

—What?

—Things were never any different before me.

—Don't be silly. It's all here.

—If Clevo made the mandate, then he put it here. It isn't true.

—Why are you upset?

—I don't like hearing that everything I believe is a . . . fib.

—I've never known the difference, I suppose. Eyes-open was never all that real to me. This isn't real, you aren't . . . this is eyes-shut. So why be upset? You and I . . . we aren't even whole people. I feel you. You wish the Zap, you fight, not much else. I'm just a shadow, even compared to you. But she is whole. She loves him. She's less a victim than either of us. So something has to have changed.

—You're saying things have gotten worse.

—If the mandate is a lie, that's all I am. You refuse to accept. I *have* to accept, or I'm even less than a shadow.

—I don't refuse to accept. It's just hard.

—You started it. You thought about love.

—You did!

—Do you know what love is?

—Reception.

They first made love in the weapons blister. It came as no surprise; if anything, they approached it so cautiously they were clumsy. She had become more and more receptive, and he had dropped his guard. It had been quick, almost frantic, far from the orchestrated and drawn-out ballet the hawks prided themselves for. There was no pretense. No need to play the roles of artists interacting. They were depending on each other. The pleasure they exchanged was nothing compared to the emotions involved.

"We're not very good with each other," Prufrax said.

Clevo shrugged. "That's because we're shy."

"Shy?"

He explained. In the past—at various times in the past,

because such differences had come and gone many times—making love had been more than a physical exchange or even an expression of comradeship. It had been the acknowledgment of a bond between people.

She listened, half-believing. Like everything else she had heard, that kind of love seemed strange, distasteful. What if one hawk was lost, and the other continued to love? It interfered with the hardfought, certainly. But she was also fascinated. Shyness—the fear of one's presentation to another. The hesitation to present truth, or the inward confusion of truth at the awareness that another might be important, more important than one thought possible. That such emotions might have existed at one time, and seem so alien now, only emphasized the distance of the past, as Clevo had tried to tell her. And that she felt those emotions only confirmed she was not as far from that past as, for dignity's sake, she might have wished.

Complex emotion was not encouraged either at the Grounds or among hawks on station. Complex emotion degraded complex performance. The simple and direct was desirable.

"But all we seem to do is talk—until now," Prufrax said, holding his hand and examining his fingers one by one. They were very little different from her own, though extended a bit from hawk fingers to give greater versatility with key instruction.

"Talking is the most human thing we can do."

She laughed. "I know what you are," she said, moving up until her eyes were even with his chest. "You're stuffy. You aren't the party type."

"Where'd you learn about parties?"

"You gave me literature to read, I read it. You're an instructor at heart. You make love by telling." She felt peculiar, almost afraid, and looked up at his face. "Not that I don't enjoy your lovemaking, like this. Physical."

"You receive well," he said. "Both ways."

"What we're saying," she whispered, "is not truth-speaking. It's amenity." She turned into the stroke of his hand through her hair. "Amenity is supposed to be decadent. That fellow who wrote about heaven and hell. He would call it a sin."

"Amenity is the recognition that somebody may see or feel differently than you do. It's the recognition of individuals. You and I, we're part of the end of all that."

"Even if you convince the overs?"

He nodded. "They want to repeat success without risk. New individuals are risky, so they duplicate past success. There will be more and more people, fewer individuals. More of you and me, less of others. The fewer individuals, the fewer stories to tell. The less history. We're part of the death of history."

She floated next to him, trying to blank her mind as she had before, to drive out the nagging awareness he was right. She thought she understood the social structure around her. Things seemed new. She said as much.

"It's a path we're taking," Clevo said. "Not a place we're at."

—It's a place *we're* at. How different are we?

—But there's so much history in here. How can it be over for us?

—I've been thinking. Do we know the last event recorded in the mandate?

—Don't, we're drifting from Prufrax now. . . .

Aryz felt himself drifting with them. They swept over countless millennia, then swept back the other way. And it became evident that as much change had been wrapped in one year of the distant past as in a thousand years of the closing entries in the mandate. Clevo's voice seemed to follow them, though they were far from his period, far from Prufrax's record.

"Tyranny is the death of history. We fought the Senexi

until we became like them. No change, youth at an end, old age coming upon us. There is no important change, merely elaborations in the pattern."

—How many times have we been here, then? How many times have we died?

Aryz wasn't sure, now. Was this the first time humans had been captured? Had he been told everything by the brood mind? Did the Senexi have no *history*, whatever that was—

The accumulated lives of living, thinking beings. Their actions, thoughts, passions, hopes.

The mandate answered even his confused, nonhuman requests. He could understand action, thought, but not passion or hope. Perhaps without those there was no *history*.

—You have no history, the mutated shape told him. There have been millions like you, even millions like the brood mind. What is the last event recorded in the brood mind that is not duplicated a thousand times over, so close they can be melded together for convenience?

—You understand that? Aryz asked the shape.

—Yes.

—How do you understand—because we made you between human and Senexi?

—Not only that.

The requests of the twin captive and shape were moving them back once more into the past, through the dim grey millennia of repeating ages. History began to manifest again, differences in the record.

On the way back to Mercior, four skirmishes were fought. Prufrax did well in each. She carried something special with her, a thought she didn't even tell Clevo, and she carried the same thought with her through their last days at the Grounds.

Taking advantage of hawk liberty, she opted a posthardfought residence just outside the Grounds, in the relatively uncrowded Daughter of Cities zone. She wouldn't be returning to fight until several issues had been decided—her status most important among them.

Clevo began making his appeal to the middle overs. He was given Grounds duty to finish his proposals. They could stay together for the time being.

The residence was sixteen square meters in area, not elegant—*natural,* as rentOpts described it. Clevo called it a "garret," inaccurately as she discovered when she looked it up in his memory blocs, but perhaps he was describing the tone.

On the last day she lay in the crook of Clevo's arm. They had done a few hours of nature sleep. He hadn't come out yet, and she looked up at his face, reached up with a hand to feel his arm.

It was different from the arms of others she had been receptive toward. It was unique. The thought amused her. There had never been a reception like theirs. This was the beginning. And if both were to be duplicated, this love, this reception, would be repeated an infinite number of times. Clevo meeting Prufrax, teaching her, opening her eyes.

Somehow, even though repetition contributed to the death of history, she was pleased. This was the secret thought she carried into fight. Each time she would survive, wherever she was, however many duplications down the line. She would receive Clevo, and he would teach her. If not now—if one or the other died—then in the future. The death of history might be a good thing. Love could go on forever.

She had lost even a rudimentary apprehension of death, even with present pleasure to live for. Her functions had sharpened. She would please him by doing all the things he could not. And if he was to enter that state she frequently found him in, that state of introspection, of reliving his own battles and of envying her activity, then that wasn't bad. All they did to each other was good.

—*Was* good

—*Was*

She slipped from his arm and left the narrow sleeping quarter, pushing through the smoke-colored air curtain to the lounge. Two hawks and an over she had never seen before were sitting there. They looked up at her.

"Under," Prufrax said.

"Over," the woman returned. She was dressed in tan and green, Grounds colors, not ship.

"May I assist?"

"Yes."

"My duty, then?"

The over beckoned her closer. "You have been receiving a researcher."

"Yes," Prufrax said. The meetings could not have been a secret on the ship, and certainly not their quartering near the Grounds. "Has that been against duty?"

"No." The over eyed Prufrax sharply, observing her perfected fightform, the easy grace with which she stood, naked, in the middle of the small compartment. "But a decision has been reached. Your status is decided now."

She felt a shiver.

"Prufrax," said the elder hawk. She recognized him from fibs, and his companion: Kumnax and Arol. Once her heroes. "You have been accorded an honor, just as your partner has. You have a valuable genetic assortment—"

She barely heard the rest. They told her she would return to fight, until they deemed she had had enough experience and background to be brought into the polinstruc division. Then her fighting would be over. She would serve better as an example, a hero.

Heroes never partnered out of function. Hawk heroes could not even partner with exhawks.

Clevo emerged from the air curtain. "Duty," the over said. "The residence is disbanded. Both of you will have separate quarters, separate duties."

They left. Prufrax held out her hand, but Clevo didn't take it. "No use," he said.

Suddenly she was filled with anger. "You'll give it up? Did I expect too much? *How strongly?*"

"Perhaps even more strongly than you," he said. "I knew the order was coming down. And still I didn't leave. That may hurt my chances with the supreme overs."

"Then at least I'm worth more than your breeding history?"

"Now you are history. History the way they make it."

"I feel like I'm dying," she said, amazement in her voice. "What is that, Clevo? What did you do to me?"

"I'm in pain, too," he said.

"You're hurt?"

"I'm confused."

"I don't believe that," she said, her anger rising again. "You knew, and you didn't do anything?"

"That would have been counter to duty. We'll be worse off if we fight it."

"So what good is your great, exalted history?"

"History is what you have," Clevo said. "I only record."

—Why did they separate them?

—I don't know. You didn't like him, anyway.

—Yes, but now . . .

—See? You're her. We're her. But shadows. She was whole.

—I don't understand.

—We don't. Look what happens to her. They took what was best out of her. Prufrax

went into battle eighteen more times before dying as

heroes often do, dying in the midst of what she did best. The question of what made her better before the separation—for she definitely was not as fine a fighter after—has not been settled. Answers fall into an extinct classification of knowledge, and there are few left to interpret, none accessible to this device.

—So she went out and fought and died. They never even made fibs about her. This killed her?

—I don't think so. She fought well enough. She died like other hawks died.

—And she might have lived otherwise.

—How can I know that, any more than you?

—They—we—met again, you know. I met a Clevo once, on my ship. They didn't let me stay with him long.

—How did you react to him?

—There was so little time, I don't know.

—Let's ask. . . .

In thousands of duty stations, it was inevitable that some of Prufrax's visions would come true, that they should meet now and then. Clevos were numerous, as were Prufraxes. Every ship carried complements of several of each. Though Prufrax was never quite as successful as the original, she was a fine type. She—

—She was never quite as successful. They took away her edge. They didn't even know it!

—They must have known.

—Then they didn't want to win!

—We don't know that. Maybe there were more important considerations.

—Yes, like killing history.

Aryz shuddered in his warming body, dizzy as if about to bud, then regained control. He had been pulled from the mandate, called to his own duty.

He examined the shapes and the human captive. There

was something different about them. How long had they been immersed in the mandate? He checked quickly, frantically, before answering the call. The reconstructed Mam had malfunctioned. None of them had been nourished. They were thin, pale, cooling.

Even the bloated mutant shape was dying; lost, like the others, in the mandate.

He turned his attention away. Everything was confusion. Was he human or Senexi now? Had he fallen so low as to understand them? He went to the origin of the call, the ruins of the temporary brood chamber. The corridors were caked with ammonia ice, burning his pod as he slipped over them. The brood mind had come out of flux bind. The emergency support systems hadn't worked well; the brood mind was damaged.

"Where have you been?" it asked.

"I assumed I would not be needed until your return from the flux bind."

"You have not been watching!"

"Was there any need? We are so advanced in time, all our actions are obsolete. The nebula is collapsed, the issue is decided."

"We do not know that. We are being pursued."

Aryz turned to the sensor wall—what was left of it—and saw that they were, indeed, being pursued. He had been lax.

"It is not your fault," the brood mind said. "You have been set a task that tainted you and ruined your function. You will dissipate."

Aryz hesitated. He had become so different, so tainted, the he actually *hesitated* at a direct command from the brood mind. But it was damaged. Without him, without what he had learned, what could it do? It wasn't reasoning correctly.

"There are facts you must know, important facts—"

Aryz felt a wave of revulsion, uncomprehending fear,

and something not unlike human anger radiate from the brood mind. Whatever he had learned and however he had changed, he could not withstand that wave.

Willingly, and yet against his will—it didn't matter—he felt himself liquefying. His pod slumped beneath him, and he fell over, landing on a pool of frozen ammonia. It burned, but he did not attempt to lift himself. Before he ended, he saw with surprising clarity what it was to be a branch ind, or a brood mind, or a human. Such a valuable insight, and it leaked out of his permea and froze on the ammonia.

The brood mind regained what control it could of the fragment. But there were no defenses worthy of the name. Calm, preparing for its own dissipation, it waited for the pursuit to conclude.

The Mam set off an alarm. The interface with the mandate was severed. Weak, barely able to crawl, the humans looked at each other in horror and slid to opposite corners of the chamber.

They were confused: which of them was the captive, which the decoy shape? It didn't seem important. They were both bone-thin, filthy with their own excrement. They turned with one motion to stars at the bloated mutant. It sat in its corner, tiny head incongruous on the huge thorax, tiny arms and legs barely functional even when healthy. It smiled wanly at them.

"We felt you," one of the Prufraxes said. "You were with us in there." Her voice was a soft croak.

"That was my place," it replied. "My only place."

"What function, what name?"

"I'm . . . I know that. I'm a researcher. In there. I knew myself in there."

They squinted at the shape. The head. Something familiar, even now. "You're a Clevo . . ."

There was noise all around them, cutting off the shape's

weak words. As they watched, their chamber was sectioned like an orange, and the wedges peeled open. The illumination ceased. Cold enveloped them.

A naked human female, surrounded by tiny versions of herself, like an angel circled by fairy kin, floated into the chamber. She was thin as a snake. She wore nothing but silver rings on her wrists and a narrow torque around her waist. She glowed blue-green in the dark.

The two Prufraxes moved their lips weakly but made no sound in the near vacuum. *Who are you?*

She surveyed them without expression, then held out her arms as if to fly. She wore no gloves, but she was of their type.

As she had done countless times before on finding such Senexi experiments—though this seemed older than most—she lifted one arm higher. The blue-green intensified, spread in waves to the mangled walls, surrounded the freezing, dying shapes. Perfect, angelic, she left the debris behind to cast its fitful glow and fade.

They had destroyed every portion of the fragment but one. They left it behind unharmed.

Then they continued, millions of them thick like mist, working the spaces between the stars, their only master the overness of the real.

They needed no other masters. They would never malfunction.

The mandate drifted in the dark and cold, its memory going on, but its only life the rapidly fading tracks where minds had once passed through it. The trails writhed briefly, almost as if alive, but only following the quantum rules of diminishing energy states. Finally, a small memory was illuminated.

Prufrax's last poem, explained the mandate reflexively.

How the fires grow! Peace passes
All memory lost.
Somehow we always miss that single door,
Dooming ourselves to circle.

Ashes to stars, lies to souls,
Let's spin round the sinks and holes.

Kill the good, eat the young.
Forever and more
You and I are never done.

The track faded into nothing. Around the mandate, the universe grew old very quickly.

The Peacemaker

by Gardner Dozois

Gardner Dozois is hardly an unknown figure in science fiction. He is the author or editor of sixteen books, including the novel Strangers, *and* The Visible Man, *a collection of short fiction. His short fiction has appeared in publications from* Playboy *and* Penthouse *to most of the leading science fiction magazines and anthologies. His critical works have been published by, among others,* Writer's Digest, Thrust, *and* Writing and Selling Science Fiction. *He has served as a judge for the World Fantasy Award, on the Nebula Award Jury, and is the genre's most distinguished multi-finalist for Nebula and Hugo Awards.*

In 1983 Dozois won the Nebula for best short story with The Peacemaker.

Roy had dreamed of the sea, as he often did. When he woke up that morning, the wind was sighing through the trees outside with a sound like the restless murmuring of surf, and for a moment he thought that he was home, back in the tidy brick house by the beach, with everything that had happened undone, and hope opened hotly inside him, like a wound.

"Mom?" he said. He sat up, straightening his legs, expecting his feet to touch the warm mass that was his dog Toby. Toby always slept curled at the foot of his bed, but already everything was breaking up and changing, slipping away, and he blinked through sleep-gummed eyes at the thin blue light coming in through the attic window, felt

92

the hardness of the old Army cot under him, and realized that he wasn't home, that there was no home anymore, that for him there could never be a home again.

He pushed the blankets aside and stood up. It was bitterly cold in the big attic room—winter was dying hard, the most terrible winter he could remember—and the rough wood planking burned his feet like ice, but he couldn't stay in bed anymore, not now.

None of the other kids were awake yet; he threaded his way through the other cots—accidently bumping against one of them so that its occupant tossed and moaned and began to snore in a higher register—and groped through cavernous shadows to the single high window. He was just tall enough to reach it, if he stood on tiptoe. He forced the window open, the old wood of its frame groaning in protest, plaster dust puffing, and shivered as the cold dawn wind poured inward, hitting him in the face, tugging with ghostly fingers at his hair, sweeping past him to rush through the rest of the stuffy attic like a restless child set free to play.

The wind smelled of pine resin and wet earth, not of salt flats and tides, and the bird-sound that rode in on that wind was the burbling of wrens and the squawking of bluejays, not the raucous shrieking of seagulls . . . but even so, as he braced his elbows against the window frame and strained up to look out, his mind still full of the broken fragments of dreams, he half-expected to see the ocean below, stretched out to the horizon, sending patient wavelets to lap against the side of the house. Instead he saw the nearby trees holding silhouetted arms up against the graying sky, the barn and the farmyard, all still lost in shadow, the surrounding fields, the weathered macadam line of the road, the forested hills rolling away into distance. Silver mist lay in pockets of low ground, retreated in wraithlike streamers up along the ridges.

Not yet. The sea had not chased him here—yet.

Somewhere out there to the east, still invisible, were the mountains, and just beyond those mountains was the sea that he had dreamed of, lapping quietly at the dusty Pennsylvania hill towns, coal towns, that were now, suddenly, seaports. There the Atlantic waited, held at bay, momentarily at least, by the humpbacked wall of the Appalachians, still perhaps forty miles from here, although closer now by leagues of swallowed land and drowned cities than it had been only three years before.

He had been down by the seawall that long-ago morning, playing some forgotten game, watching the waves move in slow oily swells, like some heavy, dull metal in liquid form, watching the tide come in . . . and come in . . . and come *in* . . . He had been excited at first, as the sea crept in, way above the high-tide line, higher than he had ever seen it before, and then, as the sea swallowed the beach entirely and began to lap patiently against the base of the seawall, he had become uneasy, and *then*, as the sea continued to rise up toward the top of the seawall itself, he had begun to be afraid. . . . The sea had just kept coming in, rising slowly and inexorably, swallowing the land at a slow walking pace, never stopping, always coming *in*, always rising higher. . . . By the time the sea had swallowed the top of the seawall and begun to creep up the short grassy slope toward his house, sending glassy fingers probing almost to his feet, he had started to scream, he had whirled and run frantically up the slope, screaming hysterically for his parents, and the sea had followed patiently at his heels. . . .

A "marine transgression," the scientists called it. Ordinary people called it, inevitably, the Flood. Whatever you called it, it had washed away the old world forever. Scientists had been talking about the possibility of such a thing for years—some of them even pointing out that it was already as warm as it had been at the peak of the last interglacial, and getting warmer—but few had suspected

just how *fast* the Antarctic ice could melt. Many times during those chaotic weeks, one scientific King Canute or
another had predicted that the worst was over, that the
tide would rise this high and no higher . . . but each time
the sea had come inexorably on, pushing miles and miles
further inland with each successive high tide, rising almost
three hundred feet in the course of one disastrous summer, drowning lowlands around the globe until there *were*
no lowlands anymore. In the United States alone, the sea
had swallowed most of the East Coast east of the Appalachians, the West Coast west of the Sierras and the Cas-
cades, much of Alaska and Hawaii, Florida, the Gulf
Coast, East Texas, taken a big wide scoop out of the lowlands of the Mississippi Valley, thin fingers of water penetrating north to Iowa and Illinois, and caused the St. Law-
rence and the Great Lakes to overflow and drown their
shorelines. The Green Mountains, the White Mountains,
the Adirondacks, the Poconos and the Catskills, the
Ozarks, the Pacific Coast Ranges—all had been transformed to archipelagos, surrounded by the invading sea.

The funny thing was . . . that as the sea pursued them
relentlessly inland, pushing them from one temporary refuge to another, he had been unable to shake the feeling
that *he* had caused the Flood: that he had done something
that day while playing atop the seawall, inadvertently
stumbled on some magic ritual, some chance combination
of gesture and word that had untied the bonds of the sea
and sent it sliding up over the land . . . that it was chasing
him, personally. . . .

A dog was barking out there now, somewhere out across
the fields toward town, but it was not *his* dog. His dog was
dead, long since dead, and its whitening skull was rolling
along the ocean floor with the tides that washed over what
had once been Brigantine, New Jersey, three hundred feet
down.

Suddenly he was covered with gooseflesh, and he

shivered, rubbing his hands over his bare arms. He returned to his cot and dressed hurriedly—no point in trying to go back to bed, Sara would be up to kick them all out of the sack in a minute or two anyway. The day had begun; he would think no further ahead than that. He had learned in the refugee camps to take life one second at a time.

As he moved around the room, he thought that he could feel hostile eyes watching him from some of the other bunks. It was much colder in here now that he had opened the window, and he had inevitably made a certain amount of noise getting dressed, but although they all valued every second of sleep they could scrounge, none of the other kids would dare to complain. The thought was bittersweet, bringing both pleasure and pain, and he smiled at it, a thin, brittle smile that was almost a grimace. No, they would watch sullenly from their bunks, and pretend to be asleep, and curse him under their breath, but they would say nothing to anyone about it. Certainly they would say nothing to *him.*

He went down through the still-silent house like a ghost, and out across the farmyard, through fugitive streamers of mist that wrapped clammy white arms around him and beaded his face with dew. His uncle Abner was there at the slit-trench before him. Abner grunted a greeting, and they stood pissing side by side for a moment in companionable silence, their urine steaming in the gray morning air.

Abner stepped backward and began to button his pants. "You start playin' with yourself yet, boy?" he said, not looking at Roy.

Roy felt his face flush. "No," he said, trying not to stammer, "no sir."

"You growin' hair already," Abner said. He swung himself slowly around to face Roy, as if his body was some ponderous machine that could only be moved and aimed by the use of pulleys and levers. The hard morning light made his face look harsh as stone, but also sallow and old. Tired, Roy thought. Unutterably weary, as though it took almost more effort than he could sustain just to stand there. Worn out, like the overtaxed fields around them. Only the eyes were alive in the eroded face; they were hard and merciless as flint, and they looked at you as if they were looking right through you to some distant thing that nobody else could see. "I've tried to explain to you about remaining pure," Abner said, speaking slowly. "About how important it is for you to keep yourself pure, not to let yourself be sullied in any way. I've tried to explain that, I hope you could understand—"

"Yes, sir," Roy said.

Abner made a groping hesitant motion with his hand, fingers spread wide, as though he were trying to sculpt meaning from the air itself. "I mean—it's important that you understand, Roy. Everything has to be *right*. I mean, everything's got to be just . . . *right* . . . or nothing else will mean anything. You got to be right in your *soul*, boy. You got to let the Peace of God into your soul. It all depends on *you* now—you got to let that Peace inside yourself, no one can do it for you. And it's so important . . . "

"Yes, sir," Roy said quietly, "I understand."

"I wish . . . " Abner said, and fell silent. They stood there for a minute, not speaking, not looking at each other. There was wood-smoke in the air now, and they heard a door slam somewhere on the far side of the house. They had instinctively been looking out across the open land to the east, and now, as they watched, the sun rose above the mountains, splitting the plum-and-ash sky open horizontally with a long wedge of red, distinguishing the rolling horizon from the lowering clouds. A lance of bright white sunlight hit their eyes, thrusting straight in at them from the edge of the world.

"You're going to make us proud, boy, I know it," Abner said, but Roy ignored him, watching in fascination as the

molten disk of the sun floated free of the horizon-line,
squinting against the dazzle until his eyes watered and his
sight blurred. Abner put his hand on the boy's shoulder.
The hand felt heavy and hot, proprietary, and Roy shook
it loose in annoyance, still not looking away from the horizon. Abner sighed, started to say something, thought better of it, and instead said, "Come on in the house, boy, and
let's get some breakfast inside you."

Breakfast—when they finally did get to sit down to it,
after the usual rambling grace and invocation by Abner—
proved to be unusually lavish. For the brethren, there
were hickory-nut biscuits, and honey, and cups of chicory;
and even the other refugee kids—who on occasion during
the long bitter winter had been fed as close to nothing at
all as law and appearances would allow—got a few slices of
fried fatback along with their habitual cornmeal mush.
Along with his biscuits and honey, Roy got wild turkey
eggs, Indian potatoes, and a real pork chop. There was a
good deal of tension around the big table that morning:
Henry and Luke were stern-faced and tense, Raymond
was moody and preoccupied, Albert actually looked
frightened; the refugee kids were round-eyed and silent,
doing their best to make themselves invisible; the jolly Mrs.
Crammer was as jolly as ever, shoveling her food in with
gusto; but the grumpy Mrs. Zeigler, who was feared and
disliked by all the kids, had obviously been crying, and ate
little or nothing. Abner's face was set like rock, his eyes
were hard and bright, and he looked from one to another
of the brethren, as if daring them to question his leader-
ship and spiritual guidance. Roy ate with good appetite
unperturbed by the emotional convection currents that
were swirling around him, calmly but deliberately concentrating on mopping up every morsel of food on his plate—
in the last couple of months he had put back some of the
weight he had lost, although by the old standards, the ones
his Mom would have applied four years ago, he was still

painfully thin. At the end of the meal, Mrs. Reardon came in from the kitchen and, beaming with the well-justified pride of someone who is about to do the impossible, presented Roy with a small, rectangular object wrapped in shiny brown paper. He was startled for a second, but yes, by God, it *was:* a Hershey bar, the first one he'd seen in years. A black market item, of course, difficult to get hold of in the impoverished East these days, and probably expensive as hell. Even some of the brethren were looking at him enviously now, and the refugee kids were frankly gaping. As he picked up the Hershey bar and slowly and caressingly peeled the wrapper back, exposing the pale chocolate beneath, one of the other kids actually began to drool.

After breakfast, the other refugee kids—"wetbacks," the townspeople sometimes called them, with elaborate irony—were divided into two groups. One group would help the brethren work Abner's farm that day, while the larger group would be loaded onto an ox-drawn dray (actually an old flatbed truck, with the cab knocked off) and sent out around the countryside to do what pretty much amounted to slave labor: road work, heavy farm work, helping with the quarrying or the timbering, rebuilding houses and barns and bridges damaged or destroyed in the chaotic days after the Flood. The federal government—or what was left of the federal government, trying desperately, and not always successfully, to keep a battered and Balkanizing country from flying completely apart, struggling to put the Humpty Dumpty that was America back together again—the federal government paid Abner (and others like him) a yearly allowance in federal scrip or promise-of-merchandise notes for giving room and board to refugees from the drowned lands . . . but times being as tough as they were, no one was going to complain if Abner also helped ease the burden of their upkeep by hiring them out locally to work for whomever could come up with the scrip, or sufficient barter goods, or an attractive work-swap offer; what was left of the state and town governments also used them on occasion (and the others like them, adult or child), gratis, for work-projects "for the common good, during this time of emergency . . . "

Sometimes, hanging around the farm with little or nothing to do, Roy almost missed going out on the work-crews, but only almost: he remembered too well the backbreaking labor performed on scanty rations . . . the sickness, the accidents, the staggering fatigue . . . the blazing sun and the swarms of mosquitoes in summer, the bitter cold in winter, the snow, the icy wind . . . He watched the dray go by, seeing the envious and resentful faces of kids he had once worked beside—Stevie, Enrique, Sal—turn towards him as it passed, and, reflexively, he opened and closed his hands. Even two months of idleness and relative luxury had not softened the thick and roughened layers of callus that were the legacy of several seasons spent on the crews. . . .No, boredom was infinitely preferable.

By mid-morning, a small crowd of people had gathered in the road outside the farmhouse. It was hotter now; you could smell the promise of summer in the air, in the wind, and the sun that beat down out of a cloudless blue sky had a real sting to it. It must have been uncomfortable out there in the open, under that sun, but the crowd made no attempt to approach—they just stood there on the far side of the road and watched the house, shuffling their feet, occasionally muttering to each other in voices that, across the road, were audible only as a low wordless grumbling.

Roy watched them for a while from the porch door; they were townspeople, most of them vaguely familiar to Roy, although none of them belonged to Abner's sect, and he knew none of them by name. The refugee kids saw little of the townspeople, being kept carefully segregated for the most part. The few times that Roy had gotten into town he had been treated with icy hostility—and God help the wetback kid who was caught by the town kids on a deserted stretch of road! For that matter, even the brethren tended to keep to themselves, and were snubbed by certain segments of town society, although the sect had increased its numbers dramatically in recent years, nearly tripling in strength during the past winter alone; there were new chapters now in several of the surrounding communities.

A gaunt-faced woman in the crowd outside spotted Roy, and shook a thin fist at him. "Heretic!" she shouted. "Blasphemer!" The rest of the crowd began to buzz ominously, like a huge angry bee. She spat at Roy, her face contorting and her shoulders heaving with the ferocity of her effort, although she must have known that the spittle had no chance of reaching him. "Blasphemer!" she shouted again. The veins stood out like cords in her scrawny neck.

Roy stepped back into the house, but continued to watch from behind the curtained front windows. There was shouting inside the house as well as outside—the brethren had been cloistered in the kitchen for most of the morning, arguing, and the sound and ferocity of their argument carried clearly through the thin plaster walls of the crumbling old house. At last the sliding door to the kitchen slammed open, and Mrs. Zeigler strode out into the parlor, accompanied by her two children and her scrawny, pasty-faced husband, and followed by two other families of brethren—about nine people altogether. Most of them were carrying suitcases, and a few had backpacks and bundles. Abner stood in the kitchen doorway and watched them go, his anger evident only in the whiteness of his knuckles as he grasped the doorframe. "*Go*, then," Abner said scornfully. "We spit you up out of our mouths! Don't ever think to come back!" He swayed in the doorway, his voice tremulous with hate. "We're better off without you, you hear? You *hear* me? We don't *need* the weak-willed and the short-sighted."

Mrs. Zeigler said nothing, and her steps didn't slow or

falter, but her homely hatchet-face was streaked with tears. To Roy's astonishment—for she had a reputation as a harridan—she stopped near the porch door and threw her arms around him. "Come with us," she said, hugging him with smothering tightness, "Roy, *please* come with us! You can, you know—we'll find a place for you, everything will work out fine." Roy said nothing, resisting the impulse to squirm—he was uncomfortable in her embrace; in spite of himself, it touched some sleeping corner of his soul he had thought was safely bricked over years before, and for a moment he felt trapped and panicky, unable to breathe, as though he were in sudden danger of wakening from a comfortable dream into a far more terrible and less desirable reality. "Come *with* us," Mrs. Zeigler said again, more urgently, but Roy shook his head gently and pulled away from her. "You're a goddamned fool then!" she blazed, suddenly angry, her voice ringing harsh and loud, but Roy only shrugged, and gave her his wistful, ghostly smile. "Damn it—" she started to say, but her eyes filled with tears again, and she whirled and hurried out of the house, followed by the other members of her party. The children— wetbacks were kept pretty much segregated from the children of the brethren as well, and he had seen some of these kids only at meals—looked at Roy with wide, frightened eyes as they passed.

Abner was staring at Roy now, from across the room; it was a hard and challenging stare, but there was also a trace of desperation in it, and in that moment Abner seemed uncertain and oddly vulnerable. Roy stared back at him serenely, unblinkingly meeting his eyes, and after a while some of the tension went out of Abner, and he turned and stumbled out of the room, listing to one side like a church steeple in the wind.

Outside, the crowd began to buzz again as Mrs. Zeigler's party filed out of the house and across the road. There was much discussion and arm waving and head shaking when the two groups met, someone occasionally gesturing back toward the farmhouse. The buzzing grew louder, then gradually died away. At last, Mrs. Zeigler and her group set off down the road for town, accompanied by some of the locals. They trudged away dispiritedly down the center of the dusty road, lugging their shabby suitcases, only a few of them looking back.

Roy watched them until they were out of sight, his face still and calm, and continued to stare down the road after them long after they were gone.

About noon, a carload of reporters arrived outside, driving up in one of the bulky new methane burners that were still rarely seen east of Omaha. They circulated through the crowd of townspeople, pausing briefly to take photographs and ask questions, working their way toward the house, and Roy watched them as if they were unicorns, strange remnants from some vanished cycle of creation. Most of the reporters were probably from State College or the new state capital at Altoona—places where a few small newspapers were again being produced—but one of them was wearing an armband that identified him as a bureau man for one of the big Denver papers, and that was prob-ably where the money for the car had come from. It was strange to be reminded that there were still areas of the country that were . . . not unchanged, no place in the world could claim that . . . and not rich, not by the old standards of affluence anyway . . . but, at any rate, better off than *here*. The whole western part of the country— from roughly the ninety-fifth meridian on west to approxi-mately the one-twenty-second—had been untouched by the flooding, and although the west had also suffered se-verely from the collapse of the national economy and the consequent social upheavals, at least much of their indus-trial base had remained intact. Denver—one of the few large American cities built on ground high enough to have been safe from the rising waters—was the new federal capital, and, if poorer and meaner, it was also bigger and busier than ever.

Abner went out to herd the reporters inside and away from the unbelievers, and after a moment or two Roy could hear Abner's voice going out there, booming like a church organ. By the time the reporters came in, Roy was sitting at the dining room table, flanked by Raymond and Aaron, waiting for them.

They took photographs of him sitting there, while he stared calmly back at them, and they took photographs of him while he politely refused to answer questions, and then Aaron handed him the pre-prepared papers, and he signed them, and repeated the legal formulas that Aaron had taught him, and they took photographs of that too. And then—able to get nothing more out of him, and made slightly uneasy by his blank composure and the remoteness of his eyes—they left.

Within a few more minutes, as though everything were over, as though the departure of the reporters had drained all possible significance from anything else that might still happen, most of the crowd outside had drifted away also, only one or two people remaining behind to stand quietly waiting, like vultures, in the once-again empty road.

Lunch was a quiet meal. Roy ate heartily, taking seconds of everything, and Mrs. Crammer was as jovial as ever, but everyone else was subdued, and even Abner seemed shaken by the schism that had just sundered his church. After the meal, Abner stood up and began to pray aloud. The brethren sat resignedly at the table, heads partially bowed, some listening, some not. Abner was holding his arms up toward the big blackened rafter of the ceiling, sweat runneling his face, when Peter came hurriedly in from outside and stood hesitating in the doorway, trying to catch Abner's eye. When it became obvious that Abner was going to keep right on ignoring him, Peter shrugged, and said in a loud flat voice, "Abner, the sheriff is here."

Abner stopped praying. He grunted, a hoarse, exhausted sound, the kind of sound a baited bear might make when, already pushed beyond the limits of endurance, someone jabs it yet again with a spear. He slowly lowered his arms and was still for a long moment, and then he shuddered, seeming to shake himself back to life. He glanced speculatively—and, it almost seemed, beseechingly—at Roy, and then straightened his shoulders and strode from the room.

They received the sheriff in the parlor, Raymond and Aaron and Mrs. Crammer sitting in the battered old armchairs, Roy sitting unobtrusively to one side on the stool from a piano that no longer worked, Abner standing a little to the fore with his arms locked behind him and his boots planted solidly on the oak planking, as if he were on the bridge of a schooner that was heading into a gale. County Sheriff Sam Braddock glanced at the others—his gaze lingering on Roy for a moment—and then ignored them, addressing himself to Abner as if they were alone in the room. "Mornin', Abner," he said.

"Mornin', Sam," Abner said quietly. "You here for some reason other than just t'say hello, I suppose."

Braddock grunted. He was a short, stocky, grizzled man with iron-gray hair and a tired face. His uniform was shiny and old and patched in a dozen places, but clean, and the huge old revolver strapped to his hip looked worn but serviceable. He fidgeted with his shapeless old hat, turning it around and around in his fingers—he was obviously embarrassed, but he was determined as well, and at last he said, "The thing of it is, Abner, I'm here to talk you out of this damned tomfoolery."

"Are you, now?" Abner said.

"We'll do whatever we damn well want to do—" Raymond burst out, shrilly, but Abner waved him to silence. Braddock glanced lazily at Raymond, then looked back at Abner, his tired old face settling into harder lines. "I'm not going to allow it," he said, more harshly. "We don't want this kind of thing going on in this county."

Abner said nothing.

"There's not a thing you can do about it, sheriff," Aaron said, speaking a bit heatedly, but keeping his melodious voice well under control. "It's all perfectly legal, all the way down the line."

"Well, now," Braddock said, "I don't know about that . . ."

"Well, I *do* know, sheriff," Aaron said calmly. "As a legally sanctioned and recognized church, we are protected by law all the way down the line. There is ample precedent, most of it recent, most of it upheld by appellate decisions within the last year: Carlton *versus* the State of Vermont, Trenholm *versus* the State of West Virginia, the Church of Souls *versus* the State of New York. There was that case up in Tylersville, just last year. Why, the Freedom of Worship Act *alone* . . ."

Braddock sighed, tacitly admitting that he knew Aaron was right—perhaps he had hoped to bluff them into obeying. "The 'Flood Congress' of '93," Braddock said, with bitter contempt. "They were so goddamned panic-stricken and full of sick chatter about Armageddon that you could've rammed *any* nonsense down their throats. That'a bad law, a pisspoor law . . ."

"Be that as it may, sheriff, you have no authority whatsoever—"

Abner suddenly began to speak, talking with a slow heavy deliberateness, musingly, almost reminiscently, ignoring the conversation he was interrupting—and indeed, perhaps he had not even been listening to it. "My grandfather lived right here on this farm, and *his* father before him—you know that, Sam? *They* lived by the old ways, and they survived and prospered. Greatgranddad, there wasn't hardly anything he needed from the outside world, anything he needed to *buy*, except maybe nails and such-like, and he could've made them himself too, if he'd needed to. Everything they needed, everything they ate, or wore, or used, they got from the woods, or from out of the soil of this farm, right here. *We* don't know how to do that anymore. We forgot the old ways, we turned our faces away, which is why the Flood came on us as a Judgement, a Judgement and a scourge, a scouring, a winnowing. The Old Days have come back again, and we've forgotten so goddamned *much*, we're almost helpless now that there's no goddamned K-mart down the goddamned street. We've got to go back to the old ways, or we'll pass from the earth, and be seen no more in it . . ." He was sweating now, staring earnestly at Braddock, as if to compel him by force of will alone to share the vision. "But it's so *hard*, Sam. . . . We have to *work* at relearning the old ways, we have to reinvent them as we go, step by step . . ."

"Some things we were better off without," Braddock said grimly.

"Up at Tylersville, they *doubled* their yield last harvest. Think what that could mean to a county as hungry as this one has been—"

Braddock shook his iron-gray head, and held up one hand, as if he were directing traffic. "I'm telling you, Abner, the town won't stand for this—I'm bound to warn you that some of the boys just might decide to go outside the law with this thing." He paused. "And, unofficially of course, I just might be inclined to give them a hand . . ."

Mrs. Crammer laughed. She had been sitting quietly and taking all of this in, smiling good-naturedly from time to time, and her laugh was a shocking thing in that stuffy little room, harsh as a crow's caw. "You'll do *nothing*, Sam Braddock," she said jovially. "And neither will anybody else. More than half the county's with us already, nearly all the country folk, and a good part of the town, too." She smiled pleasantly at him, but her eyes were small and hard. "Just you remember, we *know* where *you* live, Sam Braddock. And we know where your sister lives, too, and your sister's child, over to Framington . . ."

"Are you threatening an officer of the law?" Braddock said, but he said it in a weak voice, and his face, when he turned it away to stare at the floor, looked sick and old. Mrs. Crammer laughed again, and then there was silence.

Braddock kept his face turned down for another long moment, and then he put his hat back on, squashing it down firmly on his head, and when he looked up he pointedly ignored the brethren and addressed his next remark to Roy. "You don't have to stay with these people, son," he said. "*That's* the law, too." He kept his eyes fixed steadily on Roy. "You just say the word, son, and I'll take you straight out of here, right now." His jaw was set, and he touched the butt of his revolver, as if for encouragement. "They can't stop us. How about it?"

"No, thank you," Roy said quietly. "I'll stay."

That night, while Abner wrung his hands and prayed aloud, Roy sat half dozing before the parlor fire, unconcerned, watching the firelight throw Abner's gesticulating shadow across the whitewashed walls. There was something in the wine they kept giving him, Roy knew, maybe somebody's saved-up Quāāludes, but he didn't need it. Abner kept exhorting him to let the Peace of God into his heart, but he didn't need that either. He didn't need anything. He felt calm and self-possessed and remote, disassociated from everything that went on around him, as if he were looking down on the world through the wrong end of a telescope, feeling only a mild scientific interest as he watched the tiny mannequins swirl and pirouette. . . . Like watching television with the sound off. If this was the Peace of God, it had settled down on him months ago, during the dead of that terrible winter, while he had struggled twelve hours a day to load foundation stone in the face of icestorms and the razoring wind, while they had all, wetbacks and brethren alike, come close to starving. About the same time that word of the goings-on at Tylersville had started to seep down from the brethren's parent church upstate, about the same time that Abner, who until then had totally ignored their kinship, had begun to talk to him in the evenings about the old ways. . . .

Although perhaps the great dead cold had started to settle in even earlier, that first day of the new world, while they were driving off across foundering Brigantine, the water already up over the hubcaps of the Toyota, and he had heard Toby barking frantically somewhere behind them. . . . His dad had died that day, died of a heart attack as he fought to get them onto an overloaded boat that would take them across to the "safety" of the New Jersey mainland. His mother had died months later in one of the sprawling refugee camps, called "Floodtowns," that had sprung up on high ground everywhere along the new coastlines. She had just given up—sat down in the mud, rested her head on her knees, closed her eyes, and died. Just like that. Roy had seen the phenomenon countless times in the Floodtowns, places so festeringly horrible that even life on Abner's farm, with its Dickensian bleakness, forced labor, and short rations, had seemed—and was—a distinct change for the better. It was odd, and wrong, and sometimes it bothered him a little, but he hardly ever thought of his mother and father anymore—it was as if his mind shut itself off every time he came to those memories; he had never even cried for them, but all he had to do was close his eyes and he could see Toby, or his cat Basil running toward him and meowing with his tail held up over his back like a flag, and grief would come up like black bile at the back of his throat. . . .

It was still dark when they left the farmhouse. Roy and Abner and Aaron walked together, Abner carrying a large tattered carpetbag. Hank and Raymond ranged ahead with shotguns, in case there was trouble, but the last of the afternoon's gawkers had been driven off hours before by the cold, and the road was empty, a dim charcoal line through the slowly-lightening darkness. No one spoke, and there was no sound other than the sound of boots crunching on gravel. It was chilly again that morning, and Roy's bare feet burned against the macadam, but he trudged along stoically, ignoring the bite of cinders and pebbles. Their breath steamed faintly against the paling stars. The fields stretched dark and formless around them to either side of the road, and once they heard the rustling of some unseen animal fleeing away from them through the stubble. Mist flowed slowly down the road to meet them, sending out gleaming silver fingers to curl around their legs.

The sky was graying to the east, where the sea slept behind the mountains. Roy could imagine the sea rising higher and higher until it found its patient way around the roots of the hills and came spilling into the tableland beyond, flowing steadily forward like the mist, spreading out into a placid sheet of water that slowly swallowed the town, the farmhouse, the fields, until only the highest branches of the trees remained, held up like the beckoning arms of the drowned, and then they too would slide slowly, peacefully, beneath the water. . . .

A bird was crying out now, somewhere in the darkness, and they were walking through the fields, away from the road, cold mud squelching underfoot, the dry stubble crackling around them. Soon it would be time to sow the spring wheat, and after that, the corn. . . .

They stopped. Wind sighed through the dawn, muttering in the throat of the world. Still no one had spoken. Then hands were helping him remove the old bathrobe he'd been wearing. . . . Before leaving the house, he had been bathed, and annointed with a thick fragrant oil, and with a tiny silver scissors Mrs. Reardon had clipped a lock of his hair for each of the brethren.

Suddenly he was naked, and he was being urged forward again, his feet stumbling and slow.

They had made a wide ring of automobile flares here, the flares spitting and sizzling luridly in the wan dawn light, and in the center of the ring, they had dug a hollow in the ground.

He lay down in the hollow, feeling his naked back and buttocks settle into the cold mud, feeling it mat the hair on the back of his head. The mud made little sucking noises as he moved his arms and legs, settling in, and then he stretched out and lay still. The dawn breeze was cold, and he shivered in the mud, feeling it take hold of him like a giant's hand, tightening around him, pulling him down with a grip old and cold and strong . . .

They gathered around him, seeming, from his low perspective, to tower miles into the sky. Their faces were harsh and angular, gouged with lines and shadows that made them look like something from a stark old woodcut. Abner bent down to rummage in the carpetbag, his harsh woodcut face close to Roy's for a moment, and when he straightened up again he had the big fine-honed hunting knife in his hand.

Abner began to speak now, groaning out the words in a loud, harsh voice, but Roy was no longer listening. He watched calmly as Abner lifted the knife high into the air, and then he turned his head to look east, as if he could somehow see across all the intervening miles of rock and farmland and forest to where the sea waited behind the mountains . . .

Is this enough? he thought disjointedly, ignoring the towering scarecrow figures that were swaying in closer over him, straining his eyes to look east, to where the Pres-

ence lived . . . speaking now only to that Presence, to the
sea, to that vast remorseless deity, bargaining with it can-
nily, hopefully, shrewdly, like a country housewife at market, proffering it the fine rich red gift of his death. Is this
enough? Will this do?

Will you stop now?

ʃlouJ Birdʃ

by Ian Watson

Ian Watson, a graduate of Oxford University, lives with his wife and daughter in North Hamptonshire, Great Britain. He has taught in Japan and Tanzania. His first science fiction novel, The Embedding, *won the French Prix Apollo and was runner-up for the John W. Campbell Memorial Award; his second novel in the field,* The Jonah Kit, *won the British Science Fiction Association Award. He is also the author of* The Martian Inca, Alien Embassay, Miracle Visitors, God's World, *and* Chekhov's Journey. *His most recent novel,* The Book of the River, *the first volume of a triology in progress, was serialized in* The Magazine of Fantasy and Science Fiction. *He is a member of the Campaign for Nuclear Disarmament and of the growing British organization BAND (Book Action for Nuclear Disarmament).*

Ian Watson is the British regional director of the Science Fiction Writers of America and the European editor of the SFWA Bulletin.

Slow Birds *was nominated for the 1983 Nebula for best novelette.*

It was Mayday, and the skate-sailing festival that year was being held at Tuckerton.

By late morning, after the umpires had been out on the glass plain setting red flags around the circuit, cumulous clouds began to fill a previously blue sky, promising ideal conditions for the afternoon's sport. No rain; so that the glass wouldn't be an inch deep in water as last year at Atherton. No dazzling glare to blind the spectators, as the year before that at Buckby. And a breeze verging on brisk without ever becoming fierce: perfect to speed the com-

petitors' sails along without lifting people off their feet and
tumbling them, as four years previously at Edgewood
when a couple of broken ankles and numerous bruises had
been sustained.

After the contest there would be a pig roast; or rather
the succulent fruits thereof, for the pig had been turning
slowly on its spit these past thirty-six hours. And there
would be kegs of Old Codger Ale to be cracked. But right
now Jason Babbidge's mind was mainly occupied with
checking out his glass-skates and his fine crocus-yellow
hand-sail.

As high as a tall man, and of best old silk, only patched
in a couple of places, the sail's fore-spar of flexible ash was
bent into a bow belly by a strong hemp cord. Jason plucked
this thoughtfully like a harpist, testing the tension. Already a fair number of racers were out on the glass, showing off their paces to applause. Tuckerton folk mostly, they
were—acting as if they owned the glass hereabouts and
knew it more intimately than any visitors could. Not that it
was in any way different from the same glass over Atherton way.

Jason's younger brother Daniel whistled appreciatively
as a Tuckerton man carrying purple silk executed perfect
circles at speed, his sail shivering as he tacked.

"Just look at him, Jay!"

"What, Bob Marchant? He took a pratfall last year.
Where's the use in working up a sweat before the whistle
blows?"

By now a couple of sisters from Buckby were out too
with matching black sails, skating figure-eights around
each other, risking collision by a hair's breadth.

"Go on, Jay," urged young Daniel. "Show 'em."

Contestants from the other villages were starting to
flood on to the glass as well, but Jason noticed how Max
Tarnover was standing not so far away, merely observing
these antics with a wise smile. Master Tarnover of Tucker-

ton, last year's victor at Atherton despite the drenching spray. . . . Taking his cue from this, and going one better, Jason ignored events on the glass and surveyed the crowds instead.

He noticed Uncle John Babbidge chatting intently to an Edgewood man over where the silver band was playing; which was hardly the quietest place to talk, so perhaps they were doing business. Meanwhile on the green beyond the band the children of five villages buzzed like flies from hoop-la to skittles to bran tub, to apples in buckets of water. And those grownups who weren't intent on the band or the practice runs or on something else, such as gossip, besieged the craft and produce stalls. There must be going on for a thousand people at the festival, and the village beyond looked deserted. Rugs and benches and half-barrels had even been set out near the edge of the glass for the old folk of Tuckerton.

As the band lowered their instruments for a breather after finishing *The Floral Dance,* a bleat of panic cut across the chatter of many voices. A farmer had just vaulted into a tiny sheep-pen where a lamb almost as large as its shorn, protesting dam was ducking beneath her to suckle and hide. Laughing, the farmer hauled it out and hoisted it by its neck and back legs to guess its weight, and maybe win a prize.

And now Jason's mother was threading her way through the crowd, chewing the remnants of a pasty.

"Best of luck, son!" She grinned.

"I've told you, Mum," protested Jason. "It's bad luck to say 'good luck'."

. "Oh, luck yourself! What's luck, anyway?" She prodded her Adam's apple as if to press the last piece of meat and potatoes on its way down, though really she was indicating that her throat was bare of any charm or amulet.

"I suppose I'd better make a move." Kicking off his sandals, Jason sat to lace up his skates. With a helping

hand from Daniel he rose and stood knock-kneed, blades
cutting into the turf while the boy hoisted the sails across
his shoulders. Jason gripped the leather straps on the bow-
string and the spine-spar.

"Okay." He waggled the sail this way and that. "Let's go,
then. I won't blow away."

But just as he was about to proceed down on to the glass,
out upon the glass less than a hundred yards away a slow
bird appeared.

It materialized directly in front of one of the Buckby
sisters. Unable to veer, she had no choice but to throw
herself backwards. Crying out in frustration, and perhaps
hurt by her fall, she skidded underneath the slow bird,
sledging supine upon her now snapped and crumpled sail.

They were called slow birds because they flew through
the air—at the stately pace of three feet per minute.

They looked a little like birds, too, though only a little.
Their tubular metal bodies were rounded at the head and
tapering to a finned point at the tail, with two stubby wings
midway. Yet these wings could hardly have anything to do
with suspending their bulk in the air; the girth of a bird
was that of a horse, and its length twice that of a man lying
full length. Perhaps those wings controlled orientation or
trim.

In color they were a silvery grey; though this was only
the color of their outer skin, made of a soft metal like lead.
Quarter of an inch beneath this coating their inner skins
were black and stiff as steel. The noses of the birds were all
scored with at least a few scrape marks due to encounters
with obstacles down the years; slow birds always kept the
same height above ground—underbelly level with a man's
shoulders—and they would bank to avoid substantial
buildings or mature trees, but any frailer obstructions they
would push on through. Hence the individual patterns of
scratches. However, a far easier way of telling them apart

was by the graffiti carved on so many of their flanks; initials entwined in hearts, dates, place names, fragments of messages. These amply confirmed how very many slow birds there must be in all—something of which people could not otherwise have been totally convinced. For no one could keep track of a single slow bird. After each one had appeared—over hill, down dale, in the middle of a pasture or half way along a village street—it would fly onward slowly for any length of time between an hour and a day, covering any distance between a few score yards and a full mile. And vanish again. To reappear somewhere else unpredictably: far away or close by, maybe long afterwards or maybe soon.

Usually a bird would vanish, to reappear again.

Not always, though. Half a dozen times a year, within the confines of this particular island country, a slow bird would reach its journey's end.

It would destroy itself, and all the terrain around it for a radius of two and a half miles, fusing the landscape instantly into a sheet of glass. A flat, circular sheet of glass. A polarized, limited zone of annihilation. Scant yards beyond its rim a person might escape unharmed, only being deafened and dazzled temporarily.

Hitherto no slow bird had been known to explode so as to overlap an earlier sheet of glass. Consequently many towns and villages clung close to the borders of what had already been destroyed, and news of a fresh glass plain would cause farms and settlements to spring up there. Even so, the bulk of people still kept fatalistically to the old historic towns. They assumed that a slow bird wouldn't explode in their midst during their own lifetimes. And if it did, what would they know of it? Unless the glass happened merely to bisect a town—in which case, once the weeping and mourning was over, the remaining citizenry could relax and feel secure.

True, in the long term the whole country from coast to

coast and from north to south would be a solid sheet of
glass. Or perhaps it would merely be a checkerboard, of
circles touching circles: a glass mosaic. With what in between? Patches of desert dust, if the climate dried up due
to reflections from the glass. Or floodwater, swampland.
But that day was still far distant: a hundred years away,
two hundred, three. So people didn't worry too much.
They had been used to this all their lives long, and their
parents before them. Perhaps one day the slow birds
would stop coming. And going. And exploding. Just as
they had first started, once. Certainly the situation was no
different, by all accounts, anywhere else in the world. Only
the seas were clear of slow birds. So maybe the human race
would have to take to rafts one day. Though by then, with
what would they build them? Meanwhile, people got by;
and most had long ago given up asking why. For there was
no answer.

   The girl's sister helped her rise. No bones broken, it
seemed. Only an injury to dignity; and to her sail.
   The other skaters had all coasted to a halt and were
staring resentfully at the bird in their midst. Its belly and
sides were almost bare of graffiti; seeing this, a number of
youths hastened on to the glass, clutching penknives, rusty
nails and such. But an umpire waved them back angrily.
   "Shoo! Be off with you!" His gaze seemed to alight on
Jason, and for a fatuous moment Jason imagined that it
was himself to whom the umpire was about to appeal; but
the man called, "Master Tarnover!" instead, and Max
Tarnover duck-waddled past then glided out over the
glass, to confer.
   Presently, the umpire cupped his hands. "We're delaying
the start for half an hour," he bellowed. "Fair's fair: young
lady ought to have a chance to fix her sail, seeing as it
wasn't her fault."
   Jason noted a small crinkle of amusement on Tarnover's

face; for now either the other competitors would have to carry on prancing around tiring themselves with extra practice which none of them needed, or else troop off the glass for a recess and lose some psychological edge. In fact almost everyone opted for a break and some refreshments.

"Luck indeed!" snorted Mrs. Babbidge, as Max Tarnover clumped back their way.

Tarnover paused by Jason. "Frankly I'd say her sail's a wreck," he confided. "But what can you do? The Buckby lot would have been bitching on otherwise. 'Oh, she could have won. If she'd had ten minutes to fix it.' Bloody hunk of metal in the way." Tarnover ran a lordly eye over Jason's sail "What price skill, then?"

Daniel Babbidge regarded Tarnover with a mixture of hero worship and hostile partisanship on his brother's behalf. Jason himself only nodded and said, "Fair enough." He wasn't certain whether Tarnover was acting generously—or with patronizing arrogance. Or did this word in his ear mean that Tarnover actually saw Jason as a valid rival for the silver punch-bowl this year round?

Obviously young Daniel did not regard Jason's response as adequate. He piped up: "So where do *you* think the birds go, Master Tarnover, when they aren't here?"

A good question: quite unanswerable, but Max Tarnover would probably feel obliged to offer an answer if only to maintain his pose of worldly wisdom. Jason warmed to his brother, while Mrs. Babbidge, catching on, cuffed the boy softly.

"Now don't you go wasting Master Tarnover's time. Happen he hasn't given it a moment's thought, all his born days."

"Oh, but I have," Tarnover said.

"Well?" the boy insisted.

"Well . . . maybe they don't go anywhere at all."

Mrs. Babbidge chuckled, and Tarnover flushed.

"What I mean is, maybe they just stop being in one place then suddenly they're in the next place."

"If only you could skate like that!" Jason laughed. "Bit slow, though . . . Everyone would still pass you by at the last moment."

"They must go somewhere," young Dan said doggedly. "Maybe it's somewhere we can't see. Another sort of place, with other people. Maybe it's them that builds the birds."

"Look, freckleface, the birds don't come from Russ, or 'Merica, or anywhere else. So where's this other place?"

"Maybe it's right here, only we can't see it."

"And maybe pigs have wings." Tarnover looked about to march towards the cider and perry stall; but Mrs. Babbidge interposed herself smartly.

"Oh, as to that, I'm sure our sow Betsey couldn't fly, wings or no wings. Just hanging in the air like that, and so heavy."

"Weighed a bird recently, have you?"

"They look heavy, Master Tarnover."

Tarnover couldn't quite push his way past Mrs. Babbidge, not with his sail impeding him. He contented himself with staring past her, and muttering, "If we've nothing sensible to say about them, in my opinion it's better to shut up."

"But it isn't better," protested Daniel. "They're blowing the world up. Bit by bit. As though they're at war with us."

Jason felt humorously inventive. "Maybe that's it. Maybe these other people of Dan's are at war with us—only they forgot to mention it. And when they've glassed us all, they'll move in for the holidays. And skate happily for ever more."

"Damn long war, if that's so," growled Tarnover. "Been going on over a century now."

"Maybe that's why the birds fly so slowly," said Daniel. "What if a year to us is like an hour to those people? That's why the birds don't fall. They don't have time to."

Tarnover's expression was almost savage. "And what if the birds come only to punish us for our sins? What if they're simply a miraculous proof—"

"—that the Lord cares about us? And one day He'll forgive us? Oh goodness," and Mrs. Babbidge beamed, "surely you aren't one of *them*? A bright lad like you. Me, I don't even put candles in the window or tie knots in the bedsheets anymore to keep the birds away." She ruffled her younger son's mop of red hair. "Every one dies sooner or later, Dan. You'll get used to it, when you're properly grown up. When it's time to die, it's time to die."

Tarnover looked furiously put out; though young Daniel also seemed distressed in a different way.

"And when you're thirsty, it's time for a drink!" Spying an opening, and his opportunity, Tarnover sidled quickly around Mrs. Babbidge and strode off. She chuckled as she watched him go.

"That's put a kink in his sail!"

Forty-one other contestants, besides Jason and Tarnover, gathered between the starting flags, though not the girl who had fallen. Despite all best efforts she was out of the race, and sat morosely watching.

Then the Tuckerton umpire blew his whistle, and they were off.

The course was in the shape of a long bloomer loaf. First, it curved gently along the edge of the glass for three quarters of a mile, then bent sharply around in a half circle on to the straight, returning towards Tuckerton. At the end of the straight, another sharp half circle brought it back to the starting—and finishing—line. Three circuits in all were to be skate-sailed before the victory whistle blew. Much more than this, and the lag between leaders and stragglers could lead to confusion.

By the first turn Jason was ahead of the rest of the field, and all his practice since last year was paying off. His skates raced over the glass. The breeze thrust him convincingly. As he rounded the end of the loaf, swinging his sail to a new pitch, he noted Max Tarnover hanging back in fourth place. Determined to increase his lead, Jason leaned so close to the flag on the entry to the straight that he almost tipped it. Compensating, he came poorly on to the straight, losing a few yards. By the time Jason swept over the finishing line for the first time, to cheers from Atherton villagers, Tarnover was in third position; though he was making no very strenuous effort to overhaul, Jason realized that Tarnover was simply letting him act as pacemaker.

But a skate-sailing race wasn't the same as a foot race, where a pacemaker was generally bound to drop back eventually. Jason pressed on. Yet by the second crossing of the line Tarnover was ten yards behind, moving without apparent effort as though he and his sail and the wind and the glass were one. Noting Jason's glance, Tarnover grinned and put on a small burst of speed to push the front-runner to even greater efforts. And as he entered on the final circuit Jason also noted the progress of the slow bird, off to his left, now midway between the long curve and the straight, heading in the general direction of Edgewood. Even the laggards ought to clear the final straight before the thing got in their way, he calculated.

This brief distraction was a mistake. Tarnover was even closer behind him now, his sail pitched at an angle which must have made his wrists ache. Already he was drifting aside to overhaul Jason. And at this moment Jason grasped how he could win: by letting Tarnover think that he was pushing Jason beyond his capacity—so that Tarnover would be fooled into overexerting himself too soon.

"Can't catch me!" Jason called into the wind, guessing that Tarnover would misread this as braggadocio and assume that Jason wasn't really thinking ahead. At the same time Jason slackened his own pace slightly, hoping that his rival would fail to notice, since this was at odds with his own boast. Pretending to look panicked, he let Tarnover overtake—and saw how Tarnover continued to trip his sail strenuously even though he was actually moving a little slower than before. Without realizing it, Tarnover had his angle wrong; he was using unnecessary wrist action.

Tarnover was in the lead now. Immediately all psychological pressure lifted from Jason. With ease and grace he stayed a few yards behind, just where he could benefit from the 'eye' of air in Tarnover's wake. And thus he remained till half way down the final straight, feeling like a kestrel hanging in the sky with a mere twitch of its wings before swooping.

He held back; held back. Then suddenly changing the cant of his sail he did swoop—into the lead again.

It was a mistake. It had been a mistake all along. For as Jason sailed past, Tarnover actually laughed. Jerking his brown and orange silk to an easier, more efficient pitch, Tarnover began to pump his legs, skating like a demon. Already he was ahead again. By five yards. By ten. And entering the final curve.

As Jason tried to catch up in the brief time remaining, he knew how he had been fooled; though the knowledge came too late. So cleverly had Tarnover fixed Jason's mind on the stance of the sails, by holding his own in such a way—a way, too, which deliberately created that convenient eye of air—that Jason had quite neglected the contribution of his legs and skates, taking this for granted, failing to monitor it from moment to moment. It only took moments to recover and begin pumping his own legs too, but those few moments were fatal. Jason crossed the finish line one yard behind last year's victor; who was this year's victor too.

As he slid to a halt, bitter with chagrin, Jason was well aware that it was up to him to be gracious in defeat rather than let Tarnover seize that advantage, too.

He called out, loud enough for everyone to hear: "Magnificent, Max! Splendid skating! You really caught me on the hop there."

Tarnover smiled for the benefit of all onlookers.

"What a noisy family you Babbidges are," he said softly; and skated off to be presented with the silver punch-bowl again.

Much later that afternoon, replete with roast pork and awash with Old Codger Ale, Jason was waving an empty beer mug about as he talked to Bob Marchant in the midst of a noisy crowd. Bob, who had fallen so spectacularly the year before. Maybe that was why he had skated diffidently today and been one of the laggards.

The sky was heavily overcast, and daylight too was failing. Soon the homeward trek would have to start.

One of Jason's drinking and skating partners from Atherton, Sam Partridge, thrust his way through.

"Jay! That brother of yours: he's out on the glass. He's scrambled up on the back of the bird. He's riding it."

"*What?*"

Jason sobered rapidly, and followed Partridge with Bob Marchant tagging along behind.

Sure enough, a couple of hundred yards away in the gloaming Daniel was perched astride the slow bird. His red hair was unmistakable. By now a lot of other people were beginning to take notice and point him out. There were some ragged cheers, and a few angry protests.

Jason clutched Partridge's arm. "Somebody must have helped him up. Who was it?"

"Haven't.the foggiest. That boy needs a good walloping."

"Daniel *Babbidge!*" Mrs. Babbidge was calling nearby. She too had seen. Cautiously she advanced on to the glass, wary of losing her balance.

Jason and company were soon at her side. "It's all right,

Mum," he assured her. "I'll fetch the little . . . perisher."

Courteously Bob Marchant offered his arm and escorted Mrs. Babbidge back on the rough ground again. Jason and Partridge stepped flat-foot out across the vitrified surface accompanied by at least a dozen curious spectators.

"Did anyone spot who helped him up?" Jason demanded of them. No one admitted it.

When the group was a good twenty yards from the bird, everyone but Jason halted. Pressing on alone, Jason pitched his voice so that only the boy would hear.

"Slide off," he ordered grimly. "I'll catch you. Right monkey you've made of your mother and me."

"No," whispered Daniel. He clung tight, hands splayed like suckers, knees pressed to the flanks of the bird as though he was a jockey. "I'm going to see where it goes."

"Goes? Hell, I'm not going to waste time arguing. Get down!" Jason gripped an ankle and tugged, but this action only served to pull him up against the bird. Beside Dan's foot a heart with the entwined initials 'ZB' and 'EF' was carved. Turning away, Jason shouted, "Give me a hand, you lot! Come on someone, bunk me up!"

Nobody volunteered, not even Partridge.

"It won't bite you! There's no harm in touching it. Any kid knows that." Angrily he flat-footed back towards them. "Damn it all, Sam."

So now Partridge did shuffle forward, and a couple of other men too. But then they halted, gaping. Their expression puzzled Jason momentarily—till Sam Partridge gestured; till Jason swung round.

The air behind was empty.

The slow bird had departed suddenly. Taking its rider with it.

Half an hour later only the visitors from Atherton and their hosts remained on Tuckerton green. The Buckby,

Edgewood and Hopperton contingents had set off for home. Uncle John was still consoling a snivelling Mrs. Babbidge. Most faces in the surrounding crowd looked sympathetic, though there was a certain air of resentment, too, among some Tuckerton folk that a boy's prank had cast this black shadow over their Mayday festival.

Jason glared wildly around the onlookers. "Did nobody see who helped my brother up?" he cried. "Couldn't very well have got up himself, could he? Where's Max Tarnover? Where is he?"

"You aren't accusing Master Tarnover, by any chance?" growled a beefy farmer with a large wart on his cheek. "Sour grapes, Master Babbidge! Sour grapes is what that sounds like, and we don't like the taste of those here."

"Where is he, dammit?"

Uncle John laid a hand on his nephew's arm. "Jason, lad. Hush. This isn't helping your Mum."

But then the crowd parted, and Tarnover sauntered through, still holding the silver punch-bowl he had won.

"Well, Master Babbidge?" he enquired. "I hear you want a word with me."

"Did you see who helped my brother onto that bird? Well, did you?"

"I didn't see," replied Tarnover coolly.

It had been the wrong question, as Jason at once realized. For if Tarnover had done the deed himself, how could he possibly have watched himself do it?

"Then did you—"

"Hey up," objected the same farmer. "You've asked him, and you've had his answer."

"And I imagine your brother has had his answer too," said Tarnover. "I hope he's well satisfied with it. Naturally I offer my heartfelt sympathies to Mrs. Babbidge. If indeed the boy *has* come to any harm. Can't be sure of that, though, can we?"

"Course we can't!"

Jason tensed, and Uncle John tightened his grip on him. "*No*, lad. There's no use."

It was a sad and quiet long walk homeward that evening for the three remaining Babbidges, though a fair few Atherton folk behind sang blithely and tipsily, nonetheless. Occasionally Jason looked around for Sam Partridge, but Sam Partridge seemed to be successfully avoiding them.

The next day, May the second, Mrs. Babbidge rallied and declared it to be a "sorting out" day; which meant a day for handling all Daniel's clothes and storybooks and old toys lovingly before setting them to one side out of sight. Jason himself she packed off to his job at the saw-mill, with a flea in his ear for hanging around her like a whipped hound.

And as Jason worked at trimming planks that day the same shamed, angry frustrated thoughts skated round and round a single circuit in his head:

"In my book he's a murderer . . . You don't give a baby a knife to play with. He was cool as a cucumber afterwards. Not shocked, no. Smug . . ."

Yet what could be done about it? The bird might have hung around for hours more. Except that it hadn't . . .

Set out on a quest to find Daniel? But how? And where? Birds dodged around. Here, there and everywhere. No rhyme or reason to it. So what a useless quest that would be!

A quest to prove that Dan was alive. And if he were alive, then Tarnover hadn't killed him.

"In my book he's a murderer . . ." Jason's thoughts churned on impotently. It was like skating with both feet tied together.

Three days later a slow bird was sighted out Edgeway way. Jim Mitchum, the Edgewood thatcher, actually sought Jason out at the sawmill to bring him the news. He'd been coming over to do a job, anyway.

No doubt his visit was an act of kindness, but it filled Jason with guilt quite as much as it boosted his morale. For now he was compelled to go and see for himself, when obviously there was nothing whatever to discover. Downing tools, he hurried home to collect his skates and sail, and sped over the glass to Edgewood.

The bird was still there; but it was a different bird. There was no carved heart with the love-tangled initials 'ZB' and 'EF'.

And four days after that, mention came from Buckby of a bird spotted a few miles west of the village on the main road to Harborough. This time Jason borrowed a horse and rode. But the mention had come late; the bird had flown on a day earlier. Still, he felt obliged to search the area of the sighting for a fallen body or some other sign.

And the week after that a bird vanished only a mile from Atherton itself; this one vanished even as Jason arrived on the scene . . .

Then one night Jason went down to the Wheatsheaf. It was several weeks, in fact, since he had last been in the alehouse; now he meant to get drunk, at the long bar under the horse brasses.

Sam Partridge, Ned Darrow and Frank Yardley were there boozing; and an hour or so later Ned Darrow was offering beery advice.

"Look, Jay, where's the use in you dashing off every time someone spots a ruddy bird? Keep that up and you'll make a ruddy fool of yourself. And what if a bird pops up in Tuckerton? Bound to happen sooner or later. Going to rush off there too, are you, with your tongue hanging out?"

"All this time you're taking off work," said Frank Yardley. "You'll end up losing the job. Get on living is my advice."

"Don't know about that," said Sam Partridge unexpectedly. "Does seem to me as man ought to get his own

back. Supposing Tarnover did do the dirty on the Babbidges—"

"What's there to suppose about it?" Jason broke in angrily.

"Easy on, Jay. I was going to say as Babbidges are Atherton people. So he did the dirty on us all, right?"

"Thanks to some people being a bit slow in their help."

Sam flushed. "Now don't you start attacking everyone
right and left. No one's perfect. Just remember who your
real friends are, that's all."

"Oh, I'll remember, never fear."

Frank inclined an empty glass from side to side. "Right.
Whose round is it?"

One thing led to another, and Jason had a thick head the
next morning.

In the evening Ned banged on the Babbidge door.

"Bird on the glass, Sam says to tell you," he announced.
"How about going for a spin to see it?"

"I seem to recall last night you said I was wasting my
time."

"Ay, running around all over the country. But this is just
for a spin. Nice evening, like. Mind, if you don't want to
bother . . . Then we can all have a few jars in the Wheatsheaf afterwards."

The lads must really have missed him over the past few
weeks. Quickly Jason collected his skates and sail.

"But what about your supper?" asked his mother.
"Sheep's head broth."

"Oh, it'll keep, won't it? I might as well have a pasty or
two in the Wheatsheaf."

"Happen it's better you get out and enjoy yourself," she
said. "I'm quite content. I've got things to mend."

Twenty minutes later Jason, Sam, and Ned were skim-
ming over the glass two miles out. The sky was crimson

with banks of stratus, and a river of gold ran clear along
the horizon: foul weather tomorrow, but a glory this evening. The glassy expanse flowed with red and gold reflections: a lake of blood, fire, and molten metal. They did not
at first spot the other solitary sail-skater, nor he them, till
they were quite close to the slow bird.

Sam noticed first. "Who's that, then?"

The other sail was brown and orange. Jason recognized
it easily. "It's Tarnover!"

"Now's your chance to find out, then," said Ned.

"Do you mean that?"

Ned grinned. "Why not? Could be fun. Let's take him."

Pumping their legs, the three sail-skaters sped apart to
outflank Tarnover—who spied them and began to turn.
All too sharply, though. Or else he may have run into a
slick of water on the glass. To Jason's joy Max Tarnover,
champion of the five villages, skidded.

They caught him. This done, it didn't take the strength
of an ox to stop a skater from going anywhere else, however much he kicked and struggled. But Jason hit Tarnover on the jaw, knocking him senseless.

"What the hell you do that for?" asked Sam, easing Tarnover's fall on the glass.

"How else do we get him up on the bird?"

Sam stared at Jason, then nodded slowly.

It hardly proved the easiest operation to hoist a limp
and heavy body on to a slowly moving object while standing on a slippery surface; but after removing their skates
they succeeded. Before too long Tarnover lay sprawled
atop, legs dangling. Quickly with his pocket knife Jason
cut the hemp cord from Tarnover's sail and bound his
ankles together, running the tether tightly underneath the
bird.

Presently Tarnover awoke, and struggled groggily erect.
He groaned, rocked sideways, recovered his balance.

"Babbidge . . . Partridge, Ned Darrow. . . ? What the hell are you up to?"

Jason planted hands on hips. "Oh, we're just playing a little prank, same as you did on my brother Dan. Who's missing now; maybe forever, thanks to you."

"I never—"

"Admit it, then we might cut you down."

"And happen we mightn't," said Ned. "Not till the Wheatsheaf closes. But look on the bright side: happen we might."

Tarnover's legs twitched as he tested the bonds. He winced. "I honestly meant your brother no harm."

Sam smirked. "Nor do we mean you any. Ain't our fault if a bird decides to fly off. Anyway, only been here an hour or so. Could easily be here all night. Right, lads?"

"Right," said Ned. "And I'm thirsty. Race you? Last ones buys?"

"He's admitted he did it," said Jason. "You heard him."

"Look, I'm honestly very sorry if—"

"Shut up," said Sam. "You can stew for a while, seeing as how you've made the Babbidges stew. You can think about how sorry you really are." Partridge hoisted his sail.

It was not exactly how Jason had envisioned his revenge. This seemed like an anticlimax. Yet, to Tarnover no doubt it was serious enough. The champion was sweating slightly . . . Jason hoisted his sail, too. Presently the men skated away . . . to halt by unspoken agreement a quarter of a mile away. They stared back at Tarnover's little silhouette upon his metal steed.

"Now if it was me," observed Sam, "I'd shuffle myself along till I fell off the front . . . Rub you a bit raw, but that's how to do it."

"No need to come back, really," said Ned. "Hey, what's he trying?"

The silhouette had ducked. Perhaps Tarnover had panicked and wasn't thinking clearly, but it *looked* as if he

was trying to lean over far enough to unfasten the knot
beneath, or free one of his ankles. Suddenly the distant
figure inverted itself. It swung right round the bird, and
Tarnover's head and chest were hanging upside down, his
arms flapping. Or perhaps Tarnover had hoped the cord
would snap under his full weight; but snap it did not. And
once he was stuck in that position there was no way he
could recover himself upright again, or do anything about
inching along to the front of the bird.

Ned whistled. "He's messed himself up now, and no mistake. He's ruddy crucified himself."

Jason hesitated before saying it: "Maybe we ought to go
back? I mean, a man can die hanging upside-down too
long . . . Can't he?" Suddenly the whole episode seemed
unclean, unsatisfactory.

"Go back?" Sam Partridge fairly snarled at him. "You
were the big mouth last night. And whose idea was it to tie
him to the bird? You wanted him taught a lesson, and he's
being taught one. We're only trying to oblige you, Jay."

"Yes, I appreciate that."

"You made enough fuss about it. He isn't going to wilt
like a bunch of flowers in the time it takes us to swallow a
couple of pints."

And so they skated on, back to the Wheatsheaf in Atherton.

At ten thirty, somewhat the worse for wear, the three
men spilled out of the alehouse into Sheaf Street. A quarter moon was dodging from rift to rift in the cloudy sky,
shedding little light.

"I'm for bed," said Sam. "Let the sod wriggle his way
off."

"And who cares if he don't?" said Ned. "That way,
nobody'll know. Who wants an enemy for life? Do you,
Jay? This way you can get on with things. Happen Tarnover'll bring your brother back from wherever it is."

Shouldering his sail and swinging his skates, Ned wandered off up Sheaf Street.

"But," said Jason. He felt as though he had blundered into a midden. There was a reek of sordidness about what had taken place. The memory of Tarnover hanging upside-down had tarnished him.

"But what?" said Sam.

Jason made a show of yawning. "Nothing. See you." And he set off homeward.

But as soon as he was out of sight of Sam he slipped down through Butcher's Row in the direction of the glass alone. It was dark out there with no stars and only an occasional hint of moonlight, yet the breeze was steady and there was nothing to trip over on the glass. The bird wouldn't have moved more than a hundred yards. Jason made good speed.

The slow bird was still there. But Tarnover wasn't with it; its belly was barren of any hanged man.

As Jason skated to a halt, to look closer, figures arose in the darkness from where they had been lying flat upon the glass, covered by their sails. Six figures. Eight. Nine. All had lurked within two or three hundred yards of the bird, though not too close—nor any in the direction of Atherton. They had left a wide corridor open, which now they closed.

As the Tuckerton men moved in on him, Jason stood still, knowing that he had no chance.

Max Tarnover skated up, accompanied by that same beefy farmer with the wart.

"I did come back for you," began Jason.

The farmer spoke, but not to Jason. "Did he now? That's big of him. Could have saved his time, what with Tim Earnshaw happening along—when Master Tarnover was gone a long time. So what's to be done with him, eh?"

"Tit for tat, I'd say," said another voice.

"Let him go and look for his kid brother," offered a third. "Instead of sending other folk on his errands. What a nerve."

Tarnover himself said nothing; he just stood in the night silently.

So, presently, Jason was raised on to the back of the bird and his feet were tied tightly under it. But his wrists were bound together too, and for good measure the cord was linked through his belt.

Within a few minutes all the skaters had sped away towards Tuckerton.

Jason sat. Remembering Sam's words he tried to inch forward, but with both hands fastened to his waist this proved impossible; he couldn't gain purchase. Besides, he was scared of losing his balance as Tarnover had.

He sat and thought of his mother. Maybe she would grow alarmed when he didn't come home. Maybe she would go out and rouse Uncle John . . . And maybe she had gone to bed already.

But maybe she would wake in the night and glance into his room and send help. With fierce concentration he tried to project thoughts and images of himself at her, two miles away.

An hour wore on, then two; or so he supposed from the moving of the moon-crescent. He wished he could slump forward and sleep. That might be best; then he wouldn't know anything. He still felt drunk enough to pass out, even with his face pressed against metal. But he might easily slide to one side or the other in his sleep.

How could his mother survive a double loss? It seemed as though a curse had descended on the Babbidge family. But of course that curse had a human name; and the name was Max Tarnover. So for a while Jason damned him and imagined retribution by all the villagers of Atherton. A bloody feud. Cottages burnt. Perhaps a rape. Deaths even. No Mayday festival ever again.

But would Sam and Ned speak up? And would Atherton folk be sufficiently incensed, sufficiently willing to destroy the harmony of the five villages in a world where other things were so unsure? Particularly as some less than sympathetic soul might say that Jason, Sam, and Ned had started it all.

Jason was so involved in imagining a future feud between Atherton and Tuckerton that he almost forgot he was astride a slow bird. There was no sense of motion, no feeling of going anywhere. When he recollected where he was, it actually came as a shock.

He was riding a bird.

But for how long?

It had been around, what, six hours now? A bird could stay for a whole day. In which case he had another eighteen hours left to be rescued in. Or if it only stayed for half a day, that would take him through to morning. Just.

He found himself wondering what was underneath the metal skin of the bird. Something which could turn five miles of landscape into a sheet of glass, certainly. But other things too. Things that let it ignore gravity. Things that let it dodge in and out of existence. A brain of some kind, even?

"Can you hear me, bird?" he asked it. Maybe no one had ever spoken to a slow bird before.

The slow bird did not answer.

Maybe it couldn't, but maybe it could hear him, even so. Maybe it could obey orders.

"Don't disappear with me on your back," he told it. "Stay here. Keep on flying just like this."

But since it was doing just that already, he had no idea whether it was obeying him or not.

"Land, bird. Settle down onto the glass. Lie still."

It did not. He felt stupid. He knew nothing at all about the bird. Nobody did. Yet somewhere, someone knew. Unless the slow birds did indeed come from God, as miracles, to punish. To make men God-fearing. But why should a God want to be feared? Unless God was insane, in which case the birds might well come from Him.

They were something irrational, something from elsewhere, something which couldn't be understood by their victims any more than an ant colony understood the gardener's boot, exposing the white eggs to the sun and the sparrows.

Maybe something had entered the seas from elsewhere the previous century, something that didn't like land dwellers. Any of them. People or sheep, birds or worms or plants . . . It didn't seem likely. Salt water would rust steel, but for the first time in his life Jason thought about it intently.

"Bird, what are you? Why are you here?"

Why, he thought, is anything here? Why is there a world and sky and stars? Why shouldn't there simply be nothing for ever and ever?

Perhaps that was the nature of death: nothing for ever and ever. And one's life was like a slow bird. Appearing then vanishing, with nothing before and nothing after.

An immeasurable period of time later, dawn began to streak the sky behind him, washing it from black to grey. The greyness advanced slowly overhead as thick clouds filtered the light of the rising but hidden sun. Soon there was enough illumination to see clear all around. It must be five o'clock. Or six. But the grey glass remained blankly empty.

Who am I? wondered Jason, calm and still. Why am I conscious of a world? Why do people have minds, and think thoughts? For the first time in his life he felt that he was really thinking—and thinking had no outcome. It led nowhere.

He was, he realized, preparing himself to die. Just as all the land would die, piece by piece, fused into glass. Then no one would think thoughts any more, so that it wouldn't matter if a certain Jason Babbidge had ceased thinking at half past six one morning late in May. After all, the same thing happened every night when you went to sleep, didn't it? You stopped thinking. Perhaps everything would be purer and cleaner afterwards. Less untidy, less fretful: a pure ball of glass. In fact, not fretful at all, even if all the stars in the sky crashed into each other, even if the earth was swallowed by the sun. Silence, forever: once there was no one about to hear.

Maybe this was the message of the slow birds. Yet people only carved their initials upon them. And hearts. And the names of places which had been vitrified in a flash; or else which were going to be.

I'm becoming a philosopher, thought Jason in wonder.

He must have shifted into some hyperconscious state of mind, full of lucid clarity, though without immediate awareness of his surroundings, for he was not fully aware that help had arrived until the cord binding his ankles was cut and his right foot thrust up abruptly, toppling him off the other side of the bird into waiting arms.

Sam Patridge, Ned Darrow, Frank Yardley, and Uncle John, and Brian Sefton from the sawmill—who ducked under the bird brandishing a knife, and cut the other cord to free his wrists.

They retreated quickly from the bird, pulling Jason with them. He resisted feebly. He stretched an arm towards the bird.

"It's all right, lad," Uncle John soothed him.

"No, I want *to go*," he protested.

"Eh?"

At that moment the slow bird, having hung around long enough, vanished; and Jason stared at where it had been, speechless.

In the end his friends and uncle had to lead him away from that featureless spot on the glass, as though he was an idiot, someone touched by imbecility.

But Jason did not long remain speechless.

Presently he began to teach. Or preach. One or the other. And people listened; at first in Atherton, then in other places too.

He had learned wisdom from the slow bird, people said of him. He had communed with the bird during the night's vigil on the glass.

His doctrine of nothingness and silence spread, taking root in fertile soil, where there was soil remaining rather than glass—which was in most places, still. A paradox, perhaps: how eloquently he spoke—about being silent! But in so doing he seemed to make the silence of the glass lakes sing; and to this people listened with a new ear.

Jason traveled throughout the whole island. And this was another paradox, for what he taught was a kind of passivity, a blissful waiting for a death that was more than merely personal, a death which was also the death of the sun and stars and of all existence, a cosmic death which transfigured individual mortality. And sometimes he even sat on the back of a bird that happened by, to speak to a crowd—as though chancing fate or daring, begging the bird to take him away. But he never sat for more than an hour, then he would scramble down, trembling but quietly radiant. So besides being known as "The Silent Prophet," he was also known as "The Man who rides the Slow Birds."

On balance, it could have been said that he worked great psychological good for the communities that survived; and his words even spread overseas. His mother died proud of him—so he thought—though there was always an element of wistful reserve in her attitude . . .

Many years later, when Jason Babbidge was approaching sixty, and still no bird had ever borne him away, he settled back in Atherton in his old home—to which pilgrims of silence would come, bringing prosperity to the village and particularly to the Wheatsheaf; managed now by the daughter of the previous landlord.

And every Mayday the skate-sailing festival was still held, but now always on the glass at Atherton. No longer was it a race and a competition; since in the end the race of life could not be won. Instead it had become a pageant, a glass ballet, a re-enactment of the events of many years ago—a passion play performed by the four remaining villages. Tuckerton and all its folk had been glassed ten years before by a bird which destroyed itself so that the circle of annihilation exactly touched that edge of the glass where Tuckerton had stood till then.

One morning, the day before the festival, a knock sounded on Jason's door. His housekeeper, Martha Prestidge, was out shopping in the village so Jason answered.

A boy stood there. With red hair, and freckles.

For a moment Jason did not recognize the boy. But then he saw that it was Daniel. Daniel, unchanged. Or maybe grown up a little. Maybe a year older.

"Dan . . . ?"

The boy surveyed Jason bemusedly: his balding crown, his sagging girth, his now spindly legs, and the heavy stick with a stylized bird's head on which he leaned, gripping it with a liver-spotted hand.

"Jay," he said after a moment, "I've come back."

"Back? But. . . ."

"I know what the birds are now! They *are* weapons. Missiles. Tens and hundreds of thousands of them. There's a war going on. But it's like a game as well: a board game run by machines. Machines that think. It's only been going on for a few days in their time. The missiles shunt to and fro through time to get to their destination. But they can't shunt in the time of that world, because of cause and effect. So here's where they do their shunting. In our world. The other possibility-world."

"This is nonsense. I won't listen."

"But you must, Jay! It can be stopped for us before it's too late. I know how. Both sides can interfere with each other's missiles and explode them out of sight—that's here—if they can find them fast enough. But the war over there's completely out of control. There's a winning pattern to it, but this only matters to the machines any longer, and they're buried away underground. They build the birds at a huge rate with material from the Earth's crust, and launch them into other-time automatically."

"Stop it, Dan."

"I fell off the bird over there—but I fell into a lake, so I wasn't killed, only hurt. There are still some pockets of land left, around the Bases. They patched me up, the people there. They're finished, in another few hours of their time—though it's dozens of years to us. I brought them great hope, because it meant that all life isn't finished. Just theirs. Life can go on. What we have to do is build a machine that will stop their machines finding the slow birds over here. By making interference in the air. There are waves. Like waves of light, but you can't see them."

"You're raving."

"Then the birds will still shunt here. But harmlessly. Without glassing us. And in a hundred years time, or a few hundred, they'll even stop coming at all, because the winning pattern will be all worked out by then. One of the war machines will give up, because it lost the game. Oh, I know it ought to be able to give up right now! But there's an element of the irrational programmed into the machines' brains too, so they don't give up too soon. When they do, everyone will be long dead there on land—and some surviving people think the war machines will start glassing the ocean floor as a final strategy before they're through. But we can build an air-wave-maker. They've locked the knowledge in my brain. It'll take us a few years to mine the right metals and tool up and provide a power source . . ."

Young Daniel ran out of breath briefly. He gasped. "They had a prototype slow bird. They sat me on it and sent me into other-time again. They managed to guide it. It emerged just ten miles from here. So I walked home."

"Prototype? Air-waves? Power source? What are these?"

"I can tell you."

"Those are just words. Fanciful babble. Oh, for this babble of the world to still itself!"

"Just give me time, and I'll—"

"Time? You desire time? The mad ticking of men's minds instead of the great pure void of eternal silence? You reject acceptance? You want us to swarm forever aimlessly, deafening ourselves with our noisy chatter?"

"Look . . . I suppose you've had a long, tough life, Jay. Maybe I shouldn't have come here first."

"Oh, but you should indeed, my impetuous fool of a brother. And I do not believe my life has been ill-spent."

Daniel tapped his forehead. "It's all in here. But I'd better get it down on paper. Make copies and spread it around—just in case Atherton gets glassed. Then somebody else will know how to build the transmitter. And life can go on. Over there they think maybe the human race is the only life in the whole universe. So we have a duty to go on existing. Only, the others have destroyed themselves arguing about which way to exist. But we've still got time enough. We can build ships to sail through space to the stars. I know a bit about that too. I tell you, my visit brought them real joy in their last hours, to know this was all still possible after all."

"Oh, Dan." And Jason groaned. Patriarch-like, he raised his staff and brought it crashing down on Daniel's skull.

He had imagined that he mightn't really notice the blood amidst Daniel's bright red hair. But he did.

The boy's body slumped in the doorway. With an effort Jason dragged it inside, then with an even greater effort up the oak stairs to the attic where Martha Prestidge hardly ever went. The corpse might begin to smell after a while, but it could be wrapped up in old blankets and such.

However, the return of his housekeeper down below distracted Jason. Leaving the body on the floor he hastened out, turning the key in the lock and pocketing it.

It had become the custom to invite selected guests back to the Babbidge house following the Mayday festivities, so Martha Prestidge would be busy all the rest of the day cleaning and cooking and setting the house to rights. As was the way of the housekeepers, she hinted that Jason would get under her feet, so off he walked down to the glass and out onto its perfect flatness to stand and meditate. Villagers and visitors spying the lone figure out there nodded gladly. Their prophet was at peace, presiding over their lives. And over their deaths.

The skate-sailing masque, the passion play, was enacted as brightly and gracefully as ever the next day.

It was May the third before Jason could bring himself to go up to the attic again, carrying sacking and cord. He unlocked the door.

But apart from a dark stain of dried blood the floorboards were bare. There was only the usual jumble stacked around the walls. The room was empty of any corpse. And the window was open.

So he hadn't killed Daniel after all. The boy had recovered from the blow. Wild emotions stirred in Jason, disturbing his usual composure. He stared out of the window as though he might discover the boy lying below on the cobbles. But of Daniel there was no sign. He searched around Atherton like a haunted man, asking no questions but looking everywhere piercingly. Finding no clue, he ordered a horse and cart to take him to Edgewood. From there he traveled all around the glass, through Buckby and Hopperton; and now he asked wherever he went,

"Have you seen a boy with red hair?" The villagers told each other that Jason Babbidge had had another vision.

As well he might have, for within the year from far away news began to spread of a new teacher, with a new message. This new teacher was only a youth, but he had also ridden a slow bird—much farther than the Silent Prophet had ever ridden one.

However, it seemed that this young teacher was somewhat flawed, since he couldn't remember all the details of his message, of what he had been told to say. Sometimes he would beat his head with his fists in frustration, till it seemed that blood would flow. Yet perversely this touch of theatre appealed to some restless, troublesome streak in his audiences. They believed him because they saw his anguish, and it mirrored their own suppressed anxieties.

Jason Babbidge spoke zealously to oppose the rebellious new ideas, exhausting himself. All the philosophical beauty he had brought into the dying world seemed to hang in the balance; and reluctantly he called for a "crusade" against the new teacher, to defend his own dream of Submission.

Two years later, he might well have wished to call his words back, for their consequence was that people were tramping across the countryside in between the zones of annihilation armed with pitchforks and billhooks, cleavers and sickles. Villages were burnt; many hundreds were massacred; and there were rapes—all of which seemed to recall an earlier nightmare of Jason's from before the time of his revelation.

In the third year of this seemingly endless skirmish between the Pacificists and the Survivalists Jason died, feeling bitter beneath his cloak of serenity; and by way of burial his body was roped to a slow bird. Loyal mourners accompanied the bird in silent procession until it vanished hours later. A short while after that, quite suddenly at the Battle of Ashton Glass, it was all over, with victory for the Survivalists led by their young red-haired champion, who it was noted bore a striking resemblance to old Jason Babbidge, so that it almost seemed as though two basic principles of existence had been at contest in the world: two aspects of the selfsame being, two faces of one man.

Fifty years after that, by which time a full third of the land was glass and the climate was worsening, the Survival College in Ashton at last invented the promised machine; and from then on slow birds continued to appear and fly and disappear as before, but now none of them exploded.

And a hundred years after that all the slow birds vanished from the Earth. Somewhere, a war was over, logically and finally.

But by then, from an Earth four-fifths of whose land surface was desert or swamp—in between necklaces of barren shining glass—the first starship would arise into orbit.

It would be called *Slow Bird*. For it would fly to the stars, slowly. Slowly in human terms; two generations it would take. But that was comparatively fast.

A second starship would follow it; called *Daniel*.

Though after that massive and exhausting effort, there would be no more starships. The remaining human race would settle down to cultivate what remained of their garden in amongst the dunes and floods and acres of glass. Whether either starship would find a new home as habitable even as the partly glassed Earth, would be merely an article of faith.

On his deathbed, eighty years of age, in Ashton College lay Daniel who had never admitted to a family name.

The room was almost indecently overcrowded, though well if warmly ventilated by a wind whipping over Ashton

Glass, and bright-lit by the silvery blaze reflecting from that vitrified expanse.

The dying old man on the bed beneath a single silken sheet was like a bird himself now: shrivelled with thin bones, a beak of a nose, beady eyes, and a rooster's comb of red hair on his head.

He raised a frail hand as if to summon those closest even closer. Actually it was to touch the old wound in his skull which had begun to ache fiercely of late as though it was about to burst open or cave in, unlocking the door of memory—notwithstanding that no one now needed the key hidden there, since his Collegians had discovered it independently, given the knowledge that it existed.

Faces leaned over him: confident, dedicated faces.

"They've stopped exploding, then?" he asked, forgetfully.

"Yes, yes, years ago!" they assured him.

"And the stars—?"

"We'll build the ships. We'll discover how."

His hand sank back on to the sheet. "Call one of them—"

"Yes?"

"*Daniel.* Will you?"

They promised him this.

"That way . . . my spirit . . . "

"Yes?"

". . . will fly . . ."

"Yes?"

". . . into the silence of space."

This slightly puzzled the witnesses of his death; for they could not know that Daniel's last thought was that, when the day of the launching came, he and his brother might at last be reconciled.

Blood Music

by Greg Bear

It is not often that a writer takes two Nebula Awards in one year. Only five writers have done it since 1965, the first year the Nebulas were awarded by the Science Fiction Writers of America: Roger Zelazny, Samuel R. Delaney, Robert Silverberg, Ursula K. LeGuin, and Connie Willis. In 1984 Greg Bear joined this distinguished list, winning the novella prize with Hardfought *and the novelette award with* Blood Music, *which follows.*

There is a principle in nature I don't think anyone has pointed out before. Each hour, a myriad of trillions of little live things—bacteria, microbes, "animalcules"—are born and die, not counting for much except in the bulk of their existence and the accumulation of their tiny effects. They do not perceive deeply. They don't suffer much. A hundred billion, dying, would not begin to have the same importance as a single human death.

Within the ranks of magnitude of all creatures, small as microbes or great as humans, there is an equality of "elan," just as the branches of a tall tree, gathered together, equal the bulk of the limbs below, and all the limbs equal the bulk of the trunk.

That, at least is the principle. I believe Vergil Ulam was the first to violate it.

It had been two years since I'd last seen Vergil. My memory of him hardly matched the tan, smiling, well-dressed

146

gentleman standing before me. We had made a lunch appointment over the phone the day before, and now faced
each other in the wide double doors of the employees'
cafeteria at the Mount Freedom Medical Center.

"Vergil?" I asked. "My God, Vergil!"

"Good to see you, Edward." He shook my hand firmly.
He had lost ten or twelve kilos and what remained seemed
tighter, better proportioned. At university, Vergil had
been the pudgy, shock-haired, snaggle-toothed whiz kid
who hot-wired doorknobs, gave us punch that turned our
piss blue, and never got a date except with Eileen Terma-
gent, who shared many of his physical characteristics.

"You look fantastic," I said. "Spend a summer in Cabo
San Lucas?"

We stood in line at the counter and chose our food.
"The tan," he said, picking out a carton of chocolate milk,
"is from spending three months under a sun lamp. My
teeth were straightened just after I last saw you. I'll explain
the rest, but we need a place to talk where no one will listen
close."

I steered him to the smoker's corner, where three die-
hard puffers were scattered among six tables.

"Listen, I mean it," I said as we unloaded our trays.
"You've changed. You're looking good."

"I've changed more than you know." His tone was mo-
tion-picture ominous, and he delivered the line with a the-
atrical lift of his brows. "How's Gail?"

Gail was doing well, I told him, teaching nursery school.
We'd married the year before. His gaze shifted down to his
food—pineapple slice and cottage cheese, piece of banana
cream pie—and he said, his voice almost cracking, "Notice
something else?"

I squinted in concentration. "Uh."

"Look closer."

"I'm not sure. Well, yes, you're not wearing glasses. Con-
tacts?"

"No. I don't need them anymore."

"And you're a snappy dresser. Who's dressing you now? I hope she's as sexy as she is tasteful."

"Candice isn't—wasn't responsible for the improvement in my clothes," he said. "I just got a better job, more money to throw around. My taste in clothes is better than my taste in food, as it happens." He grinned the old Vergil self-deprecating grin, but ended it with a peculiar leer. "At any rate, she's left me, I've been fired from my job, I'm living on savings."

"Hold it," I said. "That's a bit crowded. Why not do a linear breakdown? You got a job. Where?"

"Genetron Corp.," he said. "Sixteen months ago."

"I haven't heard of them."

"You will. They're putting out common stock in the next month. It'll shoot off the board. They've broken through with MABs. Medical—"

"I know what MABs are," I interrupted. "At least in theory. Medically Applicable Biochips."

"They have some that work."

"What?" It was my turn to lift my brows.

"Microscopic logic circuits. You inject them into the human body, they set up shop where they're told and troubleshoot. With Dr. Michael Bernard's approval."

That was quite impressive. Bernard's reputation was spotless. Not only was he associated with the genetic engineering biggies, but he had made news at least once a year in his practice as a neurosurgeon before retiring. Covers on *Time, Mega, Rolling Stone.*

"That's supposed to be secret—stock, breakthrough, Bernard, everything." He looked around and lowered his voice. "But you do whatever the hell you want. I'm through with the bastards."

I whistled. "Make me rich, huh?"

"If that's what you want. Or you can spend some time with me before rushing off to your broker."

"Of course." He hadn't touched the cottage cheese or

pie. He had, however, eaten the pineapple slice and drunk the chocolate milk. "So tell me more."

"Well, in med school I was training for lab work. Biochemical research. I've always had a bent for computers, too. So I put myself through my last two years—".

"By selling software packages to Westinghouse," I said.

"It's good my friends remember. That's how I got involved with Genetron, just when they were starting out. They had big money backers, all the lab facilities I thought anyone would ever need. They hired me, and I advanced rapidly.

"Four months and I was doing my own work. I made some breakthroughs," he tossed his hand nonchalantly, "then I went off on tangents they thought were premature. I persisted and they took away my lab, handed it over to a certifiable flatworm. I managed to save part of the experiment before they fired me. But I haven't exactly been cautious . . . or judicious. So now it's going on outside the lab."

I'd always regarded Vergil as ambitious, a trifle cracked and not terribly sensitive. His relations with authority figures had never been smooth. Science, for him, was like the woman you couldn't possibly have, who suddenly opens her arms to you, long before you're ready for mature love—leaving you afraid you'll forever blow the chance, lose the prize, screw up royally. Apparently, he had. "Outside the lab? I don't get you."

"Edward, I want you to examine me. Give me a thorough physical. Maybe a cancer diagnostic. Then I'll explain more."

"You want a five-thousand-dollar exam?"

"Whatever you can do. Ultrasound, NMR, thermogram, everything."

"I don't know if I can get access to all that equipment. NMR full-scan has only been here a month or two. Hell, you couldn't pick a more expensive way—"

"Then ultrasound. That's all you'll need."

"Vergil, I'm an obstetrician, not a glamour-boy lab-tech. OB-GYN, butt of all jokes. If you're turning into a woman, maybe I can help you."

He leaned forward, almost putting his elbow into the pie, but swinging wide at the last instant by scant millimeters. The old Vergil would have hit it square. "Examine me closely and you'll . . . " He narrowed his eyes and shook his head. "Just examine me."

"So I make an appointment for ultrasound. Who's going to pay?"

"I'm on Blue Shield." He smiled and held up a medical credit card. "I messed with the personnel files at Genetron. Anything up to a hundred thousand dollars medical, they'll never check, never suspect."

He wanted secrecy, so I made arrangements. I filled out his forms myself. As long as everything was billed properly, most of the examination could take place without official notice. I didn't charge for my services. After all, Vergil had turned my piss blue. We were friends.

He came in late at night. I wasn't normally on duty then, but I stayed late, waiting for him on the third floor of what the nurses called the Frankenstein wing. I sat on an orange plastic chair. He arrived, looking olive-colored under the fluorescent lights.

He stripped, and I arranged him on the table. I noticed, first off, that his ankles looked swollen. But they weren't puffy. I felt them several times. They seemed healthy, but looked odd. "Hm," I said.

I ran the paddles over him, picking up areas difficult for the big unit to hit, and programmed the data into the imaging system. Then I swung the table around and inserted it into the enameled orifice of the ultrasound diagnostic unit, the hum-hole, so-called by the nurses.

I integrated the data from the hum-hole with that from the paddle sweeps and rolled Vergil out, then set up a video frame. The image took a second to integrate, then flowed into a pattern showing Vergil's skeleton.

Three seconds of that—my jaw gaping—and it switched to his thoracic organs, then his musculature, and finally, vascular system and skin.

"How long since the accident?" I asked, trying to take the quiver out of my voice.

"I haven't been in an accident," he said. "It was deliberate."

"Jesus, they beat you, to keep secrets?"

"You don't understand me, Edward. Look at the images again. I'm not damaged."

"Look, there's thickening here," I indicated the ankles, "and your ribs—that crazy zig-zag pattern of interlocks. Broken sometime, obviously. And—"

"Look at my spine," he said. I rotated the image in the video frame.

Buckminister Fuller, I thought. It was fantastic. A cage of triangular projections, all interlocking in ways I couldn't begin to follow, much less understand. I reached around and tried to feel his spine with my fingers. He lifted his arms and looked off at the ceiling.

"I can't find it," I said. "It's all smooth back there." I let go of him and looked at his chest, then prodded his ribs. They were sheathed in something tough and flexible. The harder I pressed, the tougher it became. Then I noticed another change.

"Hey," I said. "You don't have any nipples." There were tiny pigment patches, but no nipple formations at all.

"See?" Vergil asked, shrugging on the white robe, "I'm being rebuilt from the inside out."

In my reconstruction of those hours, I fancy myself saying, "So tell me about it." Perhaps mercifully, I don't remember what I actually said.

He explained with his characteristic circumlocutions.

Listening was like trying to get to the meat of a newspaper article through a forest of sidebars and graphic embellishments.

I simplify and condense.

Genetron had assigned him to manufacturing prototype biochips, tiny circuits made out of protein molecules. Some were hooked up to silicon chips little more than a micrometer in size, then sent through rat arteries to chemically keyed locations, to make connections with the rat tissue and attempt to monitor and even control lab-induced pathologies.

"*That* was something," he said.

"We recovered the most complex microchip by sacrificing the rat, then debriefed it—hooked the silicon portion up to an imaging system. The computer gave us bar graphs, then a diagram of the chemical characteristics of about eleven centimeters of blood vessel . . . then put it all together to make a picture. We zoomed down eleven centimeters of rat artery. You never saw so many scientists jumping up and down, hugging each other, drinking buckets of bug juice." Bug juice was lab ethanol mixed with Dr. Pepper.

Eventually, the silicon elements were eliminated completely in favor of nucleoproteins. He seemed reluctant to explain in detail, but I gathered they found ways to make huge molecules—as large as DNA, and even more complex—into electrochemical computers, using ribosome-like structures as "encoders" and "readers," and RNA as "tape." Vergil was able to mimic reproductive separation and reassembly in his nuceloproteins, incorporating program changes at key points by switching nucleotide pairs. "Genetron wanted me to switch over to supergene engineering, since that was the coming thing everywhere else. Make all kinds of critters, some out of our imagination. But I had different ideas." He twiddled his finger around his ear and made theremin sounds. "Mad scientist time,

right?" He laughed, then sobered. "I injected my best nucleoproteins into bacteria to make duplication and compounding easier. Then I started to leave them inside, so
the circuits could interact with the cells. They were heu-
ristically programmed; they taught themselves more than
I programmed them. The cells fed chemically coded information to the computers, the computers processed it and
made decisions, the cells became smart. I mean, smart as
planaria, for starters. Imagine an *E. coli* as smart as a
planarian worm!"

I nodded. "I'm imagining."

"Then I really went off on my own. We had the equipment, the techniques; and I knew the molecular language.
I could make really dense, really complicated biochips by
compounding the nucleoproteins, making them into little
brains. I did some research into how far I could go, theo-
retically. Sticking with bacteria, I could make a biochip
with the computing capacity of a sparrow's brain. Imagine
how jazzed I was! Then I saw a way to increase the complexity a thousandfold, by using something we regarded as
a nuisance—quantum chit-chat between the fixed elements of the circuits. Down that small, even the slightest
change could bomb a biochip. But I developed a program
that actually predicted and took advantage of electron tun-
neling. Emphasized the heuristic aspects of the computer,
used the chit-chat as a method of increasing complexity."

"You're losing me," I said.

"I took advantage of randomness. The circuits could
repair themselves, compare memories and correct faulty
elements. The whole schmeer. I gave them basic instructions: Go forth and multiply. Improve. By God, you
should have seen some of the cultures a week later! It was
amazing. They were evolving all on their own, like little
cities. I destroyed them all. I think one of the petri dishes
would have grown legs and walked out of the incubator if
I'd kept feeding it."

"You're kidding." I looked at him. "You're not kidding."

"Man, they *knew* what it was like to improve! They knew where they had to go, but they were just so limited, being in bacteria bodies, with so few resources."

"How smart were they?"

"I couldn't be sure. They were associating in clusters of a hundred to two hundred cells, each cluster behaving like an autonomous unit. Each cluster might have been as smart as a rhesus monkey. They exchanged information through their pili, passed on bits of memory and compared notes. Their organization was obviously different from a group of monkeys. Their world was so much simpler, for one thing. With their abilities, they were masters of the petri dishes. I put phages in with them; the phages didn't have a chance. They used every option available to change and grow."

"How is that possible?"

"What?" He seemed surprised I wasn't accepting everything at face value.

"Cramming so much into so little. A rhesus monkey is not your simple little calculator, Vergil."

"I haven't made myself clear," he said, obviously irritated. "I was using nucleoprotein computers. They're like DNA, but all the information can interact. Do you know how many nucleotide pairs there are in the DNA of a single bacteria?"

It had been a long time since my last biochemistry lesson. I shook my head.

"About two million. Add in the modified ribosome structures—fifteen thousand of them, each with a molecular weight of about three million—and consider the combinations and permutations. The RNA is arranged like a continuous loop paper tape, surrounded by ribosomes ticking off instructions and manufacturing protein chains . . ." His eyes were bright and slightly moist. "Besides, I'm not saying every cell was a distinct entity. They cooperated."

"How many bacteria in the dishes you destroyed?"

"Billions. I don't know." He smirked. "You got it, Edward. Whole planetsful of *E. coli.*"

"But they didn't fire you then?"

"No. They didn't know what was going on, for one thing. I kept compounding the molecules, increasing their size and complexity. When bacteria were too limited, I took blood from myself, separated out white cells, and injected them with the new biochips. I watched them, put them through mazes and little chemical problems. They were whizzes. Time is a lot faster at that level—so little distance for the messages to cross, and the environment is much simpler. Then I forgot to store a file under my secret code in the lab computers. Some managers found it and guessed what I was up to. Everybody panicked. They thought we'd have every social watchdog in the country on our backs because of what I'd done. They started to destroy my work and wipe my programs. Ordered me to sterilize my white cells. Christ." He pulled the white robe off and started to get dressed. "I only had a day or two. I separated out the most complex cells—"

"How complex?"

"They were clustering in hundred-cell groups, like the bacteria. Each group as smart as a ten-year-old kid, maybe." He studied my face for a moment. "Still doubting? Want me to run through how many nucleotide pairs there are in a mammalian cell? I tailored my computers to take advantage of the white cells' capacity. Ten billion nucleotide pairs, Edward. Ten E-fucking ten. And they don't have a huge body to worry about, taking up most of their thinking time."

"Okay," I said. "I'm convinced. What did you do?"

"I mixed the cells back into a cylinder of whole blood

and injected myself with it." He buttoned the top of his shirt and smiled thinly at me. "I'd programmed them with every drive I could, talked as high a level as I could using just enzymes and such. After that, they were on their own."

"You programmed them to go forth and multiply, improve?" I repeated.

"I think they developed some characteristics picked up by the biochips in their *E. coli* phases. The white cells could talk to each other with extruded memories. They also certainly found ways to ingest other types of cells and alter them without killing them."

"You're crazy."

"You can see the screen! Edward, I haven't been sick since. I used to get colds all the time. I've never felt better."

"They're inside you, finding things, changing them."

"And by now, each cluster is as smart as you or I."

"You're absolutely nuts."

He shrugged. "They fired me. They thought I was going to get revenge for what they did to my work. They ordered me out of the labs, and I haven't had a real chance to see what's been going on inside me until now. Three months."

"So . . ." My mind was racing. "You lost weight because they improved your fat metabolism. Your bones are stronger, your spine has been completely rebuilt—"

"No more backaches even if I sleep on my old mattress."

"Your heart looks different."

"I didn't know about the heart," he said, examining the frame image from a few inches. "About the fat—I was thinking about that. They could increase my brown cells, fix up the metabolism. I haven't been as hungry lately. I haven't changed my eating habits that much—I still want the same old junk—but somehow I get around to eating only what I need. I don't think they know what my brain is yet. Sure, they've got all the glandular stuff—but they don't have the *big* picture, if you see what I mean. They don't know *I'm* in there. But boy, they sure did figure out what my reproductive organs are."

I glanced at the image and shifted my eyes away.

"Oh, they look pretty normal," he said, hefting his scrotum obscenely. He snickered. "But how else do you think I'd land a real looker like Candice? She was just after a one-night stand with a techie. I looked okay then, no tan but trim, with good clothes. She'd never screwed a techie before. Joke time, right? But my little geniuses kept us up half the night. I think they made improvements each time. I felt like I had a goddamned fever."

His smile vanished. "But then one night my skin started to crawl. It really scared me. I thought things were getting out of hand. I wondered what they'd do when they crossed the blood-brain barrier and found out about *me*—about the brain's real function. So I began a campaign to keep them under control. I figured, the reason they wanted to get into the skin was the simplicity of running circuits across a surface. Much easier than trying to maintain chains of communication in and around muscles, organs, vessels. The skin was much more direct. So I bought a quartz lamp." He caught my puzzled expression. "In the lab, we'd break down the protein in biochip cells by exposing them to ultraviolet light. I alternated sunlamp with quartz treatments. Keeps them out of my skin, so far as I can tell, and gives me a nice tan."

"Give you skin cancer, too," I commented.

"They'll probably take care of that. Like police."

"Okay. I've examined you, you've told me a story I still find hard to believe . . . what do you want me to do?"

"I'm not as nonchalant as I act, Edward. I'm worried. I'd like to find some way to control them before they find out about my brain. I mean, think of it, they're in the trillions by now, each one smart. They're cooperating to some extent. I'm probably the smartest thing on the planet, and they haven't even begun to get their act together yet. I don't really want them to take over." He laughed very unpleasantly. "Steal my soul, you know? So think of some treatment to block them. Maybe we can starve the little buggers. Just think on it." He buttoned his shirt. "Give me a call." He handed me a slip of paper with his address and phone number. Then he went to the keyboard and erased the image on the frame, dumping the memory of the examination. "Just you," he said. "Nobody else for now. And please . . . hurry."

It was three o'clock in the morning when Vergil walked out of the examination room. He'd allowed me to take blood samples, then shaken my hand—his palm damp, nervous—and cautioned me against ingesting anything from the specimens.

Before I went home, I put the blood through a series of tests. The results were ready the next day.

I picked them up during my lunch break in the afternoon, then destroyed all the samples. I did it like a robot. It took me five days and nearly sleepless nights to accept what I'd seen. His blood was normal enough, though the machines diagnosed the patient as having an infection. High levels of leucocytes—white blood cells—and histamines. On the fifth day, I believed.

Gail was home before I, but it was my turn to fix dinner. She slipped one of the school's disks into the home system and showed me video art her nursery kids had been creating. I watched quietly, ate with her in silence.

I had two dreams, part of my final acceptance. The first that evening—which had me up thrashing in my sheets—I witnessed the destruction of the planet Krypton, Superman's home world. Billions of superhuman geniuses went screaming off in walls of fire. I related the destruction to my sterilizing the samples of Vergil's blood.

The second dream was worse. I dreamed that New York City was raping a woman. By the end of the dream, she was giving birth to little embryo cities, all wrapped up in translucent sacs, soaked with blood from the difficult labor.

I called him on the morning of the sixth day. He answered on the fourth ring. "I have some results," I said. "Nothing conclusive. But I want to talk with you. In person."

"Sure," he said. "I'm staying inside for the time being." His voice was strained; he sounded tired.

Vergil's apartment was in a fancy high-rise near the lake shore. I took the elevator up, listening to little advertising jingles and watching dancing holograms display products, empty apartments for rent, the building's hostess discussing social activities for the week.

Vergil opened the door and motioned me in. He wore a checked robe with long sleeves and carpet slippers. He clutched an unlit pipe in one hand, his fingers twisting it back and forth as he walked away from me and sat down, saying nothing.

"You have an infection," I said.

"Oh?"

"That's all the blood analyses tell me. I don't have access to the electron microscopes."

"I don't think it's really an infection," he said. "After all, they're my own cells. Probably something else . . . some sign of their presence, of the change. We can't expect to understand everything that's happening."

I removed my coat. "Listen," I said, "you have me worried now." The expression on his face stopped me: a kind of frantic beatitude. He squinted at the ceiling and pursed his lips.

"Are you stoned?" I asked.

He shook his head, then nodded once, very slowly. "Listening," he said.

"To what?"

"I don't know. Not sounds . . . exactly. Like music. The

heart, all the blood vessels, friction of blood along the arteries, veins. Activity. Music in the blood." He looked at me plaintively. "Why aren't you at work?"

"My day off. Gail's working."

"Can you stay?"

I shrugged. "I suppose." I sounded suspicious. I was glancing around the apartment, looking for ashtrays, packs of papers.

"I'm not stoned, Edward," he said. "I may be wrong, but I think something big is happening. I think they're finding out who I am."

I sat down across from Vergil, staring at him intently. He didn't seem to notice. Some inner process was involving him. When I asked for a cup of coffee, he motioned to the kitchen. I boiled a pot of water and took a jar of instant from the cabinet. With cup in hand, I returned to my seat. He was twisting his head back and forth, eyes open. "You always knew what you wanted to be, didn't you?" he asked.

"More or less."

"A gynecologist. Smart moves. Never false moves. I was different. I had goals, but no direction. Like a map without roads, just places to be. I didn't give a shit for anything, anyone but myself. Even science. Just a means. I'm surprised I got so far. I even hated my folks."

He gripped his chair arms.

"Something wrong?" I asked.

"They're talking to me," he said. He shut his eyes.

For an hour he seemed to be asleep. I checked his pulse, which was strong and steady, felt his forehead—slightly cool—and made myself more coffee. I was looking through a magazine, at a loss what to do, when he opened his eyes again. "Hard to figure exactly what time is like for them," he said. "It's taken them maybe three, four days to figure out language, key human concepts. Now they're on to it. On to me. Right now."

"How's that?"

He claimed there were thousands of researchers hooked up to his neurons. He couldn't give details. "They're damned efficient, you know," he said. "They haven't screwed me up yet."

"We should get you into the hospital now."

"What in hell could they do? Did you figure out any way to control them? I mean, they're my own cells."

"I've been thinking. We could starve them. Find out what metabolic differences—"

"I'm not sure I want to be rid of them," Vergil said. "They're not doing any harm."

"How do you know?"

He shook his head and held up one finger. "Wait. They're trying to figure out what space is. That's tough for them: They break distances down into concentrations of chemicals. For them, space is like intensity of taste."

"Vergil—"

"Listen! Think, Edward!" His tone was excited but even. "Observe! Something big is happening inside me. They talk to each other across the fluid, through membranes. They tailor something—viruses?—to carry data stored in nucleic acid chains. I think they're saying 'RNA.' That makes sense. That's one way I programmed them. But plasmid-like structures, too. Maybe that's what your machines think is a sign of infection—all their chattering in my blood, packets of data. Tastes of other individuals. Peers. Superiors. Subordinates."

"Vergil, I'm listening, but I still think you should be in a hospital."

"This is my show, Edward," he said. "I'm their universe. They're amazed by the new scale." He was quiet again for a time. I squatted by his chair and pulled up the sleeve to his robe. His arm was criss-crossed with white lines. I was

about to go to the phone and call for an ambulance when
he stood and stretched. "Do you realize," he said, "how
many body cells we kill each time we move?"

"I'm going to call for an ambulance," I said.

"No, you aren't." His tone stopped me. "I told you, I'm
not sick, this is my show. Do you know what they'd do to
me in a hospital? They'd be like cavemen trying to fix a
computer the same way they fix a stone axe. It would be a
farce."

"Then what the hell am I doing here?" I asked, getting
angry. "I can't do anything. I'm one of those cavemen."

"You're a friend," Vergil said, fixing his eyes on me. I
had the impression I was being watched by more than just
Vergil. "I want you here to keep me company." He
laughed. "But I'm not exactly alone."

He walked around the apartment for two hours,
fingering things, looking out windows, making himself
lunch slowly and methodically. "You know, they can actually feel their own thoughts," he said about noon. "I mean,
the cytoplasm seems to have a will of its own, a kind of
subconscious life counter to the rationality they've only
recently acquired. They hear the chemical 'noise' or whatever of the molecules fitting and unfitting inside."

At two o'clock, I called Gail to tell her I would be late. I
was almost sick with tension but I tried to keep my voice
level. "Remember Vergil Ulam? I'm talking with him right
now."

"Everything okay?" she asked.

Was it? Decidedly not. "Fine," I said.

"Culture!" Vergil said, peering around the kitchen wall
at me. I said good-bye and hung up the phone. "They're
always swimming in that bath of information. Contribut-
ing to it. It's a kind of gestalt thing, whatever. The hierarchy is absolute. They send tailored phages after cells that
don't interact properly. Viruses specified to individuals or
groups. No escape. One gets pierced by the virus, the cell

blebs outward, it explodes and dissolves. But it's not just a dictatorship. I think they effectively have more freedom than in a democracy. I mean, they vary so differently from individual to individual. Does that make sense? They vary in different ways than we do."

"Hold it," I said, gripping his shoulders. "Vergil, you're pushing me close to the edge. I can't take this much longer. I don't understand, I'm not sure I believe—"

"Not even now?"

"Okay, let's say you're giving me the right interpretation. Giving it to me straight. Have you bothered to figure out the consequences yet? What all this means, where it might lead?"

He walked into the kitchen and drew a glass of water from the tap, then returned and stood next to me. His expression had changed from childish absorption to sober concern. "I've never been very good at that."

"Are you afraid?"

"I was. Now I'm not sure." He fingered the tie of his robe. "Look, I don't want you to think I went around you, over your head or something. But I met with Michael Bernard yesterday. He put me through his private clinic, took specimens. Told me to quit the lamp treatments. He called this morning, just before you did. He says it all checks out. And he asked me not to tell anybody." He paused and his expression became dreamy again. "Cities of cells," he continued. "Edward, they push pili-like tubes through the tissues, spread information—"

"Stop it!" I shouted. "Checks out? What checks out?"

"As Bernard puts it, I have 'severely enlarged macrophages' throughout my system. And he concurs on the anatomical changes."

"What does he plan to do?"

"I don't know. I think he'll probably convince Genetron to re-open the lab."

"Is that want you want?"

"It's not just having the lab again. I want to show you. Since I stopped the lamp treatments. I'm still changing." He undid his robe and let it slide to the floor. All over his body, his skin was crisscrossed with white lines. Along his back, the lines were starting to form ridges.

"My God," I said.

"I'm not going to be much good anywhere else but the lab soon. I won't be able to go out in public. Hospitals wouldn't know what to do, as I said."

"You're . . . you can talk to them, tell them to slow down," I said, aware how ridiculous that sounded.

"Yes, indeed I can, but they don't necessarily listen."

"I thought you were their god or something."

"The ones hooked up to my neurons aren't the big wheels. They're researchers, or at least serve the same function. They know I'm here, what I am, but that doesn't mean they've convinced the upper levels of the hierarchy."

"They're disputing?"

"Something like that. It's not all that bad, anyway. If the lab is reopened, I have a home, a place to work." He glanced out the window, as if looking for someone. "I don't have anything left but them. They aren't afraid, Edward. I've never felt so close to anything before." The beatific smile again. "I'm responsible for them. Mother to them all."

"You have no way of knowing what they're going to do." He shook his head.

"No, I mean it. You say they're like a civilization—"

"Like a thousand civilizations."

"Yes, and civilizations have been known to screw up. Warfare, the environment—"

I was grasping at straws, trying to restrain a growing panic. I wasn't competent to handle the enormity of what was happening. Neither was Vergil. He was the last person I would have called insightful and wise about large issues.

"But I'm the only one at risk."

"You don't know that. Jesus, Vergil, look what they're *doing* to you!"

"To me, all to me!" he said. "Nobody else."

I shook my head and held up my hands in a gesture of defeat. "Okay, so Bernard gets them to reopen the lab, you move in, become a guinea pig. What then?"

"They treat me right. I'm more than just good old Vergil Ulam now. I'm a goddamned galaxy, a super-mother."

"Super-host, you mean." He conceded the point with a shrug.

I couldn't take any more. I made my exit with a few flimsy excuses, then sat in the lobby of the apartment building, trying to calm down. Somebody had to talk some sense into him. Who would he listen to? He had gone to Bernard . . .

And it sounded as if Bernard were not only convinced, but very interested. People of Bernard's stature didn't coax the Vergil Ulams of the world along, not unless they felt it was to their advantage.

I had a hunch, and I decided to play it. I went to a pay phone, slipped in my credit card, and called Genetron.

"I'd like you to page Dr. Michael Bernard," I told the receptionist.

"Who's calling, please?"

"This is his answering service. We have an emergency call and his beeper doesn't seem to be working."

A few anxious minutes later, Bernard came on the line. "Who the hell is this?" he asked quietly. "I don't have an answering service."

"My name is Edward Milligan. I'm a friend of Vergil Ulam's. I think we have some problems to discuss."

We made an appointment to talk the next morning.

I went home and tried to think of excuses to keep me off the next day's hospital shift. I couldn't concentrate on medicine, couldn't give my patients anywhere near the attention they deserved.

Guilty, angry, afraid.

That was how Gail found me. I slipped on a mask of calm and we fixed dinner together. After eating, holding on to each other, we watched the city lights come on in late twilight through the bayside window. Odd winter starlings pecked at the yellow lawn in the last few minutes of light, then flew away with a rising wind which made the windows rattle.

"Something's wrong," Gail said softly. "Are you going to tell me, or just act like everything's normal?"

"It's just me," I said. "Nervous. Work at the hospital."

"Oh, lord," she said, sitting up. "You're going to divorce me for that Baker woman." Mrs. Baker weighed three hundred and sixty pounds and hadn't known she was pregnant until her fifth month.

"No," I said, listless.

"Rapturous relief," Gail said, touching my forehead lightly. "You know this kind of introspection drives me crazy."

"Well, it's nothing I can talk about yet, so . . ." I patted her hand.

"That's disgustingly patronizing," she said, getting up. "I'm going to make some tea. Want some?" Now she was miffed, and I was tense with not telling.

Why not just reveal all? I asked myself. An old friend was turning himself into a galaxy.

I cleared away the table instead. That night, unable to sleep, I looked down on Gail in bed from my sitting position, pillow against the wall, and tried to determine what I knew was real, and what wasn't.

I'm a doctor, I told myself. A technical, scientific profession. I'm supposed to be immune to things like future shock.

Vergil Ulam was turning into a galaxy.

How would it feel to be topped off with a trillion Chinese? I grinned in the dark, and almost cried at the same time. What Vergil had inside him was unimaginably stranger than Chinese. Stranger than anything I—or Vergil—could easily understand. Perhaps ever understand.

But I knew what was real. The bedroom, the city lights faint through gauze curtains. Gail sleeping. Very important. Gail, in bed, sleeping.

The dream came again. This time the city came in through the window and attacked Gail. It was a great, spiky lighted-up prowler and it growled in a language I couldn't understand, made up of auto horns, crowd noises, construction bedlam. I tried to fight it off, but it got to her—and turned into a drift of stars, sprinkling all over the bed, all over everything. I jerked awake and stayed up until dawn, dressed with Gail, kissed her, savored the reality of her human, unviolated lips.

And went to meet with Bernard. He had been loaned a suite in a big downtown hospital; I rode the elevator to the sixth floor, and saw what fame and fortune could mean.

The suite was tastefully furnished, fine serigraphs on wood-paneled walls, chrome and glass furniture, cream-colored carpet, Chinese brass, and wormwood-grain cabinets and tables.

He offered me a cup of coffee, and I accepted. He took a seat in the breakfast nook, and I sat across from him, cradling my cup in moist palms. He wore a dapper gray suit and had graying hair and a sharp profile. He was in his mid sixties and he looked quite a bit like Leonard Bernstein.

"About our mutual acquaintance," he said. "Mr. Ulam. Brilliant. And, I won't hesitate to say, courageous."

"He's my friend. I'm worried about him."

Bernard held up one finger. "Courageous—and a bloody damned fool. What's happening to him should never have been allowed. He may have done it under duress, but that's no excuse. Still, what's done is done. He's talked to you, I take it."

I nodded. "He wants to return to Genetron."

"Of course. That's where all his equipment is. Where his home probably will be while we sort this out."

"Sort it out—how? Why?" I wasn't thinking too clearly. I had a slight headache.

"I can think of a large number of uses for small, super-dense computer elements with a biological base. Can't you? Genetron has already made breakthroughs, but this is something else again."

"What do you envision?"

Bernard smiled. "I'm not really at liberty to say. It'll be revolutionary. We'll have to get him in lab conditions. Animal experiments have to be conducted. We'll start from scratch, of course. Vergil's . . . um . . . colonies can't be transferred. They're based on his white blood cells. So we have to develop colonies that won't trigger immune reactions in other animals."

"Like an infection?" I asked.

"I suppose there are comparisons. But Vergil is not infected."

"My tests indicate he is."

"That's probably the bits of data floating around in his blood, don't you think?"

"I don't know."

"Listen, I'd like you to come down to the lab after Vergil is settled in. Your expertise might be useful to us."

Us. He was working with Genetron hand in glove. Could he be objective? "How will you benefit from all this?"

"Edward, I have always been at the forefront of my profession. I see no reason why I shouldn't be helping here. With my knowledge of brain and nerve functions, and the research I've been conducting in neurophysiology—"

"You could help Genetron hold off an investigation by the government," I said.

"That's being very blunt. Too blunt, and unfair."

"Perhaps. Anyway, yes: I'd like to visit the lab when Vergil's settled in. If I'm still welcome, bluntness and all." He looked at me sharply. I wouldn't be playing on *his* team; for a moment, his thoughts were almost nakedly apparent.

"Of course," Bernard said, rising with me. He reached out to shake my hand. His palm was damp. He was as nervous as I was, even if he didn't look it.

I returned to my apartment and stayed there until noon, reading, trying to sort things out. Reach a decision. What was real, what I needed to protect.

There is only so much change anyone can stand: innovaton, yes, but slow application. Don't force. Everyone has the right to stay the same until they decide otherwise.

The greatest thing in science since . . .

And Bernard would force it. Genetron would force it. I couldn't handle the thought. "Neo-Luddite," I said to myself. A filthy accusation.

When I pressed Vergil's number on the building security panel, Vergil answered almost immediately. "Yeah," he said. He sounded exhilarated now. "Come on up. I'll be in the bathroom. Door's unlocked."

I entered his apartment and walked through the hallway to the bathroom. Vergil was in the tub, up to his neck in pinkish water. He smiled vaguely at me and splashed his hands. "Looks like I slit my wrists, doesn't it?" he said softly. "Don't worry. Everything's fine now. Genetron's going to take me back. Bernard just called." He pointed to the bathroom phone and intercom.

I sat down on the toilet and noticed the sunlamp fixture standing unplugged next to the linen cabinets. The bulbs sat in a row on the edge of the sink counter. "You're sure that's what you want," I said, my shoulders slumping.

"Yeah, I think so," he said. "They can take better care of me. I'm getting cleaned up, go over there this evening. Bernard's picking me up in his limo. Style. From here on in, everything's style."

The pinkish color in the water didn't look like soap. "Is that bubble bath?" I asked. Some of it came to me in a rush then and I felt a little weaker; what had occurred to me was just one more obvious and necessary insanity.

"No," Vergil said. I knew that already.

"No," he repeated, "it's coming from my skin. They're not telling me everything, but I think they're sending out scouts. Astronauts." He looked at me with an expression that didn't quite equal concern; more like curiosity as to how I'd take it.

The confirmation made my stomach muscles tighten as if waiting for a punch. I had never even considered the possibility until now, perhaps because I had been concentrating on other aspects. "Is this the first time?" I asked.

"Yeah," he said. He laughed. "I've half a mind to let the little buggers down the drain. Let them find out what the world's really about."

"They'd go everywhere," I said.

"Sure enough."

"How . . . how are you feeling?"

"I'm feeling pretty good now. Must be billions of them." More splashing with his hands. "What do you think? Should I let the buggers out?"

Quickly, hardly thinking, I knelt down beside the tub. My fingers went for the cord on the sunlamp and I plugged it in. He had hot-wired doorknobs, turned my piss blue, played a thousand dumb practical jokes and never grown up, never grown mature enough to understand that he was just brilliant enough to really affect the world; he would never learn caution.

He reached for the drain knob. "You know, Edward, I—"

He never finished. I picked up the fixture and dropped

it into the tub, jumping back at the flash of steam and sparks. Vergil screamed and thrashed and jerked and then everything was still, except for the low, steady sizzle and the smoke wafting from his hair.

I lifted the toilet lid and vomited. Then I clenched my nose and went into the living room. My legs went out from under me and I sat abruptly on the couch.

After an hour, I searched through Vergil's kitchen and found bleach, ammonia, and a bottle of Jack Daniel's. I returned to the bathroom, keeping the center of my gaze away from Vergil. I poured first the booze, then the bleach, then the ammonia into the water. Chlorine started bubbling up and I left, closing the door behind me.

The phone was ringing when I got home. I didn't answer. It could have been the hospital. It could have been Bernard. Or the police. I could envision having to explain everything to the police. Genetron would stonewall; Bernard would be unavailable.

I was exhausted, all my muscles knotted with tension and whatever name one can give to the feelings one has after—

Committing genocide?

That certainly didn't seem real. I could not believe I had just murdered a hundred trillion intelligent beings. Snuffed a galaxy. It was laughable. But I didn't laugh.

It was not at all hard to believe I had just killed one human being, a friend. The smoke, the melted lamp rods, the drooping electrical outlet and smoking cord.

Vergil.

I had dunked the lamp into the tub with Vergil.

I felt sick. Dreams, cities raping Gail (and what about his girlfriend, Candice?). Letting the water filled with them out. Galaxies sprinkling over us all. What horror. Then again, what potential beauty—a new kind of life, symbiosis and transformation.

Had I been through enough to kill them all? I had a

moment of panic. Tomorrow, I thought, I will sterilize his apartment. Somehow, I didn't even think of Bernard.

When Gail came in the door, I was asleep on the couch. I came to, groggy, and she looked down at me.

"You feeling okay?" she asked, perching on the edge of the couch. I nodded.

"What are you planning for dinner?" My mouth wasn't working properly. The words were mushy. She felt my forehead.

"Edward, you have a fever," she said. "A very high fever."

I stumbled into the bathroom and looked in the mirror. Gail was close behind me. "What is it?" she asked.

There were lines under my collar, around my neck. White lines, like freeways. They had already been in me a long time, days.

"Damp palms," I said. So obvious.

I think we nearly died. I struggled at first, but in minutes I was too weak to move. Gail was just as sick within an hour.

I lay on the carpet in the living room, drenched in sweat. Gail lay on the couch, her face the color of talcum, eyes closed, like a corpse in an embalming parlor. For a time I thought she was dead. Sick as I was, I raged—hated, felt tremendous guilt at my weakness, my slowness to understand all the possibilities. Then I no longer cared. I was too weak to blink, so I closed my eyes and waited.

There was a rhythm in my arms, my legs. With each pulse of blood, a kind of sound welled up within me, like an orchestra thousands strong, but not playing in unison; playing whole seasons of symphonies at once. Music in the blood. The sound became harsher, but more coordinated, wave-trains finally cancelling into silence, then separating into harmonic beats.

The beats semed to melt into me, into the sound of my own heart.

First, they subdued our immune responses. The war—and it was a war, on a scale never before known on Earth, with trillions of combatants—lasted perhaps two days.

By the time I regained enough strength to get to the kitchen faucet, I could feel them working on my brain, trying to crack the code and find the god within the protoplasm. I drank until I was sick, then drank more moderately and took a glass to Gail. She sipped at it. Her lips were cracked, her eyes bloodshot and ringed with yellowish crumbs. There was some color in her skin. Minutes later, we were eating feebly in the kitchen.

"What in hell was *that?*" was the first thing she asked. I didn't have the strength to explain. I peeled an orange and shared it with her. "We should call a doctor," she said. But I knew we wouldn't. I was already receiving messages; it was becoming apparent that any sensation of freedom we had was illusory.

The messages were simple at first. Memories of commands, rather than the commands themselves, manifested themselves in my thoughts. We were not to leave the apartment—a concept which seemed quite abstract to those in control, even if undesirable—and we were not to have contact with others. We would be allowed to eat certain foods, and drink tap water, for the time being.

With the subsidence of the fevers, the transformations were quick and drastic. Almost simultaneously, Gail and I were immobilized. She was sitting at the table, I was kneeling on the floor. I was able barely to see her in the corner of my eye.

Her arm was developing pronounced ridges.

They had learned inside Vergil; their tactics within the two of us were very different. I itched all over for about two hours—two hours in hell—before they made the breakthrough and found me. The effort of ages on their timescale paid off and they communicated smoothly and directly with this great, clumsy intelligence which had once controlled their universe.

They were not cruel. When the concept of discomfort and its undesirability was made clear, they worked to alleviate it. They worked too effectively. For another hour, I was in a sea of bliss, out of all contact with them.

With dawn the next day, we were allowed freedom to move again; specifically, to go to the bathroom. There were certain waste products they could not deal with. I voided those—my urine was purple—and Gail followed suit. We looked at each other vacantly in the bathroom. Then she managed a slight smile. "Are they talking to you?" she asked. I nodded. "Then I'm not crazy."

For the next twelve hours, control seemed to loosen on some levels. During that time, I managed to pencil the majority of this manuscript. I suspect there was another kind of war going on in me. Gail was capable of our previous limited motion, but no more.

When full control resumed, we were instructed to hold each other. We did not hesitate.

"Eddie . . ." she whispered. My name was the last sound I ever heard from outside.

Standing, we grew together. In hours, our legs expanded and spread out. Then extensions grew to the windows to take in sunlight, and to the kitchen to take water from the sink. Filaments soon reached to all corners of the room, stripping paint and plaster from the walls, fabric and stuffing from the furniture.

By the next dawn, the transformation was complete.

I no longer have any clear view of what we look like. I suspect we resemble cells—large, flat and filamented cells, draped purposefully across most of the apartment. The great shall mimic the small.

I have been asked to carry on recording, but soon that

will not be possible. Our intelligence fluctuates daily as we are absorbed into the minds within. Each day, our individuality declines. We are, indeed, great clumsy dinosaurs. Our memories have been taken over by billions of them, and our personalities have been spread through the transformed blood.

Soon there will be no need for centralization.

I am informed that already the plumbing has been invaded. People throughout the building are undergoing transformation.

Within the old time frame of weeks, we will reach the lakes, rivers, and seas in force.

I can barely begin to guess the results. Every square inch of the planet will teem with thought. Years from now, perhaps much sooner, they will subdue their own individuality—what there is of it.

New creatures will come, then. The immensity of their capacity for thought will be inconceivable.

All my hatred and fear is gone now.

I leave them—us—with only one question.

How many times has this happened, elsewhere? Travellers never came through space to visit the Earth. They had no need.

They had found universes in grains of sand.

Homefaring

by Robert Silverberg

*Robert Silverberg served as the second president of the Science Fiction
Writers of America (1967–1968) and has always been one of the
organization's most active members in addition to producing more
works of fiction and nonfiction than one can easily count. He holds
four Nebula and two Hugo Awards; and originated and for ten years
edited the New Dimensions series of original anthologies. His latest
novel is an epic fantasy,* Gilgamesh the King.

Herewith Homefaring, *a nominee for the 1983 Nebula for best
novella.*

McCulloch was beginning to molt. The sensation, ines-
capable and unarguable, horrified him—it felt exactly as
though his body was going to split apart, which it was—
and yet it was also completely familiar, expected, welcome.
Wave after wave of keen and dizzying pain swept through
him. Burrowing down deep in the sandy bed, he waved his
great claws about, lashed his flat tail against the pure white
sand, scratched frantically with quick worried gestures of
his eight walking-legs.

He was frightened. He was calm. He had no idea what
was about to happen to him. He had done this a hundred
times before.

The molting prodrome had overwhelming power. It
blotted from his mind all questions, and, after a moment,
all fear. A white line of heat ran down his back—no, down

176

the top of his carapace—from a point just back of his head to the first flaring segments of his tail-fan. He imagined that all the sun's force, concentrated through some giant glass lens, was being inscribed in a single track along his shell. And his soft inner body was straining, squirming, expanding, filling the carapace to overflowing. But still that rigid shell contained him, refusing to yield to the pressure. To McCulloch it was much like being inside a wet-suit that was suddenly five times too small.

—*What is the sun? What is glass? What is a lens? What is a wet-suit?*

The questions swarmed suddenly upward in his mind like little busy many-legged creatures springing out of the sand. But he had no time for providing answers. The molting prodrome was developing with astounding swiftness, carrying him along. The strain was becoming intolerable. In another moment he would surely burst. He was writhing in short angular convulsions. Within his claws, his tissues now were shrinking, shriveling, drawing back within the ferocious shell-hulls, but the rest of him was continuing inexorably to grow larger.

He had to escape from this shell, or it would kill him. He had to expel himself somehow from this impossibly constricting container. Digging his front claws and most of his legs into the sand, he heaved, twisted, stretched, pushed. He thought of himself as being pregnant with himself, struggling fiercely to deliver himself of himself.

Ah. The carapace suddenly began to split.

The crack was only a small one, high up near his shoulders—*shoulders?*—but the imprisoned substance of him surged swiftly toward it, widening and lengthening it, and in another moment the hard horny covering was cracked from end to end. *Ah. Ah.* That felt so good, that release from constraint! Yet McCulloch still had to free himself. Delicately he drew himself backward, withdrawing leg

after leg from its covering in a precise, almost fussy way, as
though he were pulling his arms from the sleeves of some
incredibly ancient and frail garment.

Until he had his huge main claws free, though, he knew
he could not extricate himself from the sundered shell.
And freeing the claws took extreme care. The front limbs
still were shrinking, and the limy joints of the shell seemed
to be dissolving and softening, but nevertheless he had to
pull each claw through a passage much narrower than
itself. It was easy to see how a hasty move might break a
limb off altogether.

He centered his attention on the task. It was a little like
telling his wrists to make themselves small, so he could
slide them out of handcuffs.

—*Wrists? Handcuffs? What are those?*

McCulloch paid no attention to that baffling inner voice.
Easy, easy, there—ah—yes, there, like that! One claw was
free. Then the other, slowly, carefully. Done. Both of them
retracted. The rest was simple: some shrugging and wig-
gling, exhausting but not really challenging, and he succeeded in extending the breach in the carapace until he
could crawl backward out of it. Then he lay on the sand
beside it, weary, drained, naked, soft, terribly vulnerable.
He wanted only to return to the sleep out of which he had
emerged into this nightmare of shellsplitting.

But some force within him would not let him slacken
off. A moment to rest, only a moment. He looked to his
left, toward the discarded shell. Vision was difficult—there
were peculiar, incomprehensible refraction effects that
broke every image into thousands of tiny fragments—but
despite that, and despite the dimness of the light, he was
able to see that the shell, golden-hued with broad arrow-
shaped red markings, was something like a lobster's, yet
even more intricate, even more bizarre. McCulloch did not
understand why he had been inhabiting a lobster's shell.

Obviously because he was a lobster; but he was not a lobster. That was so, was it not? Yet he was under water. He lay on fine white sand, at a depth so great he could not make out any hint of sunlight overhead. The water was warm, gentle, rich with tiny tasty creatures and with a swirling welter of sensory data that swept across his receptors in bewildering abundance.

He sought to learn more. But there was no further time for resting and thinking now. He was unprotected. Any passing enemy could destroy him while he was like this. Up, up, seek a hiding-place: that was the requirement of the moment.

First, though, he paused to devour his old shell. That too seemed to be the requirement of the moment; so he fell upon it with determination, seizing it with his clumsy-looking but curiously versatile front claws, drawing it toward his busy, efficient mandibles. When that was accomplished—no doubt to recycle the lime it contained, which he needed for the growth of his new shell—he forced himself up and began a slow scuttle, somehow knowing that the direction he had taken was the right one.

Soon came the vibrations of something large and solid against his sensors—a wall, a stone mass rising before him—and then, as he continued, he made out with his foggy vision the sloping flank of a dark broad cliff rising vertically from the ocean floor. Festoons of thick, swaying red and yellow water plants clung to it, and a dense stippling of rubbery-looking finger-shaped sponges, and a crawling, gaping, slithering host of crabs and mollusks and worms, which vastly stirred McCulloch's appetite. But this was not a time to pause to eat, lest he be eaten. Two enormous green anemones yawned nearby, ruffling their voluptuous membranes seductively, hopefully. A dark shape passed overhead, huge, tubular, tentacular, menacing. Ignoring the thronging populations of the rock,

McCulloch picked his way over and around them until he came to the small cave, the McCulloch-sized cave, that was his goal.

Gingerly he backed through its narrow mouth, knowing there would be no room for turning around once he was inside. He filled the opening nicely, with a little space left over. Taking up a position just within the entrance, he blocked the cave-mouth with his claws. No enemy could enter now. Naked though he was, he would be safe during this vulnerable period.

For the first time since his agonizing awakening, McCulloch had a chance to halt: rest, regroup, consider.

It seemed a wise idea to be monitoring the waters just outside the cave even while he was resting, though. He extended his antennae a short distance into the swarming waters, and felt at once the impact, again, of a myriad sensory inputs, all the astounding complexity of the reef-world. Most of the creatures that moved slowly about on the face of the reef were simple ones, but McCulloch could feel, also, the sharp pulsations of intelligence coming from several points not far away: the anemones, so it seemed, and that enormous squid-like thing hovering overhead. Not intelligence of a kind that he understood, but that did not trouble him: for the moment, understanding could wait, while he dealt with the task of recovery from the exhausting struggles of his molting. Keeping the antennae moving steadily in slow sweeping circles of surveillance, he began systematically to shut down the rest of his nervous system, until he had attained the rest state that he knew—how?—was optimum for the rebuilding of his shell. Already his soft new carapace was beginning to grow rigid as it absorbed water, swelled, filtered out and utilized the lime. But he would have to sit quietly a long while before he was fully armored once more.

He rested. He waited. He did not think at all.

* * *

After a time his repose was broken by that inner voice, the one that had been trying to question him during the wildest moments of his molting. It spoke without sound, from a point somewhere within the core of his torpid consciousness.

—*Are you awake?*

—*I am now,* McCulloch answered irritably.

—*I need definitions. You are a mystery to me. What is a McCulloch?*

—*A man.*

—*That does not help.*

—*A male human being.*

—*That also has no meaning.*

—*Look, I'm tired. Can we discuss these things some other time?*

—*This is a good time. While we rest, while we replenish ourself.*

—Ourselves, McCulloch corrected.

—Ourself *is more accurate.*

—*But there are two of us.*

—*Are there? Where is the other?*

McCulloch faltered. He had no perspective on his situation, none that made any sense.—*One inside the other, I think. Two of us in the same body. But definitely two of us. McCulloch and not-McCulloch.*

—*I concede the point. There are two of us. You are within me. Who are you?*

—*McCulloch.*

—*So you have said. But what does that mean?*

—*I don't know.*

The voice left him alone again. He felt its presence nearby, as a kind of warm node somewhere along his spine, or whatever was the equivalent of his spine, since he did not think invertebrates had spines. And it was fairly clear to him that he was an invertebrate.

He had become, it seemed, a lobster, or, at any rate, something lobster-like. Implied in that was transition: *he had become.* He had once been something else. Blurred, tantalizing memories of the something else that he once had been danced in his consciousness. He remembered hair, fingers, fingernails, flesh. Clothing: a kind of removable exoskeleton. Eyelids, ears, lips: shadowy concepts all, names without substance, but there was a certain elusive reality to them, a volatile, tricky plausibility. Each time he tried to apply one of those concepts to himself—"fingers," "hair," "man," "McCulloch"—it slid away, it would not stick. Yet all the same those terms had some sort of relevance to him.

The harder he pushed to isolate that relevance, though, the harder it was to maintain his focus on any part of that soup of half-glimpsed notions in which his mind seemed to be swimming. The thing to do, McCulloch decided, was to go slow, try not to force understanding, wait for comprehension to seep back into his mind. Obviously he had had a bad shock, some major trauma, a total disorientation. It might be days before he achieved any sort of useful integration.

A gentle voice from outside his cave said, "I hope that your growing has gone well."

Not a voice. He remembered voice: vibration of the air against the eardrums. No air here, maybe no eardrums. This was a stream of minute chemical messengers spurting through the mouth of the little cave and rebounding off the thousands of sensory filaments on his legs, tentacles, antennae, carapace, and tail. But the effect was one of words having been spoken. And it was distinctly different from that other voice, the internal one, that had been questioning him so assiduously a little while ago.

"It goes extremely well," McCulloch replied: or was it the other inhabitant of his body that had framed the answer? "I grow. I heal. I stiffen. Soon I will come forth."

"We feared for you." The presence outside the cave emanated concern, warmth, intelligence. Kinship. "In the

first moments of your Growing, a strangeness came from
you."

"Strangeness is within me. I am invaded."

"Invaded? By what?"

"A McCulloch. It is a man, which is a human being."

"Ah. A great strangeness indeed. Do you need help?"

McCulloch answered, "No. I will accommodate to it."

And he knew that it was the other within himself who
was making these answers, though the boundary between
their identities was so indistinct that he had a definite sense
of being the one who shaped these words. But how could
that be? He had no idea how one shaped words by sending
squirts of body-fluid into the all-surrounding ocean-fluid.
That was not his language. His language was—

—words—

—English words—

He trembled in sudden understanding. His antennae
thrashed wildly, his many legs jerked and quivered. Images churned in his suddenly boiling mind: bright lights,
elaborate equipment, faces, walls, ceilings. People moving
about him, speaking in low tones, occasionally addressing
words to him, English words—

—*Is English what all McCullochs speak?*

—*Yes.*

—*So English is human-language?*

—*Yes. But not the only one,* said McCulloch. *I speak English,
and also German and a little—French. But other humans speak
other languages.*

—*Very interesting. Why do you have so many languages?*

—*Because—because—we are different from one another, we
live in different countries, we have different cultures—*

—*This is without meaning again. There are many creatures,
but only one language, which all speak with greater or lesser skill,
according to their destinies.*

McCulloch pondered that. After a time he replied:

—*Lobster is what you are. Long body, claws and antennae in front, many legs, flat tail in back. Different from, say, a clam. Clams have shell on top, shell on bottom, soft flesh in between, hinge connecting. You are not like that. You have lobster body. So you are lobster.*

Now there was silence from the other.

Then—after a long pause—

—*Very well. I accept the term. I am lobster. You are human. They are clams.*

—*What do you call yourselves in your own language?*

Silence.

—*What's your own name for yourself? Your individual self, the way my individual name is McCulloch and my species-name is human being?*

Silence.

—*Where am I, anyway?*

Silence, still, so prolonged and utter that McCulloch wondered if the other being had withdrawn itself from his consciousness entirely. Perhaps days went by in this unending silence, perhaps weeks: he had no way of measuring the passing of time. He realized that such units as days or weeks were without meaning now. One moment succeeded the next, but they did not aggregate into anything continuous.

At last came a reply.

—*You are in the world, human McCulloch.*

Silence came again, intense, clinging, a dark warm garment. McCulloch made no attempt to reach the other mind. He lay motionless, feeling his carapace thicken. From outside the cave came a flow of impressions of passing beings, now differentiating themselves very sharply: he felt the thick fleshy pulses of the two anemones, the sharp stabbing presence of the squid, the slow ponderous broadcast of something dark and winged, and, again and again, the bright, comforting, unmistakable output of the other lobster-creatures. It was a busy, complex world out there. The McCulloch part of him longed to leave the cave and explore it. The lobster part of him rested, content within its tight shelter.

He formed hypotheses. He had journeyed from his own place to this place, damaging his mind in the process, though now his mind seemed to be reconstructing itself steadily, if erratically. What sort of voyage? To another world? No: that seemed wrong. He did not believe that conditions so much like the ocean floor of Earth would be found on another—

Earth.

All right: significant datum. He was human, he came from Earth. And he was still on Earth. In the ocean. He was—what?—a land-dweller, an air-breather, a biped, a flesh-creature, a human. And now he was within the body of a lobster. Was that it? The entire human race, he thought, has migrated into the bodies of lobsters, and here we are on the ocean floor, scuttling about, waving our claws and feelers, going through difficult and dangerous moltings—

Or maybe I'm the only one. A scientific experiment, with me as the subject: man into lobster. That brightly lit room that he remembered, the intricate gleaming equipment all about him—that was the laboratory, that was where they had prepared him for his transmigration, and then they had thrown the switch and hurled him into the body of—

No. No. Makes no sense. Lobsters, McCulloch reflected, are low-phylum creatures with simple nervous systems, limited intelligence. Plainly the mind he had entered was a complex one. It asked thoughtful questions. It carried on civilized conversations with its friends, who came calling like ceremonious Japanese gentlemen, offering expressions of solicitude and good will.

New hypothesis: that lobsters and other low-phylum animals are actually quite intelligent, with minds roomy enough to accept the sudden insertion of a human being's entire neural structure, but we in our foolish anthropocentric way have up till now been too blind to perceive—

No. Too facile. You could postulate the secretly lofty intelligence of the world's humble creatures, all right: you could postulate anything you wanted. But that didn't make it so. Lobsters did not ask questions. Lobsters did not come calling like ceremonious Japanese gentlemen. At least, not the lobsters of the world he remembered.

Improved lobsters? Evolved lobsters? Super-lobsters of the future?

—*When am I?*

Into his dizzied broodings came the quiet disembodied internal voice of not-McCulloch, his companion:

—*Is your displacement then one of time rather than space?*

—*I don't know. Probably both. I'm a land creature.*

—*That has no meaning.*

—*I don't live in the ocean. I breathe air.*

From the other consciousness came an expression of deep astonishment tinged with skepticism.

—*Truly? That is very hard to believe. When you are in your own body you breathe no water at all?*

—*None. Not for long, or I would die.*

—*But there is so little land! And no creatures live upon it. Some make short visits there. But nothing can dwell there very long. So it has always been. And so will it be, until the time of the Molting of the World.*

McCulloch considered that. Once again he found himself doubting that he was still on Earth. A world of water? Well, that could fit into his hypothesis of having journeyed forward in time, though it seemed to add a layer of implausibility upon implausibility. How many millions of years, he wondered, would it take for nearly all the Earth to have become covered with water? And he answered himself: In about as many as it would take to evolve a species of intelligent invertebrates.

Suddenly, terribly, it all fit together. Things crystallized and clarified in his mind, and he found access to another segment of his injured and redistributed memory; and he began to comprehend what had befallen him, or, rather, what he had willingly allowed himself to undergo. With that comprehension came a swift stinging sense of total displacement and utter loss, as though he were drowning and desperately tugging at strands of seaweed in a futile attempt to pull himself back to the surface. All that was real to him, all that he was part of, everything that made sense—gone, gone, perhaps irretrievably gone, buried under the weight of uncountable millennia, vanished, drowned, forgotten, reduced to mere geology—it was unthinkable, it was unacceptable, it was impossible, and as the truth of it bore in on him he found himself choking on the frightful vastness of time past.

But that bleak sensation lasted only a moment and was gone. In its place came excitement, delight, confusion, and a feverish throbbing curiosity about this place he had entered. He was here. That miraculous thing that they had strived so fiercely to achieve had been achieved—rather too well, perhaps, but it had been achieved, and he was launched on the greatest adventure he would ever have, that anyone would ever have. This was not the moment for submitting to grief and confusion. Out of that world lost and all but forgotten to him came a scrap of verse that gleamed and blazed in his soul: *Only through time time is conquered.*

McCullouch reached toward the mind that was so close to his within this strange body.

—*When will it be safe for us to leave this cave?* he asked.

—*It is safe any time, now. Do you wish to go outside?*

—*Yes. Please.*

The creature stirred, flexed its front claws, slapped its flat tail against the floor of the cave, and in a slow ungraceful way began to clamber through the narrow opening, pausing more than once to search the waters outside for lurking enemies. McCulloch felt a quick hot burst of terror, as though he were about to enter some important meeting and had discovered too late that he was naked. Was the shell truly ready? Was he safely armored against the unknown foes outside, or would they fall upon him and tear him apart like furious shrikes? But his host did not seem to share those fears. It went plodding on and out, and in a moment more it emerged on an algae-encrusted tongue of the reef wall, a short distance below the two anemones. From each of those twin masses of rippling flesh came the same sullen pouting hungry murmurs: "Ah, come closer, why don't you come closer?"

"Another time," said the lobster, sounding almost playful, and turned away from them.

McCulloch looked outward over the landscape. Earlier, in the turmoil of his bewildering arrival and the pain and chaos of the molting prodrome, he had not had time to assemble any clear and coherent view of it. But now—despite the handicap of seeing everything with the alien perspective of the lobster's many-faceted eyes—he was able to put together an image of the terrain.

His view was a shortened one, because the sky was like a dark lid, through which came only enough light to create a cone-shaped arena spreading just a little way. Behind him was the face of the huge cliff, occupied by plant and animal life over virtually every square inch, and stretching upward until its higher reaches were lost in the dimness far overhead. Just a short way down from the ledge where he rested was the ocean floor, a broad expanse of gentle, undulating white sand streaked here and there with long widening gores of some darker material. Here and there bottom-growing plants arose in elegant billowy clumps, and McCulloch spotted occasional creatures moving among them over the sand that were much like lobsters and crabs, though with some differences. He saw also some starfish and snails and sea urchins that did not look at all unfamiliar. At higher levels he could make out a few swimming creatures: a couple of the squid-like animals—they were hulking-looking ropy-armed things, and he disliked them instinctively—and what seemed to be large jellyfish. But something was missing, and after a moment McCulloch realized what it was: fishes. There was a rich population of invertebrate life wherever he looked, but no fishes as far as he could see.

Not that he could see very far. The darkness clamped down like a curtain perhaps two or three hundred yards away. But even so, it was odd that not one fish had entered his field of vision in all this time. He wished he knew more about marine biology. Were there zones on Earth where no sea animals more complex than lobsters and crabs existed? Perhaps, but he doubted it.

Two disturbing new hypotheses blossomed in his mind. One was that he had landed in some remote future era where nothing out of his own time survived except low-phylum sea-creatures. The other was that he had not traveled to the future at all, but had arrived by mischance in some primordial geological epoch in which vertebrate life had not yet evolved. That seemed unlikely to him, though. This place did not have a prehistoric feel to him. He saw no trilobites; surely there ought to be trilobites everywhere about, and not these oversized lobsters, which he did not remember at all from his childhood visits to the natural history museum's prehistory displays.

But if this was truly the future—and the future belonged to the lobsters and squids—

That was hard to accept. Only invertebrates? What could invertebrates accomplish, what kind of civilization could lobsters build, with their hard unsupple bodies and great clumsy claws? Concepts, half-remembered or less than that, rushed through his mind: the Taj Mahal, the Gutenberg Bible, the Sistine Chapel, the Madonna of the

Rocks, the great window at Chartres. Could lobsters create those? Could squids? What a poor place this world must be, McCulloch thought sadly, how gray, how narrow, how tightly bounded by the ocean above the endless sandy floor.

—*Tell me,* he said to his host. *Are there any fishes in this sea?*

The response was what he was coming to recognize as a sigh.

—*Fishes? That is another word without meaning.*

—*A form of marine life, with an internal bony structure—*

—*With its shell* inside?

—*That's one way of putting it,* said McCulloch.

—*There are no such creatures. Such creatures have never existed. There is no room for the shell within the soft parts of the body. I can barely comprehend such an arrangement: surely there is no need for it!*

—*It can be useful, I assure you. In the former world it was quite common.*

—*The world of human beings?*

—*Yes. My world,* McCulloch said.

—*Anything might have been possible in a former world, human McCulloch. Perhaps indeed before the world's last Molting shells were worn inside. And perhaps after the next one they will be worn there again. But in the world I know, human McCulloch, it is not the practice.*

—*Ah,* McCulloch said. *Then I am even farther from home than I thought.*

—*Yes,* said the host. *I think you are very far from home indeed. Does that cause you sorrow?*

—*Among other things.*

—*If it causes you sorrow, I grieve for your grief, because we are companions now.*

—*You are very kind,* said McCulloch to his host.

The lobster asked McCulloch if he was ready to begin their journey; and when McCulloch indicated that he was, his host serenely kicked itself free of the ledge with a single powerful stoke of its tail. For an instant it hung suspended; then it glided toward the sandy bottom as gracefully as though it were floating through air. When it landed, it was with all its many legs poised delicately *en pointe,* and it stood that way, motionless, a long moment.

Then it suddenly set out with great haste over the ocean floor, running so lightfootedly that it scarcely raised a puff of sand wherever it touched down. More than once it ran right across some bottom-grubbing creature, some slug or scallop, without appearing to disturb it at all. McCulloch thought the lobster was capering in sheer exuberance, after its long internment in the cave; but some growing sense of awareness of his companion's mind told him after a time that this was no casual frolic, that the lobster was not in fact dancing but fleeing.

—*Is there an enemy?* McCulloch asked.

—*Yes. Above.*

The lobster's antennae stabbed upward at a sharp angle, and McCulloch, seeing through the other's eyes, perceived now a large looming cylindrical shape swimming in slow circles near the upper border of their range of vision. It might have been a shark, or even a whale. McCulloch felt deceived and betrayed; for the lobster had told him this was an invertebrate world, and surely that creature above him—

—*No,* said the lobster, without slowing its manic sprint. *That animal has no shell of the sort you described within its body. It is only a bag of flesh. But it is very dangerous.*

—*How will we escape it?*

—*We will not escape it.*

The lobster sounded calm, but whether it was the calm of fatalism or mere expressionlessness, McCulloch could not say: the lobster had been calm even in the first moments of McCulloch's arrival in its mind, which must surely have been alarming and even terrifying to it.

It had begun to move now in ever-widening circles. This seemed not so much an evasive tactic as a ritualistic one, now, a dance indeed. A farewell to life? The swimming creature had descended until it was only a few lobster-lengths above them, and McCulloch had a clear view of it. No, not a fish or a shark or any type of vertebrate at all, he realized, but an animal of a kind wholly unfamiliar to him, a kind of enormous worm-like thing whose meaty yellow body was reinforced externally by some sort of chitinous struts running its entire length. Fleshy vane-like fins rippled along its sides, but their purpose seemed to be more one of guidance than propulsion, for it appeared to move by guzzling in great quantities of water and expelling them through an anal siphon. Its mouth was vast, with a row of dim little green eyes ringing the scarlet lips. When the creature yawned, it revealed itself to be toothless, but capable of swallowing the lobster easily at a gulp.

Looking upward into the yawning mouth, McCulloch had a sudden image of himself elsewhere, spreadeagled under an inverted pyramid of shining machinery as the countdown reached its final moments, as the technicians made ready to—
—to hurl him—
—to hurl him forward in time—
Yes. An experiment. Definitely an experiment. He could remember it now. Bleier, Caldwell, Rodrigues, Mortenson. And all the others. Gathered around him, faces tight, forced smiles. The lights. The colors. The bizarre coils of equipment. And the volunteer. The volunteer. First human subject to be sent forward in time. The various rabbits and mice of the previous experiments, though they had apparently survived the round trip unharmed, had not been capable of delivering much of a report on their adventures. "I'm smarter than any rabbit," McCulloch had said. "Send me. I'll tell you what it's like up there." The

volunteer. All that was coming back to him in great swatches now, as he crouched here within the mind of something much like a lobster, waiting for a vast yawning predator to pounce. The project, the controversies, his coworkers, the debate over risking a human mind under the machine, the drawing of lots. McCulloch had not been the only volunteer. He was just the lucky one. "Here you go, Jim-boy. A hundred years down the time-line."

Or fifty, or eighty, or a hundred and twenty. They didn't have really precise trajectory control. They thought he might go as much as a hundred twenty years. But beyond much doubt they had overshot by a few hundred million. Was that within the permissible parameters of error?

He wondered what would happen to him if his host here were to perish. Would he die also? Would he find himself instantly transferred to some other being of this epoch? Or would he simply be hurled back instead to his own time? He was not ready to go back. He had just begun to observe, to understand, to explore—

McCulloch's host had halted its running, now, and stood quite still in what was obviously a defensive mode, body cocked and upreared, claws extended, with the huge crusher claw erect and the long narrow cutting claw opening and closing in a steady rhythm. It was a threatening pose, but the swimming thing did not appear to be greatly troubled by it. Did the lobster mean to let itself be swallowed, and then to carve an exit for itself with those awesome weapons, before the alimentary juices could go to work on its armor?

"You choose your prey foolishly," said McCulloch's host to its enemy.

The swimming creature made a reply that was unintelligible to McCulloch: vague blurry words, the clotted outspew of a feeble intelligence. It continued its unhurried downward spiral.

"You are warned," said the lobster. "You are not selecting your victim wisely."

Again came a muddled response, sluggish and incoherent, the speech of an entity for whom verbal communication was a heavy, all but impossible effort.

Its enormous mouth gaped. Its fins rippled fiercely as it
siphoned itself downward the last few yards to engulf the
lobster. McCulloch prepared himself for transition to some
new and even more unimaginable state when his host met
its death. But suddenly the ocean floor was swarming with
lobsters. They must have been arriving from all sides—
summoned by his host's frantic dance, McCulloch wondered?—while McCulloch, intent on the descent of the
swimmer, had not noticed. Ten, twenty, possibly fifty of
them arrayed themselves now beside McCulloch's host,
and as the swimmer, tail on high, mouth wide, lowered
itself like some gigantic suction-hose toward them, the lobsters coolly and implacably seized its lips in their claws.
Caught and helpless, it began at once to thrash, and from
the pores through which it spoke came bleating incoherent
cries of dismay and torment.

There was no mercy for it. It had been warned. It
dangled tail upward while the pack of lobsters methodically devoured it from below, pausing occasionally to strip
away and discard the rigid rods of chitin that formed its
superstructure. Swiftly they reduced it to a faintly visible
cloud of shreds oscillating in the water, and then small
scavenging creatures came to fall upon those, and there
was nothing at all left but the scattered rods of chitin on
the sand.

The entire episode had taken only a few moments: the
coming of the predator, the dance of McCulloch's host, the
arrival of the other lobsters, the destruction of the enemy.
Now the lobsters were gathered in a sort of convocation
about McCulloch's host, wordlessly manifesting a com-

monality of spirit, a warmth of fellowship after feasting, that seemed quite comprehensible to McCulloch. For a short while they had been uninhibited savage carnivores consuming convenient meat; now once again they were courteous, refined, cultured—Japanese gentlemen, Oxford dons, gentle Benedictine monks.

McCulloch studied them closely. They were definitely more like lobsters than like any other creature he had ever seen, very much like lobsters, and yet there were differences. They were larger. How much larger, he could not tell, for he had no real way of judging distance and size in this undersea world; but he supposed they must be at least three feet long, and he doubted that lobsters of his time, even the biggest, were anything like that in length. Their bodies were wider than those of lobsters, and their heads were larger. The two largest claws looked like those of the lobsters he remembered, but the ones just behind them seemed more elaborate, as if adapted for more delicate procedures than mere rending of food and stuffing it into the mouth. There was an odd little hump, almost a dome, midway down the lobster's back—the center of the expanded nervous system, perhaps.

The lobsters clustered solemnly about McCulloch's host and each lightly tapped its claws against those of the adjoining lobster in a sort of handshake, a process that seemed to take quite some time. McCulloch became aware also that a conversation was under way.

What they were talking about, he realized, was him.

"It is not painful to have a McCulloch within one," his host was explaining. "It came upon me at molting time, and that gave me a moment of difficulty, molting being what it is. But it was only a moment. After that my only concern was for the McCulloch's comfort."

"And it is comfortable now?"

"It is becoming more comfortable."

"When will you show it to us?"

"Ah, that cannot be done. It has no real existence, and therefore I cannot bring it forth."

"What is it, then? A wanderer? A revenant?"

"A revenant, yes. So I think. And a wanderer. It says it is a human being."

"And what is that? Is a human being a kind of McCulloch?"

"I think a McCulloch is a kind of human being."

"Which is a revenant."

"Yes, I think so."

"This is an Omen!"

"Where is its world?"

"Its world is lost to it."

"Yes, definitely an Omen."

"It lived on dry land."

"It breathed air."

"It wore its shell within its body."

"What a strange revenant!"

"What a strange world its world must have been."

"It is the former world, would you not say?"

"So I surely believe. And therefore this is an Omen."

"Ah, we shall Molt. We shall Molt."

McCulloch was altogether lost. He was not even sure when his own host was the speaker.

"Is it the Time?"

"We have an Omen, do we not?"

"The McCulloch surely was sent as a herald."

"There is no precedent."

"Each Molting, though, is without precedent. We cannot conceive what came before. We cannot imagine what comes after. We learn by learning. The McCulloch is the herald. The McCulloch is the Omen."

"I think not. I think it is unreal and unimportant."

"Unreal, yes. But not unimportant."

"The Time is not at hand. The Molting of the World is

not yet due. The human is a wanderer and a revenant, but not a herald and certainly not an Omen."

"It comes from the former world."

"It says it does. Can we believe that?"

"It breathed air. In the former world, perhaps there were creatures that breathed air."

"It says it breathed air. I think it is neither herald nor Omen, neither wanderer nor revenant. I think it is a myth and a fugue. I think it betokens nothing. It is an accident. It is an interruption."

"That is an uncivil attitude. We have much to learn from the McCulloch. And if it is an Omen, we have immediate responsibilities that must be fulfilled."

"But how can we be certain of what it is?"

May I speak? said McCulloch to his host.

—Of course.

—How can I make myself heard?

—Speak through me.

"The McCulloch wishes to be heard!"

"Hear it! Hear it!"

"Let it speak!"

McCulloch said, and the host spoke the words aloud for him, "I am a stranger here, and your guest, and so I ask you to forgive me if I give offense, for I have little understanding of your ways. Nor do I know if I am a herald or an Omen. But I tell you in all truth that I am a wanderer, and that I am sent from the former world, where there are many creatures of my kind, who breathe air and live upon the land and carry their—shells—inside their body."

"An Omen, certainly," said several of the lobsters at once. "A herald, beyond doubt."

McCulloch continued, "It was our hope to discover something of the worlds that are to come after ours. And therefore I was sent forward—"

"A herald—certainly a herald!"

"—to come to you, to go among you, to learn to know

you, and then to return to my own people, the air-people, the human people, and bring the word of what is to come. But I think that I am not the herald you expect. I carry no message for you. We could not have known that you were here. Out of the former world I bring you the blessing of those that have gone before, however, and when I go back to that world I will bear tidings of your life, of your thought, of your ways—"

"Then our kind is unknown to your world?"

McCulloch hesitated. "Creatures somewhat like you do exist in the seas of the former world. But they are smaller and simpler than you, and I think their civilization, if they have one, is not a great one."

"You have no discourse with them, then?" one of the lobsters asked.

"Very little," he said. A miserable evasion, cowardly, vile. McCulloch shivered. He imagined himself crying out, "We eat them!" and the water turning black with their shocked outbursts—and saw them instantly falling upon him, swiftly and efficiently slicing him to scraps with their claws. Through his mind ran monstrous images of lobsters in tanks, lobsters boiling alive, lobsters smothered in rich sauces, lobsters shelled, lobsters minced, lobsters rendered into bisques—he could not halt the torrent of dreadful visions. Such was our discourse with your ancestors. Such was our mode of interspecies communication. He felt himself drowning in guilt and shame and fear.

The spasm passed. The lobsters had not stirred. They continued to regard him with patience: impassive, unmoving, remote. McCulloch wondered if all that had passed through his mind just then had been transmitted to his host. Very likely; the host earlier had seemed to have access to all of his thoughts, though McCulloch did not have the same entree to the host's. And if the host knew, did all the others? What then, what then?

Perhaps they did not even care. Lobsters, he recalled,

were said to be callous cannibals, who might attack one
another in the very tanks where they were awaiting their
turns in the chef's pot. It was hard to view these detached
and aloof beings, these dons, these monks, as having that
sort of ferocity: but yet he had seen them go to work on
that swimming mouth-creature without any show of em-
barrassment, and perhaps some atavistic echo of their ancestors' appetites lingered in them, so that they would
think it only natural that McCullochs and other humans
had fed on such things as lobsters. Why should they be
shocked? Perhaps they thought that humans fed on humans, too. It was all in the former world, was it not? And
in any event it was foolish to fear that they would exact
some revenge on him for Lobster Thermidor, no matter
how appalled they might be. He wasn't here. He was nothing more than a figment, a revenant, a wanderer, a set of
intrusive neural networks within their companion's brain.
The worst they could do to him, he supposed, was to exor-
cise him, and send him back to the former world.

Even so, he could not entirely shake the guilt and the
shame. Or the fear.

Bleier said, "Of course, you aren't the only one who's
going to be in jeopardy when we throw the switch. There's
your host to consider. One entire human ego slamming
into his mind out of nowhere like a brick falling off a
building—what's it going to do to him?"

"Flip him out, is my guess," said Jake Ybarra. "You'll
land on him and he'll announce he's Napoleon, or Joan of
Arc, and they'll hustle him off to the nearest asylum. Are
you prepared for the possibility, Jim, that you're going to
spend your entire time in the future sitting in a loony-bin
undergoing therapy?"

"Or exorcism," Mortenson suggested. "If there's been
some kind of reversion to barbarism. Christ, you might
even get your host burned at the stake!"

"I don't think so," McCulloch said quietly. "I'm a lot more optimistic than you guys. I don't expect to land in a world of witch-doctors and mumbo-jumbo, and I don't expect to find myself in a place that locks people up in Bedlam because they suddenly start acting a little strange. The chances are that I *am* going to unsettle my host when I enter him, but that he'll simply get two sanity-stabilizer pills from his medicine chest and take them with a glass of water and feel better in five minutes. And then I'll explain what's happening to him."

"More than likely no explanations will be necessary," said Maggie Caldwell. "By the time you arrive, time travel will have been a going proposition for three or four generations, after all. Having a traveler from the past turn up in your head will be old stuff to them. Your host will probably know exactly what's going on from the moment you hit him."

"Let's hope so," Bleier said. He looked across the laboratory to Rodrigues. "What's the count, Bob?"

"T minus eighteen minutes."

"I'm not worried about a thing," McCulloch said.

Caldwell took his hand in hers. "Neither am I, Jim."

"Then why is your hand so cold?" he asked.

"So I'm a *little* worried," she said.

McCulloch grinned. "So am I. A little. Only a little."

"You're human, Jim. No one's ever done this before."

"It'll be a can of corn!" Ybarra said.

Bleier looked at him blankly. "What the hell does that mean, Jake?"

Ybarra said, "Archaic twentieth-century slang. It means it's going to be a lot easier than we think."

"I told you," said McCulloch, "I'm not worried."

"I'm still worried about the impact on the host," said Bleier.

"All those Napoleons and Joans of Arc that have been cluttering the asylums for the last few hundred years,"

Maggie Caldwell said, "Could it be that they're really hosts for time-travelers going backward in time?"

"You can't go backward," said Mortenson. "You know that. The round trip has to begin with a forward leap."

"Under present theory," Caldwell said. "But present theory's only five years old. It may turn out to be incomplete. We may have had all sorts of travelers out of the future jumping through history, and never even knew it. All the nuts, lunatics, inexplicable geniuses, idiot-savants—"

"Save it, Maggie," Bleier said. "Let's stick to what we understand right now."

"Oh? Do we understand anything?" McCulloch asked.

Bleier gave him a sour look. "I thought you said you weren't worried."

"I'm not. Not much. But I'd be a fool if I thought we really had a firm handle on what we're doing. We're shooting in the dark, and let's never kid ourselves about it."

"T minus fifteen," Rodrigues called.

"Try to make the landing easy on your host, Jim," Bleier said.

"I've got no reason not to want to," said McCulloch.

He realized that he had been wandering. Bleier, Maggie, Mortenson, Ybarra—for a moment they had been more real to him than the congregation of lobsters: he had heard their voices, he had seen their faces, Bleier plump and perspiring and serious, Ybarra dark and lean, Maggie with her crown of short upswept red hair blazing in the laboratory light—and yet they were all dead, a hundred million years dead, two hundred million, back there with the triceratops and the trilobite in the drowned former world, and here he was among the lobster-people. How futile all those discussions of what the world of the early twenty-second century was going to be like! Those speculations on population density, religious belief, attitudes toward science, level of technological achievement, all those late-night sessions in the final months of the project, designed to prepare him for any eventuality he might encounter while he was visiting the future—what a waste, what a needless exercise. As was all that fretting about upsetting the mental stability of the person who would receive his transtemporalized consciousness. Such qualms, such moral delicacy—all unnecessary, McCulloch knew now.

But of course they had not anticipated sending him so eerily far across the dark abysm of time, into a world in which humankind and all its works were not even legendary memories, and the host who would receive him was a calm and thoughtful crustacean capable of taking him in with only the most mild and brief disruption of its serenity.

The lobsters, he noticed now, had reconfigured themselves while his mind had been drifting. They had broken up their circle and were arrayed in a long line stretching over the ocean floor, with his host at the end of the procession. The queue was a close one, each lobster so close to the one before it that it could touch it with the tips of its antennae, which from time to time they seemed to be doing; and they all were moving in a weird kind of quasi-military lockstep, every lobster swinging the same set of walking-legs forward at the same time.

Where are we going? McCulloch asked his host.

—*The pilgrimage has begun.*

—*What pilgrimage is that?*

—*To the dry place,* said the host. *To the place of no water. To the land.*

—*Why?*

—*It is the custom. We have decided that the time of the Molting of the World is soon to come; and therefore we must make the pilgrimage. It is the end of all things. It is the coming of a newer world. You are the herald; so we have agreed.*

—*Will you explain? I have a thousand questions. I need to know more about all this,* McCulloch said.

—Soon. Soon. This is not a time for explanations.

McCulloch felt a firm and unequivocal closing of contact, an emphatic withdrawal. He sensed a hard ringing silence that was almost an absence of the host, and knew it would be inappropriate to transgress against it. That was painful, for he brimmed now with an overwhelming rush of curiosity. The Molting of the World? The end of all things? A pilgrimage to the land? *What* land? Where? But he did not ask. He could not ask. The host seemed to have vanished from him, disappearing utterly into this pilgrimage, this migration, moving in its lockstep way with total concentration and a kind of mystic intensity. McCulloch did not intrude. He felt as though he had been left alone in the body they shared.

As they marched, he concentrated on observing, since he could not interrogate. And there was much to see; for the longer he dwelled within his host, the more accustomed he grew to the lobster's sensory mechanisms. The compound eyes, for instance. Enough of his former life had returned to him now so that he remembered human eyes clearly, those two large gleaming ovals, so keen, so subtle of focus, set beneath protecting ridges of bone. His host's eyes were nothing like that: they were two clusters of tiny lenses rising on jointed, movable stalks, and what they showed was an intricately dissected view, a mosaic of isolated points of light. But he was learning somehow to translate those complex and baffling images into a single clear one, just as, no doubt, a creature accustomed to compound-lens vision would sooner or later learn to see through human eyes, if need be. And McCulloch found now that he could not only make more sense out of the views he received through his host's eyes, but that he was seeing farther, into quite distant dim recesses of this sunless undersea realm.

Not that the stalked eyes seemed to be a very important part of the lobster's perceptive apparatus. They provided nothing more than a certain crude awareness of the immediate terrain. But apparently the real work of perceiving was done mainly by the thousands of fine bristles, so minute that they were all but invisible, that sprouted on every surface of his host's body. These seemed to send a constant stream of messages to the lobster's brain: information on the texture and topography of the ocean floor, on tiny shifts in the flow and temperature of the water, of the proximity of obstacles, and much else. Some of the small hairlike filaments were sensitive to touch and others, it appeared, to chemicals; for whenever the lobster approached some other life-form, it received data on its scent—or the underwater equivalent—long before the creature itself was within visual range. The quantity and richness of these inputs astonished McCulloch. At every moment came a torrent of data corresponding to the landslide senses he remembered, smell, taste, touch; and some central processing unit within the lobster's brain handled everything in the most effortless fashion.

But there was no sound. The ocean world appeared to be wholly silent. McCulloch knew that that was untrue, that sound waves propagated through water as persistently as through air; indeed, faster. Yet the lobster seemed neither to possess nor to need any sort of auditory equipment. The sensory bristles brought in all the data it required. The "speech" of these creatures, McCulloch had long ago realized, was effected not by voice but by means of spurts of chemicals released into the water, hormones, perhaps, or amino acids, something of a distinct and readily recognizable identity, emitted in some high-redundancy pattern that permitted easy recognition and decoding despite the difficulties caused by currents and eddies. It was, McCulloch thought, like trying to communicate by printing individual letters on scraps of paper and hurling them into the wind. But it did somehow seem to work, however

clumsy a concept it might be, because of the extreme sen-
sitivity of the lobster's myriad chemoreceptors.

The antennae played some significant role also. There
were two sets of them, a pair of three-branched ones just
behind the eyes and a much longer single-branched pair
behind those. The long ones restlessly twitched and
probed inquisitively and most likely, he suspected, served
as simple balancing and coordination devices much like
the whiskers of a cat. The purpose of the smaller antennae
eluded him, but it was his guess that they were involved in
the process of communication between one lobster and
another, either by some semaphore system or in a deeper
communion beyond his still awkward comprehension.

McCulloch regretted not knowing more about the lobsters of his own era. But he had only a broad general
knowledge of natural history, extensive, fairly deep, yet
not good enough to tell him whether these elaborate sensory functions were characteristic of all lobsters or had
evolved during the millions of years it had taken to create
the water-world. Probably some of each, he decided. Very
likely even the lobsters of the former world had had much
of this scanning equipment, enough to allow them to lo-
cate their prey, to find their way around in the dark sub-
oceanic depths, to undertake their long and unerring mi-
grations. But he found it hard to believe that they could
have had much "speech" capacity, that they gathered in
solemn sessions to discuss abstruse questions of theology
and mythology, to argue gently about omens and heralds
and the end of all things. That was something that the
patient and ceaseless unfoldings of time must have
wrought.

The lobsters marched without show of fatigue: not
scampering in that dancelike way that his host had
adopted while summoning its comrades to save it from the
swimming creature, but moving nevertheless in an elegant

and graceful fashion, barely touching the ground with the tips of their legs, going onward, step by step by step, steadily and fairly swiftly.

McCulloch noticed that new lobsters frequently joined the procession, cutting in from left or right just ahead of his host, who always remained at the rear of the line; that line now was so long, hundreds of lobsters long, that it was impossible to see its beginning. Now and again one would reach out with its bigger claw to seize some passing animal, a starfish or urchin or small crab, and without missing a step would shred and devour it, tossing the unwanted husk to the cloud of planktonic scavengers that always hovered nearby. This foraging on the march was done with utter lack of self-consciousness; it was almost by reflex that these creatures snatched and gobbled as they journeyed.

And yet all the same they did not seem like mere marauding mouths. From this long line of crustaceans there emanated, McCulloch realized, a mysterious sense of community, a wholeness of society, that he did not understand but quite sharply sensed. This was plainly not a mere migration but a true pilgrimage. He thought ruefully of his earlier condescending view of these people, incapable of achieving the Taj Mahal or the Sistine Chapel, and felt abashed: for he was beginning to see that they had other accomplishments of a less tangible sort that were only barely apparent to his displaced and struggling mind.

"When you come back," Maggie said, "you'll be someone else. There's no escaping that. It's the one thing I'm frightened of. Not that you'll die making the hop, or that you'll get into some sort of terrible trouble in the future, or that we won't be able to bring you back at all, or anything like that. But that you'll have become someone else."

"I feel pretty secure in my identity," McCulloch told her.

"I know you do. God knows, you're the most stable person in the group, and that's why you're going. But even so. Nobody's ever done anything like this before. It can't help but change you. When you return, you're going to be unique among the human race."

"That sounds very awesome. But I'm not sure it'll matter that much, Mag. I'm just taking a little trip. If I were going to Paris, or Istanbul, or even Antarctica, would I come back totally transformed? I'd have had some new experiences, but—"

"It isn't the same," she said. "It isn't even remotely the same." She came across the room to him and put her hands on his shoulders, and stared deep into his eyes, which sent a little chill through him, as it always did; for when she looked at him that way there was a sudden flow of energy between them, a powerful warm rapport rushing from her to him and from him to her as though through a huge conduit, that delighted and frightened him both at once. He could lose himself in her. He had never let himself feel that way about anyone before. And this was not the moment to begin. There was no room in him for such feelings, not now, not when he was within a couple of hours of leaping off into the most unknown of unknowns. When he returned—if he returned—he might risk allowing something at last to develop with Maggie. But not on the eve of departure, when everything in his universe was tentative and conditional. "Can I tell you a little story, Jim?" she asked.

"Sure."

"When my father was on the faculty at Cal, he was invited to a reception to meet a couple of the early astronauts, two of the Apollo men—I don't remember which ones, but they were from the second or third voyage to the Moon. When he showed up at the faculty club, there were two or three hundred people there, milling around having cocktails, and most of them were people he didn't know. He walked in and looked around and within ten seconds he had found the astronauts. He didn't have to be told. He just *knew*. And this is my father, remember, who doesn't believe in ESP or anything like that. But he said they were impossible to miss, even in that crowd. You could see it on their faces, you could feel the radiance coming from them, there was an aura, there was something about their eyes. Something that said, *I have walked on the Moon, I have been to that place which is not of our world and I have come back, and now I am someone else. I am who I was before, but I am someone else also.*"

"But they went to the *Moon*, Mag!"

"And you're going to the *future*, Jim. That's even weirder. You're going to a place that doesn't exist. And you may meet yourself there—ninety-nine years old, and waiting to shake hands with you—or you might meet me, or your grandson, or find out that everyone on Earth is dead, or that everyone has turned into a disembodied spirit, or that they're all immortal superbeings, or—or—Christ, I don't know. You'll see a world that nobody alive today is supposed to see. And when you come back, you'll have that aura. You'll be transformed."

"Is that so frightening?"

"To me it is," she said.

"Why is that?"

"Dummy," she said. "Dope. How explicit do I have to be, anyway? I thought I was being obvious enough."

He could not meet her eyes. "This isn't the best moment to talk about—"

"I know. I'm sorry, Jim. But you're important to me, and you're going somewhere and you're going to become someone else, and I'm scared. Selfish and scared."

"Are you telling me not to go?"

"Don't be absurd. You'd go no matter what I told you, and I'd despise you if you didn't. There's no turning back now."

"No."

"I shouldn't have dumped any of this on you today. You don't need it right this moment."

"It's okay," he said softly. He turned until he was looking straight at her, and for a long moment he simply stared into her eyes and did not speak, and then at last he said, "Listen, I'm going to take a big fantastic improbable insane voyage, and I'm going to be a witness to God knows what, and then I'm going to come back and yes, I'll be changed—only an ox wouldn't be changed, or maybe only a block of stone—but I'll still be me, whoever *me* is. Don't worry, okay? I'll still be me. And we'll still be us."

"Whoever *us* is."

"Whoever. Jesus, I wish you were going with me, Mag!"

"That's the silliest schoolboy thing I've ever heard you say."

"True, though."

"Well, I can't go. Only one at a time can go, and it's you. I'm not even sure I'd want to go. I'm not as crazy as you are, I suspect. You go, Jim, and come back and tell me all about it."

"Yes."

"And then we'll see what there is to see about you and me."

"Yes," he said.

She smiled. "Let me show you a poem, okay? You must know it, because it's Eliot, and you know all the Eliot there is. But I was reading him last night—thinking of you, reading him—and I found this, and it seemed to be the right words, and I wrote them down. From one of the *Quartets.*"

"I think I know," he said:

" *'Time and past and future
Allow but a little consciousness—' '*

"That's a good one too," Maggie said. "But it's not the one I had in mind." She unfolded a piece of paper. "It's this:

" *'We shall not cease from exploration*

And the end of all our exploring
Will be to arrive where we started—' "
" '—*And know the place for the first time,*' " he completed.
"Yes. Exactly. To arrive where we started. And know the
place for the first time."

The lobsters were singing as they marched. That was the
only word, McCulloch thought, that seemed to apply. The
line of pilgrims now was immensely long—there must have
been thousands in the procession by this time, and more
were joining constantly—and from them arose an outpouring of chemical signals, within the narrowest of tonal
ranges, that mingled in a close harmony and amounted to
a kind of sustained chant on a few notes, swelling, filling all
the ocean with its powerful and intense presence. Once
again he had an image of them as monks, but not Benedic-
tines, now: these were Buddhist, rather, an endless line of
yellow-robed holy men singing a great Om as they made
their way up some Tibetan slope. He was awed and
humbled by it—by the intensity, and by the whole-
heartedness of the devotion. It was getting hard for him to
remember that these were crustaceans, no more than
ragged claws scuttling across the floors of silent seas; he
sensed minds all about him, whole and elaborate minds
arising out of some rich cultural matrix, and it was coming
to seem quite natural to him that these people should have
armored exoskeletons and joined eye-stalks and a dozen
busy legs.

His host had still not broken its silence, which must have
extended now over a considerable period. Just how long a
period, McCulloch had no idea, for there were no
significant alternations of light and dark down here to
indicate the passing of time, nor did the marchers ever
seem to sleep, and they took their food, as he had seen, in
a casual and random way without breaking step. But it

seemed to McCulloch that he had been effectively alone in the host's body for many days.

He was not minded to try re-enter contact with the other just yet—not until he received some sort of signal from it. Plainly the host had withdrawn into some inner sanctuary to undertake a profound meditation; and McCulloch, now that the early bewilderment and anguish of his journey through time had begun to wear off, did not feel so dependent upon the host that he needed to blurt his queries constantly into his companion's consciousness. He would watch, and wait, and attempt to fathom the mysteries of this place unaided.

The landscape had undergone a great many changes since the beginning of the march. That gentle bottom of fine white sand had yielded to a terrain of rough dark gravel, and that to one of a pale sedimentary stuff made up of tiny shells, the mortal remains, no doubt, of vast hordes of diatoms and foraminifera, that rose like clouds of snowflakes at the lobsters' lightest steps. Then came a zone where a stratum of thick red clay spread in all directions. The clay held embedded in it an odd assortment of rounded rocks and clamshells and bits of chitin, so that it had the look of some complex paving material from a fashionable terrace. And after that they entered a region where slender spires of a sharp black stone, faceted like worked flint, sprouted stalagmite-fashion at their feet. Through all of this the lobster-pilgrims marched unperturbed, never halting, never breaking their file, moving in a straight line whenever possible and making only the slightest of deviations when compelled to it by the harshness of the topography.

Now they were in a district of coarse yellow sandy globules, out of which two types of coral grew: thin angular strands of deep jet, and supple, almost mobile figures of a rich lovely salmon hue. McCulloch wondered where

on Earth such stuff might be found, and chided himself at
once for the foolishness of the thought: the seas he knew
had been swallowed long ago in the great all-
encompassing ocean that swathed the world, and the
familiar continents, he supposed, had broken from their
moorings and slipped to strange parts of the globe well
before the rising of the waters. He had no landmarks.
There was an equator somewhere, and there were two
poles, but down here beyond the reach of direct sunlight,
in this warm changeless uterine sea, neither north nor
south nor east held any meaning. He remembered other
lines:

> *Sand-strewn caverns, cool and deep*
> *Where the winds are all asleep;*
> *Where the spent lights quiver and gleam;*
> *Where the salt weed sways in the stream;*
> *Where the sea-beasts rang'd all round*
> *Feed in the ooze of their pasture-ground . . .*

What was the next line? Something about great whales
coming sailing by, sail and sail with unshut eye, round the
world for ever and aye. Yes, but there were no great
whales here, if he understood his host correctly; no dol-
phins, no sharks, no minnows; there were only these
swarming lower creatures, mysteriously raised on high,
lords of the world. And mankind? Birds and bats, horses
and bears? Gone. Gone. And the valleys and meadows?
The lakes and streams? Taken by the sea. The world lay
before him like a land of dreams, transformed. But was it,
as the poet had said, a place which hath really neither joy,
nor love, nor light, nor certitude, nor peace, nor help for
pain? It did not seem that way. For light there was merely
that diffuse faint glow, so obscure it was close to nonexistent, that filtered down through unknown fathoms. But

what was that lobster-song, that ever-swelling crescendo, if not some hymn to love and certitude and peace, and help for pain? He was overwhelmed by peace, surprised by joy, and he did not understand what was happening to him. He was part of the march, that was all. He was a member of the prilgrimage.

He had wanted to know if there was any way he could signal to be pulled back home: a panic button, so to speak. Bleier was the one he asked, and the question seemed to drive the man into an agony of uneasiness. He scowled, he tugged at his jowls, he ran his hands through his sparse strands of hair.

"No," he said finally. "We weren't able to solve that one, Jim. There's simply no way of propagating a signal backward in time."

"I didn't think so," McCulloch said. "I just wondered."

"Since we're not actually sending your physical body, you shouldn't find yourself in any real trouble. Psychic discomfort, at the worst—disorientation, emotional up-heaval, at the worst a sort of terminal homesickness. But I think you're strong enough to pull your way through any of that. And you'll always know that we're going to be yanking you back to us at the end of the experiment."

"How long am I going to be gone?"

"Elapsed time will be virtually nil. We'll throw the switch, off you'll go, you'll do your jaunt, we'll grab you back, and it'll seem like no time at all, perhaps a thousandth of a second. We aren't going to believe that you went anywhere at all, until you start telling us about it."

McCulloch sensed that Bleier was being deliberately eva-sive, not for the first time since McCulloch had been selected as the time-traveler. "It'll seem like no time at all to the people watching in the lab," he said. "But what about for me?"

"Well, of course for you it'll be a little different, because you'll have had a subjective experience in another time-frame."

"That's what I'm getting at. How long are you planning to leave me in the future? An hour? A week?"

"That's really hard to determine, Jim."

"What does that mean?"

"You know, we've sent only rabbits and stuff. They've come back okay, beyond much doubt—"

"Sure. They still munch on lettuce when they're hungry, and they don't tie their ears together in knots before they hop. So I suppose they're none the worse for wear."

"Obviously we can't get much of a report from a rabbit."

"Obviously."

"You're sounding awfully goddamned hostile today, Jim. Are you sure you don't want us to scrub the mission and start training another volunteer?" Bleier asked.

"I'm just trying to elicit a little hard info," McCulloch said. "I'm not trying to back out. And if I sound hostile, it's only because you're dancing all around my questions, which is becoming a considerable pain in the ass."

Bleier looked squarely at him and glowered. "All right. I'll tell you anything you want to know that I'm capable of answering. Which is what I think I've been doing all along. When the rabbits come back, we test them and we observe no physiological changes, no trace of ill effects as a result of having separated the psyche from the body for the duration of a time-jaunt. Christ, we can't even tell the rabbits *have* been on a time-jaunt, except that our instruments indicate the right sort of thermodynamic drain and entropic reversal, and for all we know we're kidding ourselves about that, which is why we're risking our reputations and your neck to send a human being who can tell us what the heck happens when we throw the switch. But you've seen the rabbits jaunting. You know as well as I do that they come back okay."

Patiently McCulloch said, "Yes. As okay as a rabbit ever is, I guess. But what I'm trying to find out from you, and what you seem unwilling to tell me, is how long I'm going to be up there in subjective time."

"We don't know, Jim," Bleier said.

"You don't *know*? What if it's ten years? What if it's a thousand? What if I'm going to live out an entire life-span, or whatever is considered a life-span a hundred years from now, and grow old and wise and wither away and die and then wake up a thousandth of a second later on your lab table?"

"We don't know. That's why we have to send a human subject."

"There's no way to measure subjective jaunt-time?"

"Our instruments are here. They aren't *there*. You're the only instrument we'll have there. For all we know, we're sending you off for a million years, and when you come back here you'll have turned into something out of H. G. Wells. Is that straightforward enough for you, Jim? But I don't think it's going to happen that way, and Mortenson doesn't think so either, or Ybarra for that matter. What we think is that you'll spend something between a day and a couple of months in the future, with the outside possibility of a year. And when we give you the hook, you'll be back here with virtually nil elapsed time. But to answer your first question again, there's no way you can instruct us to yank you back. You'll just have to sweat it out, however long it may be. I thought you knew that. The hook, when it comes, will be virtually automatic, a function of the thermodynamic homeostasis, like the recoil of a gun. An equal and opposite reaction: or maybe more like the snapping back of a rubber band. Pick whatever metaphor you want. But if you don't like the way any of this sounds, it's not too late for you to back out, and nobody will say a word against you. It's never too late to back out. Remember that, Jim."

McCulloch shrugged. "Thanks for leveling with me. I

appreciate that. And no, I don't want to drop out. The only thing I wonder about is whether my stay in the future is going to seem too long or too goddamned short. But I won't know that until I get there, will I? And then the time I have to wait before coming home is going to be entirely out of my hands. And out of yours too, is how it seems. But that's all right. I'll take my chances. I just wondered what I'd do if I got there and found that I didn't much like it there."

"My bet is that you'll have the opposite problem," said Bleier. "You'll like it so much you won't want to come back."

Again and again, while the pilgrims traveled onward, McCulloch detected bright flares of intelligence gleaming like brilliant pinpoints of light in the darkness of the sea. Each creature seemed to have a characteristic emanation, a glow of neural energy. The simple ones—worms, urchins, starfish, sponges—emitted dim gentle signals; but there were others as dazzling as beacons. The lobster-folk were not the only sentient life-forms down here.

Occasionally he saw, as he had in the early muddled moments of the jaunt, isolated colonies of the giant sea anemones: great flowery-looking things, rising on thick pedestals. From them came a soft alluring lustful purr, a siren crooning calculated to bring unwary animals within reach of their swaying tentacles and the eager mouths hidden within the fleshy petals. Cemented to the floor on their swaying stalks, they seemed like somber philosophers, lost in the intervals between meals in deep reflections on the purpose of the cosmos. McCulloch longed to pause and try to speak with them, for their powerful emanation appeared plainly to indicate that they possessed a strong intelligence, but the lobsters moved past the anemones without halting.

The squid-like beings that frequently passed in flotillas

overhead seemed even keener of mind: large animals, sleek and arrogant of motion, with long turquoise bodies that terminated in hawser-like arms, and enormous bulging eyes of a startling scarlet color. He found them ugly and repugnant, and did not quite know why. Perhaps it was some attitude of his host's that carried over subliminally to him; for there was an unmistakable chill among the lobsters whenever the squids appeared, and the chanting of the marchers grew more vehement, as though betokening a warning.

That some kind of frosty detente existed between the two kinds of life-forms was apparent from the regard they showed one another and from the distances they maintained. Never did the squids descend into the ocean-floor zone that was the chief domain of the lobsters, but for long spans of time they would soar above, in a kind of patient aerial surveillance, while the lobsters, striving ostentatiously to ignore them, betrayed discomfort by quickened movements of their antennae.

Still other kinds of high-order intelligence manifested themselves as the pilgrimage proceeded. In a zone of hard and rocky terrain McCulloch felt a new and distinctive mental pulsation, coming from some creature that he must not have encountered before. But he saw nothing unusual: merely a rough grayish landscape pockmarked by dense clumps of oysters and barnacles, some shaggy outcroppings of sponges and yellow seaweeds, a couple of torpid anemones. Yet out of the midst of all that unremarkable clutter came clear strong signals, produced by minds of considerable force. Whose? Not the oysters and barnacles, surely. The mystery intensified as the lobsters, without pausing in their march, interrupted their chant to utter words of greeting, and had greetings in return, drifting toward them from that tangle of marine underbrush.

"Why do you march?" the unseen speakers asked, in a voice that rose in the water like a deep slow groaning.

"We have had an Omen," answered the lobsters.

"Ah, is it the Time?"

"The Time will surely be here," the lobsters replied.

"Where is the herald, then?"

"The herald is within me," said McCulloch's host, breaking its long silence at last.

—*To whom do you speak?* McCulloch asked.

—*Can you not see? There. Before us.*

McCulloch saw only algae, barnacles, sponges, oysters.

—*Where?*

—*In a moment you will see,* said the host.

The column of pilgrims had continued all the while to move forward, until now it was within the thick groves of seaweed. And now McCulloch saw who the other speakers were. Huge crabs were crouched at the bases of many of the larger rock formations, creatures far greater in size than the largest of the lobsters; but they were camouflaged so well that they were virtually invisible except at the closest range. On their broad arching backs whole gardens grew: brilliantly colored sponges, algae in somber reds and browns, fluffy many-branched crimson things, odd complex feathery growths, even a small anemone or two, all jammed together in such profusion that nothing of the underlying crab showed except beady long-stalked eyes and glinting claws. Why beings that signalled their presence with potent telepathic outputs should choose to cloak themselves in such elaborate concealments, McCulloch could not guess: perhaps it was to deceive a prey so simple that it was unable to detect the emanations of these crabs' minds.

As the lobsters approached, the crabs heaved themselves up a little way from the rocky bottom, and shifted themselves ponderously from side to side, causing the intricate streamers and filaments and branches of the creatures growing on them to stir and wave about. It was like a forest agitated by a sudden hard gust of wind from the north.

"Why do you march, why do you march?" called the crabs. "Surely it is not yet the Time. Surely!"

"Surely it is," the lobsters replied. "So we all agree. Will you march with us?"

"Show us your herald!" the crabs cried. "Let us see the Omen!"

—*Speak to them,* said McCulloch's host.

—*But what am I to say?*

—*The truth. What else can you say?*

—*I know nothing. Everything here is a mystery to me.*

—*I will explain all things afterward. Speak to them now.*

—*Without understanding?*

—*Tell them what you told us.*

Baffled, McCulloch said, speaking through the host, "I have come from the former world as an emissary. Whether I am a herald, whether I bring an Omen, is not for me to say. In my own world I breathed air and carried my shell within my body."

"Unmistakably a herald," said the lobsters.

To which the crabs replied, "That is not so unmistakable to us. We sense a wanderer and a revenant among you. But what does that mean? The Molting of the World is not a small thing, good friends. Shall we march, just because this strangeness is come upon you? It is not enough evidence. And to march is not a small thing either, at least for us."

"We have chosen to march," the lobsters said, and indeed they had not halted at all throughout this colloquy; the vanguard of their procession was far out of sight in a black-walled canyon, and McCulloch's host, still at the end of the line, was passing now through the last few crouching-places of the great crabs. "If you mean to join us, come now."

From the crabs came a heavy outpouring of regret. "Alas, alas, we are large, we are slow, the way is long, the path is dangerous."

"Then we will leave you."

"If it is the Time, we know that you will perform the offices on our behalf. If it is not the Time, it is just as well that we do not make the pilgrimage. We are—not—certain. We—cannot—be—sure—it—is—an—Omen—"

McCulloch's host was far beyond the last of the crabs. Their words were faint and indistinct, and the final few were lost in the gentle surgings of the water.

—*They make a great error,* said McCulloch's host to him. *If it is truly the Time, and they do not join the march, it might happen that their souls will be lost. That is a severe risk: but they are a lazy folk. Well, we will perform the offices on their behalf.*

And to the crabs the host called, "We will do all that is required, have no fear!" But it was impossible, McCulloch thought, that the words could have reached the crabs across such a distance.

He and the host now were entering the mouth of the black canyon. With the host awake and talkative once again, McCulloch meant to seize the moment at last to have some answers to his questions.

—*Tell me now*—he began.

But before he could complete the thought, he felt the sea roil and surge about him as though he had been swept up in a monstrous wave. That could not be, not at this depth; but yet that irresistible force, booming toward him out of the dark canyon and catching him up, hurled him into a chaos as desperate as that of his moment of arrival. He sought to cling, to grasp, but there was no purchase; he was loose of his moorings; he was tossed and flung like a bubble on the winds.

—*Help me!* he called. *What's happening to us?*

—*To you, friend human McCulloch. To you alone. Can I aid you?*

What was that? Happening only to him? But certainly he and the lobster both were caught in this undersea tempest, both being thrown about, both whirled in the same maelstrom—

Faces danced around him. Charlie Bleier, pudgy, ear-
nest-looking. Maggie, tender-eyed, troubled. Bleier had
his hand on McCulloch's right wrist, Maggie on the other,
and they were tugging, tugging—

But he had no wrists. He was a lobster.

"Come, Jim—"

"No! Not yet!"

"Jim—Jim—"

"Stop—pulling—you're hurting—"

"Jim—"

McCulloch struggled to free himself from their grasp.
As he swung his arms in wild circles, Maggie and Bleier,
still clinging to them, went whipping about like tethered
balloons. "Let go," he shouted. "You aren't here! There's
nothing for you to hold on to! You're just hallucinations!
Let—go—!"

And then, as suddenly as they had come, they were
gone.

The sea was calm. He was in his accustomed place,
seated somewhere deep within his host's consciousness.
The lobster was moving forward, steady as ever, into the
black canyon, following the long line of its companions.

McCulloch was too stunned and dazed to attempt contact for a long while. Finally, when he felt some measure of
composure return, he reached his mind into his host's:

—*What happened?*

—*I cannot say. What did it seem like to you?*

—*The water grew wild and stormy. I saw faces out of the former
world. Friends of mine. They were pulling at my arms. You felt
nothing?*

—*Nothing,* said the host, *except a sense of your own turmoil.
We are deep here: beyond the reach of storms.*

—*Evidently I'm not.*

—*Perhaps your homefaring-time is coming. Your world is summoning you.*

Of course! The faces, the pulling at his arms—the plausibility of the host's suggestion left McCulloch trembling with dismay. Homefaring-time! Back there in the lost and inconceivable past, they had begun angling for him, casting their line into the vast gulf of time—

—*I'm not ready,* he protested. *I've only just arrived here! I know nothing yet! How can they call me so soon?*

—*Resist them, if you would remain.*

—*Will you help me?*

—*How would that be possible?*

—*I'm not sure,* McCulloch said. *But it's too early for me to go back. If they pull on me again, hold me! Can you?*

—*I can try, friend human McCulloch.*

—*And you have to keep your promise to me now.*

—*What promise is that?*

—*You said you would explain things to me. Why you've undertaken this pilgrimage. What it is I'm supposed to be the Omen of. What happens when the Time comes. The Molting of the World.*

—*Ah,* said the host.

But that was all it said. In silence it scrabbled with busy legs over a sharply creviced terrain. McCulloch felt a fierce impatience growing in him. What if they yanked him again, now, and this time they succeeded? There was so much yet to learn! But he hesitated to prod the host again, feeling abashed. Long moments passed. Two more squids appeared: the radiance of their probing minds was like twin searchlights overhead. The ocean floor sloped downward gradually but perceptibly here. The squids vanished, and another of the predatory big-mouthed swimming-things, looking as immense as a whale and, McCulloch supposed, filling the same ecological niche, came cruising down into the level where the lobsters marched, considered their numbers in what appeared to be some surprise, and swam slowly upward again and out of sight. Something else of great size, flapping enormous wings somewhat like those of a stingray but clearly just a boneless mass of chitin-strutted flesh, appeared next, surveyed the pilgrims with equally bland curiosity, and flew to the front of the line of lobsters, where McCulloch lost it in the darkness. While all of this was happening the host was quiet and inaccessible, and McCulloch did not dare attempt to penetrate its privacy. But then, as the pilgrims were moving through a region where huge, dim-witted scallops with great bright eyes nestled everywhere, waving gaudy pink and blue mantles, the host unexpectedly resumed the conversation as though there had been no interruption, saying:

—*What we call the Time of the Molting of the World is the time when the world undergoes a change of nature, and is purified and reborn. At such a time, we journey to the place of dry land, and perform certain holy rites.*

—*And these rites bring about the Molting of the World?* McCulloch asked.

—*Not at all. The Molting is an event wholly beyond our control. The rites are performed for our own sakes, not for the world's.*

—*I'm not sure I understand.*

—*We wish to survive the Molting, to travel onward into the world to come. For this reason, at a Time of Molting, we must make our observances, we must demonstrate our worth. It is the responsibility of my people. We bear the duty for all the peoples of the world.*

—*A priestly caste, is that it?* McCulloch said. *When this cataclysm comes, the lobsters go forth to say the prayers for everyone, so that everyone's soul will survive?*

The host was silent again: pondering McCulloch's terms, perhaps, translating them into more appropriate equivalents. Eventually it replied:

—*That is essentially correct.*

—*But other peoples can join the pilgrimage if they want. Those crabs. The anemones. The squids, even?*

—*We invite all to come. But we do not expect anyone but ourselves actually to do it.*

—How often has there been such a ceremony? McCulloch asked.

—I cannot say. Never, perhaps.

—Never?

—The Molting of the World is not a common event. We think it has happened only twice since the beginning of time.

In amazement McCulloch said:

—Twice since the world began, and you think it's going to happen again in your own lifetimes?

—Of course we cannot be sure of that. But we have had an Omen, or so we think, and we must abide by that. It was foretold that when the end is near, an emissary from the former world would come among us. And so it has come to pass. Is that not so?

—Indeed.

—Then we must make the pilgrimage, for if you have not brought the Omen we have merely wasted some effort, but if you are the true herald we will have forfeited all of eternity if we let your message go unheeded.

It sounded eerily familiar to McCulloch: a messianic prophecy, a cult of the millennium, an apocalyptic transfiguration. He felt for a moment as though he had landed in the ninth century instead of in some impossibly remote future epoch. And yet the host's tone was so calm and rational, the sense of spiritual obligation that the lobster conveyed was so profound, that McCulloch found nothing absurd in these beliefs. Perhaps the world *did* end from time to time, and the performing of certain rituals did in fact permit its inhabitants to transfer their souls onward into whatever unimaginable environment was to succeed the present one. Perhaps.

—Tell me, said McCulloch. *What were the former worlds like, and what will the next one be?*

—You should know more about the former worlds than I, friend human McCulloch. And as for the world to come, we may only speculate.

—But what are your traditions about those worlds?

—*The first world,* the lobster said, *was a world of fire.*

—*You can understand fire, living in the sea?*

—*We have heard tales of it from those who have been to the dry place. Above the water there is air, and in the air there hangs a ball of fire, which gives the world warmth. Is this not the case?*

McCulloch, hearing a creature of the ocean floor speak of things so far beyond its scope and comprehension, felt a warm burst of delight and admiration.

—*Yes! We call that ball of fire the sun.*

—*Ah, so that is what you mean, when you think of the sun! The word was a mystery to me, when first you used it. But I understand you much better now, do you not agree?*

—*You amaze me.*

—*The first world, so we think, was fire: it was like the sun. And when we dwelled upon that world, we were fire also. It is the fire that we carry within us to this day, that glow, that brightness, which is our life, and which goes from us when we die. After a span of time so long that we could never describe its length, the Time of the Molting came upon the fire-world and it grew hard, and gathered a cloak of air about itself, and creatures lived upon the land and breathed the air. I find that harder to comprehend, in truth, than I do the fire-world. But that was the first Molting, when the air-world emerged: that world from which you have come to us. I hope you will tell me of your world, friend human McCulloch, when there is time.*

—*So I will,* said McCulloch. *But there is so much more I need to hear from you first!*

—*Ask it.*

—*The second Molting—the disappearance of my world, the coming of yours—*

—*The tradition is that the sea existed, even in the former world, and that it was not small. At the Time of the Molting it rose and devoured the land and all that was upon it, except for one place that was not devoured, which is sacred. And then all the world was covered by water, and that was the second Molting, which brought forth the third world.*

—How long ago was that?

—How can I speak of the passing of time? There is no way to speak of that. Time passes, and lives end, and worlds are transformed. But we have no words for that. If every grain of sand in the sea were one lifetime, then it would be as many lifetimes ago as there are grains of sand in the sea. But does that help you? Does that tell you anything? It happened. It was very long ago. And now our world's turn has come, or so we think.

—And the next world? What will that be like? McCulloch asked.

—There are those who claim to know such things, but I am not one of them. We will know the next world when we have entered it, and I am content to wait until then for the knowledge.

McCulloch had a sense then that the host had wearied of this sustained contact, and was withdrawing once again from it; and, though his own thirst for knowledge was far from sated, he chose once again not to attempt to resist that withdrawal.

All this while the pilgrims had continued down a gentle incline into the great bowl of a sunken valley. Once again now the ocean floor was level, but the water was notably deeper here, and the diffused light from above was so dim that only the most rugged of algae could grow, making the landscape bleak and sparse. There were no sponges here, and little coral, and the anemones were pale and small, giving little sign of the potent intelligence that infused their larger cousins in the shallower zones of the sea.

But there were other creatures at this level that McCulloch had not seen before. Platoons of alert, mobile oysters skipped over the bottom, leaping in agile bounds on columns of water that they squirted like jets from tubes in their dark green mantles: now and again they paused in mid-leap and their shells quickly opened and closed, snapping shut, no doubt, on some hapless larval thing of the plankton too small for McCulloch, via the lobster's imperfect vision, to detect. From these oysters came bright darting blurts of mental activity, sharp and probing: they must be as intelligent, he thought, as cats or dogs. Yet from time to time a lobster, swooping with an astonishingly swift claw, would seize one of these oysters and deftly, almost instantaneously, shuck and devour it. Appetite was no respecter of intelligence in this world of needful carnivores, McCulloch realized.

Intelligent, too, in their way, were the hordes of nearly invisible little crustaceans—shrimp of some sort, he imagined—that danced in shining clouds just above the line of march. They were ghostly things perhaps an inch long, virtually transparent, colorless, lovely, graceful. Their heads bore two huge glistening black eyes; their intestines, glowing coils running the length of their bodies, were tinged with green; the tips of their tails were an elegant crimson. They swam with the aid of a horde of busy finlike legs, and seemed almost to be mocking their stolid, plodding cousins as they marched; but these sparkling little creatures also occasionally fell victim to the lobsters' inexorable claws, and each time it was like the extinguishing of a tiny brilliant candle.

An emanation of intelligence of a different sort came from bulky animals that McCulloch noticed roaming through the gravelly foothills flanking the line of march. These seemed at first glance to be another sort of lobster, larger even than McCulloch's companions: heavily armored things with many-segmented abdomens and thick paddle-shaped arms. But then, as one of them drew nearer, McCulloch saw the curved tapering tail with its sinister spike, and realized he was in the presence of the scorpions of the sea.

They gave off a deep, almost somnolent mental wave: slow thinkers but not light ones, Teutonic ponderers, grapplers with the abstruse. There were perhaps two dozen of them, who advanced upon the pilgrims and in quick one-

sided struggles pounced, stung, slew. McCulloch watched
in amazement as each of the scorpions dragged away a
victim and, no more than a dozen feet from the line of
march, began to gouge into its armor to draw forth tender
chunks of pale flesh, without drawing the slightest response from the impassive, steadily marching column of
lobsters.

They had not been so complacent when the great-
mouthed swimming thing had menaced McCulloch's host;
then, the lobsters had come in hordes to tear the attacker
apart. And whenever one of the big squids came by, the
edgy hostility of the lobsters, their willingness to do battle
if necessary, was manifest. But they seemed indifferent to
the scorpions. The lobsters accepted their onslaught as
placidly as though it were merely a toll they must pay in
order to pass through this district. Perhaps it was. McCulloch was only beginning to perceive how dense and intricate a fabric of ritual bound this submarine world together.

The lobsters marched onward, chanting in unfailing
rhythm as though nothing untoward had happened. The
scorpions, their hungers evidently gratified, withdrew and
congregated a short distance off, watching without much
show of interest as the procession went by them. By the
time McCulloch's host, bringing up the rear, had gone past
the scorpions, they were fighting among themselves in a
lazy, half-hearted way, like playful lions after a successful
hunt. Their mental emanation, sluggishly booming
through the water, grew steadily more blurred, more
vague, more toneless.

And then it was overlaid and entirely masked by the
pulsation of some new and awesome kind of mind ahead:
one of enormous power, whose output beat upon the water with what was almost a physical force, like some massive metal chain being lashed against the surface of the
ocean. Apparently the source of this gigantic output still

lay at a considerable distance, for, strong as it was, it grew stronger still as the lobsters advanced toward it, until at last it was an overwhelming clangor, terrifying, bewildering. McCulloch could no longer remain quiescent under the impact of that monstrous sound. Breaking through to the sanctuary of his host, he cried:

—*What is it?*

—*We are approaching a god,* the lobster replied.

—*A god, did you say?*

—*A divine presence, yes. Did you think we were the rulers of this world?*

In fact McCulloch had, assuming automatically that his time-jaunt had deposited him within the consciousness of some member of this world's highest species, just as he would have expected to have landed, had he reached the twenty-second century as intended, in the consciousness of a human rather than in a frog or a horse. But obviously the division between humanity and all sub-sentient species in his own world did not have an exact parallel here; many races, perhaps all of them, had some sort of intelligence, and it was becoming clear that the lobsters, though a high life-form, were not the highest. He found that dismaying and even humbling; for the lobsters seemed quite adequately intelligent to him, quite the equals—for all his early condescension to them—of mankind itself. And now he was to meet one of their gods? How great a mind was a god likely to have?

The booming of that mind grew unbearably intense, nor was there any way to hide from it. McCulloch visualized himself doubled over in pain, pressing his hands to his ears, an image that drew a quizzical shaft of thought from his host. Still the lobsters pressed forward, but even they were responding now to the waves of mental energy that rippled outward from that unimaginable source. They had at last broken ranks, and were fanning out horizontally on the broad dark plain of the ocean floor, as though deploying themselves before a place of worship. Where was the god? McCulloch, striving with difficulty to see in this nearly lightless place, thought he made out some vast shape ahead, some dark entity, swollen and fearsome, that rose like a colossal boulder in the midst of the suddenly diminutive-looking lobsters. He saw eyes like bright yellow platters, gleaming furiously; he saw a huge frightful beak; he saw what he thought at first to be a nest of writhing serpents, and then realized to be tentacles, dozens of them, coiling and uncoiling with a terrible restless energy. To the host he said:

—*Is that your god?*

But he could not hear the reply, for an agonizing new force suddenly buffeted him, one even more powerful than that which was emanating from the giant creature that sat before him. It ripped upward through his soul like a spike. It cast him forth, and he tumbled over and over, helpless in some incomprehensible limbo, where nevertheless he could still hear the faint distant voice of this lobster host:

—*Friend human McCulloch? Friend human McCulloch?*

He was drowning. He had waded incautiously into the surf, deceived by the beauty of the transparent tropical water and the shimmering white sand below, and a wave had caught him and knocked him to his knees, and the next wave had come before he could arise, pulling him under. And now he tossed like a discarded doll in the suddenly turbulent sea, struggling to get his head above water and failing, failing, failing.

Maggie was standing on the shore, calling in panic to him, and somehow he could hear her words even through the tumult of the crashing waves: "This way, Jim, swim toward me! Oh, please, Jim, this way, this way!"

Bleier was there too, Mortenson, Bob Rodrigues, the whole group, ten or fifteen people, running about wor-

riedly, beckoning to him, calling his name. It was odd that
he could see them, if he was under water. And he could
hear them so clearly, too, Bleier telling him to stand up
and walk ashore, the water wasn't deep at all, and Rodrigues saying to come in on hands and knees if he couldn't
manage to get up, and Ybarra yelling that it was getting
late, that they couldn't wait all the goddamned afternoon,
that he had been swimming long enough. McCulloch wondered why they didn't come after him, if they were so
eager to get him to shore. Obviously he was unable to help
himself.

"Look," he said, "I'm drowning, can't you see? Throw
me a line, for Christ's sake!" Water rushed into his mouth
as he spoke. It filled his lungs, it pressed against his brain.

"We can't hear you, Jim!"

"Throw me a line!" he cried again, and felt the torrents
pouring through his body. "I'm—drowning—drowning—"

And then he realized that he did not at all want them to
rescue him, that it was worse to be rescued than to drown.
He did not understand why he felt that way, but he made
no attempt to question the feeling. All that concerned him
now was preventing those people on the shore, those humans, from seizing him and taking him from the water.
They were rushing about, assembling some kind of machine to pull him in, an arm at the end of a great boom.
McCulloch signalled to them to leave him alone.

"I'm okay," he called. "I'm not drowning after all! I'm
fine right where I am!"

But now they had their machine in operation, and its
long metal arm was reaching out over the water toward
him. He turned and dived, and swam as hard as he could
away from the shore, but it was no use: the boom seemed
to extend over an infinite distance, and no matter how fast
he swam the boom moved faster, so that it hovered just
above him now, and from its tip some sort of hook was
descending—

"No—no—let me be! I don't want to go ashore!"

Then he felt a hand on his wrist: firm, reassuring, taking control. All right, he thought. They've caught me after all, they're going to pull me in. There's nothing I can do about it. They have me, and that's all there is to it. But he realized, after a moment, that he was heading not toward shore but out to sea, beyond the waves, into the calm warm depths. And the hand that was on his wrist was not a hand; it was a tentacle, thick as heavy cable, a strong sturdy tentacle lined on one side by rounded suction cups that held him in an unbreakable grip.

That was all right. Anything to be away from that wild crashing surf. It was much more peaceful out here. He could rest, catch his breath, get his equilibrium. And all the while that powerful tentacle towed him steadily seaward. He could still hear the voices of his friends on shore, but they were as faint as the cries of distant sea-birds now, and when the looked back he saw only tiny dots, like excited ants, moving along the beach. McCulloch waved at them. "See you some other time," he called, "I didn't want to come out of the water yet anyway." Better here. Much much better. Peaceful. Warm. Like the womb. And that tentacle around his wrist: so reassuring, so steady.

—*Friend human McCulloch? Friend human McCulloch?*

—*This is where I belong. Isn't it?*

—*Yes. This is where you belong. You are one of us, friend human McCulloch. You are one of us.*

Gradually the turbulence subsided, and he found himself regaining his balance. He was still within the lobster; the whole horde of lobsters was gathered around him, thousands upon thousands of them, a gentle solicitous community; and right in front of him was the largest octopus imaginable, a creature that must have been fifteen or twenty feet in diameter, with tentacles that extended an implausible distance on all sides. Somehow he did not find the sight frightening.

"He is recovered now," his host announced.

—*What happened to me?* McCulloch asked.

—*Your people called you again. But you did not want to make your homefaring, and you resisted them. And when we understood that you wanted to remain, the god aided you, and you broke free of their pull.*

—*The god?*

His host indicated the great octopus.

—*There.*

It did not seem at all improbable to McCulloch now. The infinite fullness of time brings about everything, he thought: even intelligent lobsters, even a divine octopus. He still could feel the mighty telepathic output of the vast creature, but though it had lost none of its power it no longer caused him discomfort; it was like the roaring thunder of some great waterfall, to which one becomes accustomed, and which, in time, one begins to love. The octopus sat motionless, its immense yellow eyes trained on McCulloch, its scarlet mantle rippling gently, its tentacles weaving in intricate patterns. McCulloch thought of an octopus he had once seen when he was diving in the West Indies: a small shy scuttling thing, hurrying to slither behind a gnarled coral head. He felt chastened and awed by this evidence of the magnifications wrought by the eons. A hundred million years? Half a billion? The numbers were without meaning. But that span of years had produced this creature. He sensed a serene intelligence of incomprehensible depth, benign, tranquil, all-penetrating: a god indeed. Yes. Truly a god. Why not?

The great cephalopod was partly sheltered by an overhanging wall of rock. Clustered about it were dozens of the scorpion-things, motionless, poised: plainly a guard force. Overhead swam a whole army of the big squids, doubtless

guardians also, and for once the presence of those creatures did not trigger any emotion in the lobsters, as if they
regarded squids in the service of the god as acceptable
ones. The scene left McCulloch dazed with awe. He had
never felt farther from home.

—*The god would speak with you,* said his host.

—*What shall I say?*

—*Listen, first.*

McCulloch's lobster moved forward until it stood virtually beneath the octopus's huge beak. From the octopus,
then, came an outpouring of words that McCulloch did
not immediately comprehend, but which, after a moment,
he understood to be some kind of benediction that en-
folded his soul like a warm blanket. And gradually he
perceived that he was being spoken to.

"Can you tell us why you have come all this way, human
McCulloch?"

"It was an error. They didn't mean to send me so far—
only a hundred years or less, that was all we were trying to
cross. But it was our first attempt. We didn't really know
what we were doing. And I suppose I wound up halfway
across time—a hundred million years, two hundred,
maybe a billion—who knows?"

"It is a great distance. Do you feel no fear?"

"At the beginning I did. But not any longer. This world
is alien to me, but not frightening."

"Do you prefer it to your own?"

"I don't understand," McCulloch said.

"Your people summoned you. You refused to go. You
appealed to us for aid, and we aided you in resisting your
homecalling, because it was what you seemed to require
from us."

"I'm—not ready to go home yet," he said. "There's so
much I haven't seen yet, and that I want to see. I want to
see everything. I'll never have an opportunity like this
again. Perhaps no one ever will. Besides, I have services to

perform here. I'm the herald; I bring the Omen; I'm part of this pilgrimage. I think I ought to stay until the rites have been performed. I *want* to stay until then."

"Those rites will not be performed," said the octopus quietly.

"Not performed?"

"You are not the herald. You carry no Omen. The Time is not at hand."

McCulloch did not know what to reply. Confusion swirled within him. No Omen? Not the Time?

—*It is so,* said the host. *We were in error. The god has shown us that we came to our conclusion too quickly. The time of the Molting may be near, but it is not yet upon us. You have many of the outer signs of a herald, but there is no Omen upon you. You are merely a visitor. An accident.*

McCulloch was assailed by a startlingly keen pang of disappointment. It was absurd; but for a time he had been the central figure in some apocalyptic ritual of immense significance, or at least had been thought to be, and all that suddenly was gone from him, and he felt strangely diminished, irrelevant, bereft of his bewildering grandeur. A visitor. An accident.

—*In that case I feel great shame and sorrow,* he said. *To have caused so much trouble for you. To have sent you off on this pointless pilgrimage.*

—*No blame attaches to you,* said the host. *We acted of our free choice, after considering the evidence.*

"Nor was the pilgrimage pointless," the octopus declared. "There are no pointless pilgrimages. And this one will continue."

"But if there's no Omen—if this is not the Time—"

"There are other needs to consider," replied the octopus, "and other observances to carry out. We must visit the dry place ourselves, from time to time, so that we may prepare ourselves for the world that is to succeed ours, for it will be very different from ours. It is time now for such a visit, and well past time. And also we must bring you to the dry place, for only there can we properly make you one of us."

"I don't understand," said McCulloch.

"You have asked to stay among us; and if you stay, you must become one of us, for your sake, and for ours. And that can best be done at the dry place. It is not necessary that you understand that now, human McCulloch."

—*Make no further reply,* said McCulloch's host. *The god has spoken. We must proceed.*

Shortly the lobsters resumed their march, chanting as before, though in a more subdued way, and, so it seemed to McCulloch, singing a different melody. From the context of his conversation with it, McCulloch had supposed that the octopus now would accompany them, which puzzled him, for the huge unwieldy creature did not seem capable of any extensive journey. That proved to be the case: the octopus did not go along, though the vast booming resonances of its mental output followed the procession for what must have been hundreds of miles.

Once more the line was a single one, with McCulloch's host at the end of the file. A short while after departure it said:

—*I am glad, friend human McCulloch, that you chose to continue with us. I would be sorry to lose you now.*

—*Do you mean that? Isn't it an inconvenience for you, to carry me around inside your mind?*

—*I have grown quite accustomed to it. You are part of me, friend human McCulloch. We are part of one another. At the place of the dry land we will celebrate our sharing of this body.*

—*I was lucky,* said McCulloch, *to have landed like this in a mind that would make me welcome.*

—*Any of us would have made you welcome,* responded the host.

McCulloch pondered that. Was it merely a courteous

turn of phrase, or did the lobster mean him to take the answer literally? Most likely the latter: the host's words seemed always to have only a single level of meaning, a straightforwardly literal one. So any of the lobsters would have taken him in uncomplainingly? Perhaps so. They appeared to be virtually interchangeable beings, without distinctive individual personalities, without names, even. The host had remained silent when McCulloch had asked him its name, and had not seemed to understand what kind of a label McCulloch's own name was. So powerful was their sense of community, then, that they must have little sense of private identity. He had never cared much for that sort of hive-mentality, where he had observed it in human society. But here it seemed not only appropriate but admirable.

—*How much longer will it be,* McCulloch asked, *before we reach the place of dry land?*

—*Long.*

—*Can you tell me where it is?*

—*It is in the place where the world grows narrower,* said the host.

McCulloch had realized, the moment he asked the question, that it was meaningless: what useful answer could the lobster possibly give? The old continents were gone and their names long forgotten. But the answer he had received was meaningless too: where, on a round planet, is the place where the world grows narrower? He wondered what sort of geography the lobsters understood. If I live among them a hundred years, he thought, I will probably just begin to comprehend what their perceptions are like.

Where the world grows narrower. All right. Possibly the place of the dry land was some surviving outcropping of the former world, the summit of Mount Everest, perhaps, Kilimanjaro, whatever. Or perhaps not: perhaps even those peaks had been ground down by time, and new ones had arisen—one of them, at least, tall enough to rise above the universal expanse of sea. It was folly to suppose that any shred at all of his world remained accessible: it was all down there beneath tons of water and millions of years of sediments, the old continents buried, hidden, rearranged by time like pieces scattered about a board.

The pulsations of the octopus's mind could no longer be felt. As the lobsters went tirelessly onward, moving always in that lithe skipping stride of theirs and never halting to rest or to feed, the terrain rose for a time and then began to dip again, slightly at first and then more than slightly. They entered into waters that were deeper and significantly darker, and somewhat cooler as well. In this somber zone, where vision seemed all but useless, the pilgrims grew silent for long spells for the first time, neither chanting nor speaking to one another, and McCulloch's host, who had become increasingly quiet, disappeared once more into its impenetrable inner domain and rarely emerged.

In the gloom and darkness there began to appear a strange red glow off to the left, as though someone had left a lantern hanging midway between the ocean floor and the surface of the sea. The lobsters, when that mysterious light came into view, at once changed the direction of their line of march to go veering off to the right; but at the same time they resumed their chanting, and kept one eye trained on the glowing place as they walked.

The water felt warmer here. A zone of unusual heat was spreading outward from the glow. And the taste of the water, and what McCulloch persisted in thinking of as its smell, were peculiar, with a harsh choking salty flavor. Brimstone? Ashes?

McCulloch realized that what he was seeing was an undersea volcano, belching forth a stream of red-hot lava that was turning the sea into a boiling bubbling cauldron. The sight stirred him oddly. He felt that he was looking into the pulsing ancient core of the world, the primordial

flame, the geological link that bound the otherwise vanished former worlds to this one. There awakened in him a
powerful tide of awe, and a baffling unfocused yearning
that he might have termed homesickness, except that it
was not, for he was no longer sure where his true home lay.

—*Yes,* said the host. *It is a mountain on fire. We think it is a
part of the older of the two former worlds that has endured both of
the Moltings. It is a very sacred place.*

—*An object of pilgrimage?* McCulloch asked.

—*Only to those who wish to end their lives. The fire devours all
who approach it.*

—*In my world we had many such fiery mountains,* McCulloch
said. *They often did great destruction.*

—*How strange your world must have been!*

—*It was very beautiful,* said McCulloch.

—*Surely. But strange. The dry land, the fire in the air—the
sun, I mean—the air-breathing creatures—yes, strange, very
strange. I can scarcely believe it really existed.*

—*There are times, now, when I begin to feel the same way,*
McCulloch said.

The volcano receded in the distance; its warmth could
no longer be felt; the water was dark again, and cold, and
growing colder, and McCulloch could no longer detect any
trace of that sulphurous aroma. It seemed to him that they
were moving now down an endless incline, where scarcely
any creatures dwelled.

And then he realized that the marchers ahead had
halted, and were drawn up in a long row as they had been
when they came to the place where the octopus held its
court. Another god? No. There was only blackness ahead.

—*Where are we?* he asked.

—*It is the shore of the great abyss.*

Indeed what lay before them looked like the Pit itself:
lightless, without landmark, an empty landscape. McCulloch understood now that they had been marching all this

while across some sunken continent's coastal plain, and at last they had come to—what?—the graveyard where one of Earth's lost oceans lay buried in ocean?

—*Is it possible to continue?* he asked.

—*Of course,* said the host. *But now we must swim.*

Already the lobsters before them were kicking off from shore with vigorous strokes of their tails and vanishing into the open sea beyond. A moment later McCulloch's host joined them. Almost at once there was no sense of a bottom beneath them—only a dark and infinitely deep void. Swimming across this, McCulloch thought, is like falling through time—an endless descent and no safety net.

The lobsters, he knew, were not true swimming creatures: like the lobsters of his own era they were bottom-dwellers, who walked to get where they needed to go. But they could never cross this abyss that way, and so they were swimming now, moving steadily by flexing their huge abdominal muscles and their tails. Was it terrifying to them to be setting forth into a place without landmarks like this? His host remained utterly calm, as though this were no more than an afternoon stroll.

McCulloch lost what little perception of the passage of time that he had had. Heave, stroke, onward, heave, stroke, onward, that was all, endless repetition. Out of the depths there occasionally came an upwelling of cold water, like a dull, heavy river miraculously flowing upward through air, and in that strange surging from below rose a fountain of nourishment, tiny transparent struggling creatures and even smaller flecks of some substance that must have been edible, for the lobsters, without missing a stroke, sucked in all they could hold. And swam on and on. McCulloch had a sense of being involved in a trek of epic magnitude, a once-in-many-generations thing that would be legendary long after.

Enemies roved this open sea: the free-swimming creatures that had evolved out of God only knew which kinds of worms or slugs to become the contemporary equivalents of sharks and whales. Now and again one of these huge beasts dived through the horde of lobsters, harvesting it at will. But they could eat only so much; and the survivors kept going onward.

Until at last—months, years later?—the far shore came into view; the ocean floor, long invisible, reared up beneath them and afforded support; the swimmers at last put their legs down on the solid bottom, and with something that sounded much like gratitude in their voices began once again to chant in unison as they ascended the rising flank of a new continent.

The first rays of the sun, when they came into view an unknown span of time later, struck McCulloch with an astonishing, overwhelming impact. He perceived them first as a pale greenish glow resting in the upper levels of the sea just ahead, striking downward like illuminated wands; he did not then know what he was seeing, but the sight engendered wonder in him all the same; and later, when that radiance diminished and was gone and in a short while returned, he understood that the pilgrims were coming up out of the sea. So they had reached their goal: the still point of the turning world, the one remaining unsubmerged scrap of the former Earth.

—*Yes,* said the host. *This is it.*

In that same instant McCulloch felt another tug from the past: a summons dizzying in its imperative impact. He thought he could hear Maggie Caldwell's voice crying across the time-winds: "Jim, Jim, come back to us!" and Bleier, grouchy, angered, muttering, "For Christ's sake, McCulloch, stop holding on up there! This is getting expensive!" Was it all his imagination, that fantasy of hands on his wrists, familiar faces hovering before his eyes?"

"Leave me alone," he said. "I'm still not ready."

"Will you ever be?" That was Maggie. "Jim, you'll be marooned. You'll be stranded there if you don't let us pull you back now."

"I may be marooned already," he said, and brushed the voices out of his mind with surprising ease.

He returned his attention to his companions and saw that they had halted their trek a little way short of that zone of light which now was but a quick scramble ahead of them. Their linear formation was broken once again. Some of the lobsters, marching blindly forward, were piling up in confused-looking heaps in the shallows, forming mounds fifteen or twenty lobsters deep. Many of the others had begun a bizarre convulsive dance: wild twitchy cavorting, rearing up on their back legs, waving their claws about, flicking their antennae in frantic circles.

—*What's happening?* McCulloch asked his host. *Is this the beginning of a rite?*

But the host did not reply. The host did not appear to be within their shared body at all. McCulloch felt a silence far deeper than the host's earlier withdrawals; this seemed not a withdrawal but an evacuation, leaving McCulloch in sole possession. That new solitude came rolling in upon him with a crushing force. He sent forth a tentative probe, found nothing, found less than nothing. Perhaps it's meant to be this way, he thought. Perhaps it was necessary for him to face this climactic initiation unaided, unaccompanied.

Then he noticed that what he had taken to be a weird jerky dance was actually the onset of a mass molting prodrome. Hundreds of the lobsters had been stricken simultaneously, he realized, with that strange painful sense of inner expansion, of volcanic upheaval and stress: that heaving and rearing about was the first stage of the splitting of the shell.

And all of the molters were females.

Until that instant McCulloch had not been aware of any

division into sexes among the lobsters. He had barely been able to tell one from the next; they had no individual character, no shred of uniqueness. Now, suddenly, strangely, he knew without being told that half of his companions were females, and that they were molting now because they were fertile only when they had shed their old armor, and that the pilgrimage to the place of the dry land was the appropriate time to engender the young. He had asked no questions of anyone to learn that; the knowledge was simply within him; and, reflecting on that, he saw that the host was absent from him because the host was wholly fused with him; he was the host, the host was Jim McCulloch.

He approached a female, knowing precisely which one was the appropriate one, and sang to her, and she acknowledged his song with a song of her own, and raised her third pair of legs to him, and let him plant his gametes beside her oviducts. There was no apparent pleasure in it, as he remembered pleasure from his days as a human. Yet it brought him a subtle but unmistakable sense of fulfillment, of the completion of biological destiny, that had a kind of orgasmic finality about it, and left him calm and anchored at the absolute dead center of his soul: yes, truly the still point of the turning world, he thought.

His mate moved away to begin her new Growing and the awaiting of her motherhood. And McCulloch, unbidden, began to ascend the slope that led to the land.

The bottom was fine sand here, soft, elegant. He barely touched it with his legs as he raced shoreward. Before him lay a world of light, radiant, heavenly, a bright irresistible beacon. He went on until the water, pearly-pink and transparent, was only a foot or two deep, and the domed upper curve of his back was reaching into the air. He felt no fear. There was no danger in this. Serenely he went forward—the leader, now, of the trek—and climbed out into the hot sunlight.

Robert Silverberg

It was an island, low and sandy, so small that he imagined he could cross it in a day. The sky was intensely blue and the sun, hanging close to a noon position, looked swollen and fiery. A little grove of palm trees clustered a few hundred yards inland, but he saw nothing else, no birds, no insects, no animal life of any sort. Walking was difficult here—his breath was short, his shell seemed to be too tight, his stalked eyes were stinging in the air—but he pulled himself forward, almost to the trees. Other male lobsters, hundreds of them, thousands of them, were following. He felt himself linked to each of them: his people, his nation, his community, his brothers.

Now, at that moment of completion and communion, came one more call from the past.

There was no turbulence in it this time. No one was yanking at his wrist, no surf boiled and heaved in his mind and threatened to dash him on the reefs of the soul. The call was simple and clear: *This is the moment of coming back, Jim.*

Was it? Had he no choice? He belonged here. These were his people. This was where his loyalties lay.

And yet, and yet: he knew that he had been sent on a mission unique in human history, that he had been granted a vision beyond all dreams, that it was his duty to return and report on it. There was no ambiguity about that. He owed it to Bleier and Maggie and Ybarra and the rest to return, to tell them everything.

How clear it all was! He belonged *here,* and he belonged *there,* and an unbreakable net of loyalties and responsibilities held him to both places. It was a perfect equilibrium; and therefore he was tranquil and at ease. The pull was on him; he resisted nothing, for he was at last beyond all resistance to anything. The immense sun was a drumbeat in the heavens; the fiery warmth was a benediction; he had never known such peace.

"I must make my homefaring now," he said, and released himself, and let himself drift upward, light as a bubble, toward the sun.

Strange figures surrounded him, tall and narrow-bodied, with odd fleshy faces and huge moist mouths and bulging staring eyes, and their kind of speech was a crude hubbub of sound-waves that bashed and battered against his sensibilities with painful intensity. "We were afraid the signal wasn't reaching you, Jim," they said. "We tried again and again, but there was no contact, nothing. And then just as we were giving up, suddenly your eyes were opening, you were stirring, you stretched your arms—"

He felt air pouring into his body, and dryness all around him. It was a struggle to understand the speech of these creatures who were bending over him, and he hated the reek that came from their flesh and the booming vibrations that they made with their mouths. But gradually he found himself returning to himself, like one who has been lost in a dream so profound that it eclipses reality for the first few moments of wakefulness.

"How long was I gone?" he asked.

"Four minutes and eighteen seconds," Ybarra said.

McCulloch shook his head. "Four minutes? Eighteen seconds? It was more like forty months, to me. Longer. I don't know how long."

"Where did you go, Jim? What was it like?"

"Wait," someone else said. "He's not ready for debriefing yet. Can't you see, he's about to collapse?"

McCulloch shrugged. "You sent me too far."

"How far? Five hundred years?" Maggie asked.

"Millions," he said.

Someone gasped.

"He's dazed," a voice said at his left ear.

"Millions of years," McCulloch said in a slow, steady, determinedly articulate voice. "*Millions.* The whole earth was covered by the sea, except for one little island. The people are lobsters. They have a society, a culture. They worship a giant octopus."

Maggie was crying. "Jim, oh, Jim—"

"No. It's true. I went on migration with them. Intelligent lobsters is what they are. And I wanted to stay with them forever. I felt you pulling at me, but I—didn't—want—to—go—"

"Give him a sedative, Doc," Bleier said.

"You think I'm crazy? You think I'm deranged? They were lobsters, fellows. *Lobsters.*"

After he had slept and showered and changed his clothes they came to see him again, and by that time he realized that he must have been behaving like a lunatic in the first moments of his return, blurting out his words, weeping, carrying on, crying out what surely had sounded like gibberish to them. Now he was rested, he was calm, he was at home in his own body once again.

He told them all that had befallen him, and from their faces he saw at first that they still thought he had gone around the bend: but as he kept speaking, quietly, straightforwardly, in rich detail, they began to acknowledge his report in subtle little ways, asking questions about the geography, about the ecological balance in a manner that showed him they were not simply humoring him. And after that, as it sank in upon them that he really had dwelled for a period of many months at the far end of time, beyond the span of the present world, they came to look upon him—it was unmistakable—as someone who was now wholly unlike them. In particular he saw the cold glassy stare in Maggie Caldwell's eyes.

Then they left him, for he was tiring again; and later Maggie came to see him alone, and took his hand and held it between hers, which were cold.

She said, "What do you want to do now, Jim?"

"To go back there."

"I thought you did."

"It's impossible, isn't it?" he said.

"We could try. But it couldn't ever work. We don't know what we're doing, yet, with that machine. We don't know where we'd send you. We might miss by a million years. By a billion."

"That's what I figured too."

"But you want to go back?"

He nodded. "I can't explain it. It was like being a member of some Buddhist monastery, do you see? Feeling *absolutely sure* that this is where you belong, that everything fits together perfectly, that you're an integral part of it. I've never felt anything like that before. I never will again."

"I'll talk to Bleier, Jim, about sending you back."

"No. Don't. I can't possibly get there. And I don't want to land anywhere else. Let Ybarra take the next trip. I'll stay here."

"Will you be happy?"

He smiled. "I'll do my best," he said.

When the others understood what the problem was, they saw to it that he went into re-entry therapy—Bleier had already foreseen something like that, and made preparations for it—and after a while the pain went from him, that sense of having undergone a violent separation, of having been ripped untimely from the womb. He resumed his work in the group and gradually recovered his mental balance and took an active part in the second transmission, which sent a young anthropologist named Ludwig off for two minutes and eight seconds. Ludwig did not see lobsters, to McCulloch's intense disappointment. He went sixty years in the future and came back glowing with wondrous tales of atomic fusion plants.

That was too bad, McCulloch thought. But soon he decided that it was just as well, that he preferred being the only one who had encountered the world beyond this world, probably the only human being who ever would.

He thought of that world with love, wondering about his mate and her millions of larvae, about the journey of his friends back across the great abyss, about the legends that were being spun about his visit in that unimaginably distant epoch. Sometimes the pain of separation returned, and Maggie found him crying in the night, and held him until he was whole again. And eventually the pain did not return. But still he did not forget, and in some part of his soul he longed to make his homefaring back to his true kind, and he rarely passed a day when he did not think he could hear the inaudible sound of delicate claws, scurrying over the sands of silent seas.

The 1983 Nebula Award Nominees

FOR NOVEL

Against Infinity by Gregory Benford (Timescape)
Startide Rising by David Brin (Bantam)
Tea with the Black Dragon by R. A. MacAvoy (Bantam)
The Void Captain's Tale by Norman Spinrad (Timescape)
Lyonesse by Jack Vance (Berkley)
The Citadel of the Autarch by Gene Wolfe (Timescape)

FOR NOVELLA

"Hardfought" by Greg Bear (*Isaac Asimov's Science Fiction Magazine*, February 1983)

"The Gospel According to Gamaliel Crucis" by Michael Bishop (*Isaac Asimov's Science Fiction Magazine*, November 1983)

"Her Habiline Husband" by Michael Bishop (*Universe 13*, Doubleday)

"Eszterhazy and the Autogondola-Invention" by Avram Davidson (*Amazing*, November 1983)

"Transit" by Vonda N. McIntyre (*Isaac Asimov's Science Fiction Magazine*, October 1983)

"Homefaring" by Robert Silverberg (*Amazing*, November 1983)

250   THE 1983 NEBULA AWARD NOMINEES

FOR NOVELETTE

"Blood Music" by Greg Bear (*Analog*, June 1983)
"Blind Shemmy" by Jack Dann (*Omni*, April 1983)
"The Monkey Treatment" by George R. R. Martin (*The Magazine of Fantasy & Science Fiction*, July 1983)
"Black Air" by Kim Stanley Robinson (*The Magazine of Fantasy & Science Fiction*, March 1983)
"Cicada Queen" by Bruce Sterling (*Universe 13*, Doubleday)
"Slow Birds" by Ian Watson (*The Magazine of Fantasy & Science Fiction*, June 1983)
"The Sidon in the Mirror" by Connie Willis (*Isaac Asimov's Science Fiction Magazine*, April 1983)

FOR SHORT STORY

"The Peacemaker" by Gardner Dozois (*Isaac Asimov's Science Fiction Magazine*, August 1983)
"Her Furry Face" by Leigh Kennedy (*Isaac Asimov's Science Fiction Magazine*, Mid-December, 1983)
"Cryptic" by Jack McDevitt (*Isaac Asimov's Science Fiction Magazine*, April 1983)
"Ghost Town" by Chad Oliver (*Analog*, Mid-September, 1983)
"The Geometry of Narrative" by Hilbert Schenck (*Analog*, August 1983)
"Wong's Lost and Found Emporium" by William F. Wu (*Amazing*, May 1983)

Pa/t Nebula Award Winner/

1965

BEST NOVEL: *Dune* by Frank Herbert
BEST NOVELLA: "The Saliva Tree" by Brian W. Aldiss; "He Who Shapes" by Roger Zelazny (tie)
BEST NOVELETTE: "The Doors of His Face, the Lamps of His Mouth" by Roger Zelazny
BEST SHORT STORY: " 'Repent, Harlequin!' Said the Ticktockman" by Harlan Ellison

1966

BEST NOVEL: *Flowers for Algernon* by Daniel Keyes; *Babel-17* by Samuel R. Delany (tie)
BEST NOVELLA: "The Last Castle" by Jack Vance
BEST NOVELETTE: "Call Him Lord" by Gordon R. Dickson
BEST SHORT STORY: "The Secret Place" by Richard McKenna

1967

BEST NOVEL: *The Einstein Intersection* by Samuel R. Delany
BEST NOVELLA: "Behold the Man" by Michael Moorcock
BEST NOVELETTE: "Gonna Roll the Bones" by Fritz Leiber
BEST SHORT STORY: "Aye, and Gomorrah" by Samuel R. Delany

1968

BEST NOVEL: *Rite of Passage* by Alexei Panshin
BEST NOVELLA: "Dragonrider" by Anne McCaffrey
BEST NOVELETTE: "Mother to the World" by Richard Wilson
BEST SHORT STORY: "The Planners" by Kate Wilhelm

1969

BEST NOVEL: *The Left Hand of Darkness* by Ursula K. Le Guin
BEST NOVELLA: "A Boy and His Dog" by Harlan Ellison
BEST NOVELETTE: "Time Considered as a Helix of Semi-Precious Stones" by Samuel R. Delany
BEST SHORT STORY: "Passengers" by Robert Silverberg

1970

BEST NOVEL: *Ringworld* by Larry Niven
BEST NOVELLA: "Ill Met in Lankhmar" by Fritz Leiber
BEST NOVELETTE: "Slow Sculpture" by Theodore Sturgeon
BEST SHORT STORY: No Award

1971

BEST NOVEL *A Time of Changes* by Robert Silverberg
BEST NOVELLA: "The Missing Man" by Katherine MacLean
BEST NOVELETTE: "The Queen of Air and Darkness" by Poul Anderson
BEST SHORT STORY: "Good News from the Vatican" by Robert Silverberg

1972

BEST NOVEL: *The Gods Themselves* by Isaac Asimov
BEST NOVELLA: "A Meeting with Medusa" by Arthur C. Clarke
BEST NOVELETTE: "Goat Song" by Poul Anderson
BEST SHORT STORY: "When It Changed" by Joanna Russ

1973

BEST NOVEL: *Rendezvous with Rama* by Arthur C. Clarke

BEST NOVELLA: "The Death of Doctor Island" by Gene Wolfe

BEST NOVELETTE: "Of Mist, and Grass and Sand" by Vonda N. McIntyre

BEST SHORT STORY "Love Is the Plan, the Plan Is Death" by James Tiptree, Jr.

BEST DRAMATIC PRESENTATION: *Soylent Green*

1974

BEST NOVEL: *The Dispossessed* by Ursula K. Le Guin

BEST NOVELLA: "Born with the Dead" by Robert Silverberg

BEST NOVELETTE: "If the Stars Are Gods" by Gordon Eklund and Gregory Benford

BEST SHORT STORY: "The Day Before the Revolution" by Ursula K. Le Guin

BEST DRAMATIC PRESENTATION: *Sleeper*

GRAND MASTER AWARD: Robert A. Heinlein

1975

BEST NOVEL: *The Forever War* by Joe Haldeman

BEST NOVELLA: "Home Is the Hangman" by Roger Zelazny

BEST NOVELETTE: "San Diego Lightfoot Sue" by Tom Reamy

BEST SHORT STORY: "Catch That Zeppelin!" by Fritz Leiber

BEST DRAMATIC PRESENTATION: *Young Frankenstein*

GRAND MASTER: Jack Williamson

1976

BEST NOVEL: *Man Plus* by Frederik Pohl

BEST NOVELLA: "Houston, Houston, Do You Read?" by James Tiptree, Jr.

BEST NOVELETTE: "The Bicentennial Man" by Isaac Asimov

BEST SHORT STORY: "A Crowd of Shadows" by Charles L. Grant
GRAND MASTER: Clifford D. Simak

1977

BEST NOVEL: *Gateway* by Frederik Pohl
BEST NOVELLA: "Stardance" by Spider and Jeanne Robinson
BEST NOVELETTE: "The Screwfly Solution" by Raccoona Sheldon
BEST SHORT STORY: "Jeffty Is Five" by Harlan Ellison
GRAND MASTER: Jack Williamson
SPECIAL AWARD: *Star Wars*

1978

BEST NOVEL: *Dreamsnake* by Vonda N. McIntyre
BEST NOVELLA: "The Persistence of Vision" by John Varley
BEST NOVELETTE: "A Glow of Candles, a Unicorn's Eye" by
    Charles L. Grant
BEST SHORT STORY: "Stone" by Edward Bryant
GRAND MASTER: L. Sprague de Camp

1979

BEST NOVEL: *The Fountains of Paradise* by Arthur C. Clarke
BEST NOVELLA: "Enemy Mine" by Barry Longyear
BEST NOVELETTE: "Sandkings" by George R. R. Martin
BEST SHORT STORY: "giANTS" by Edward Bryant

1980

BEST NOVEL: *Timescape* by Gregory Benford
BEST NOVELLA: "The Unicorn Tapestry" by Suzy McKee Charnas
BEST NOVELETTE: "The Ugly Chickens" by Howard Waldrop
BEST SHORT STORY: "Grotto of the Dancing Deer" by Clifford D.
    Simak

1981

BEST NOVEL: *The Claw of the Conciliator* by Gene Wolfe
BEST NOVELLA: "The Saturn Game" by Poul Anderson
BEST NOVELETTE: "The Quickening" by Michael Bishop
BEST SHORT STORY: "The Bone Flute" by Lisa Tuttle*

1982

BEST NOVEL: *No Enemy But Time* by Michael Bishop
BEST NOVELLA: "Another Orphan" by John Kessel
BEST NOVELETTE: "Fire Watch" by Connie Willis
BEST SHORT STORY: "A Letter From the Clearys" by Connie Willis

*This Nebula Award was declined by the author.